FELLA
EVER AFTER

S.O. Callahan

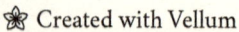 Created with Vellum

CHAPTER ONE

"She won't listen to me!"

My eyes followed the horse and rider as they took another turn around the ring. The mare was clearly feeling unsure about the young lad on her back, and he was returning those feelings with the tension I could see in each movement he made in the saddle. I drew in a breath and coughed as I moved from my position along the outside of the fence and unlatched the gate so I could step in with them. Mathew pulled the mare to a stop, causing him to lurch forward in his seat. He made a frustrated sound and hung his head back as far as it would go, face toward the sky.

"Come down from there," I told him gently as I helped him out of the saddle. I'd been working with this duo for almost three weeks, and I had to give him credit for his listening skills. He was always quick to do whatever I asked. His only fault was no fault of his own; he lacked experience and confidence. Unfortunately for all of us involved, those two things could only come with time.

Mathew inhaled deeply through his nose and sighed as he

stood next to his horse. He didn't touch her, or even acknowledge her, he just pulled the reins over her head and looked at me, waiting. I studied them carefully for a moment as I sifted through all the advice I'd ever been given. My dad had been my coach for most of my life, and now that I found myself in a similar role, I wanted to make him proud.

"How old is she?" I asked, tilting my chin up toward the mare. Mathew turned to look at her finally, shrugging his shoulders.

"I don't know." His gaze returned to mine. I nodded, keeping my face neutral.

"She's four. Practically a baby." I reached out to stroke the wide, white blaze that stretched down the length of her face. Her ears pricked toward me and then relaxed again, listening to the boy at her side. "I'll bet you didn't know much when you were four, either." I turned my focus to him again. "And on top of that, you both speak a different language. She doesn't know your words. Someday she might recognize a few of them, and remember that the sound of them means she should behave a certain way. But her language is touch."

Mathew didn't say anything as he looked at his horse again. His brows drew together as his eyes trailed over the side of her face and neck. "Touch?" he echoed with uncertainty.

"Every move you make in the saddle means something to her. Every squeeze of your legs, each shift in your weight. When you become a skilled rider, it'll be as if you and your horse become one living thing, moving together, and even thinking together." This was something I had learned first-hand as a wee child. I waited for Mathew's reaction to see if it meant anything to him at eleven. When he didn't respond at all, I decided to try a different approach. I walked back to the gate and opened it, holding it for them. "Bring her along," I instructed, and he did.

The mare followed him out and didn't react to the catch of the gate closing behind her. She was a sound animal, steady even at her young age, and she was gorgeous yet. Black with four white stockings to match the blaze down her face. I knew Mathew's father had paid a lot of money for her before I ever laid eyes on her. The day they came to tour our stables, Wally had informed me that she was from the same breeder that Henry's family used. They'd found the most prestigious name to provide their son's new horse, and then they'd come looking for the renowned Walshe facilities.

After our win in the championship match, my brother William had been fielding inquiries left and right about the spaces we had available for boarding. It had quickly become more than any of us ever expected. I was secretly happy for the rest of my family because it forced William to put a pause on his frequent business travels.

I had been working one of Henry's horses when Mathew showed up with his father. Wally had called me over to speak with them after they watched me for several minutes. I'd seen the intimidation in the lad's face as he gazed up at Henry's stunning gelding from his position outside of the fence. We exchanged pleasantries before I answered questions about our season, the rest of the players on our team, and my own experience with horses. I was trying to sell our business the way I knew William would expect me to. I hadn't realized I was actually selling myself.

"And how much will the lessons be?" Mr. Galligher asked this like it had already been discussed. I shot a sidelong glance at Wally, but he didn't even pause before he responded.

"That'll be a question for Mr. William, sir, I ain't in charge of the payments."

I found Wally on his way to the paddock after I'd finished with Henry's horse. He immediately swiped his cap off his bald head and clutched it in his outstretched hand, one finger pointed at me, as if it would keep him safe from whatever I was about to say. I followed him as he picked up speed to keep some distance between us.

"I already know what you're—"

"Lessons?!" I cut him off, stalking after him. "What is he talking about, Wally?"

"He didn't give much of a choice, lad. It's part of what he talked about with William and me, and William didn't say no." He flopped his cap back down on his head and adjusted it so it would stay put as he pushed the gate open, sliding the rough rope from his shoulder. "Three days a week for an hour. You can manage that." I stopped at the gate as it shut in front of me with a harsh click. Wally kept walking and I let our conversation fall there. I brought my hands up to rub my face slowly and sighed out a few coughs.

That's how I found myself walking down our pale dirt road with Mathew and his new mare. We were silent for only a short time before he spoke. "What are we doing?"

"You're spending time with your horse." It made him laugh. I grinned, because it did sound silly, but it was more important than he knew. "You should talk to her. Introduce yourself."

He laughed again, quieter this time, but I could tell he was considering it.

"What do I say?"

"I'll go first," I told him. I studied the way her unclipped mane shifted and shone in the sunlight that was peeking through the afternoon clouds overhead. I made a show of clearing my throat before I spoke, keeping the situation light. "My name is Peter. I'm glad you've come to stay with us here. We have the best grass for you to eat, and I'll tell you a little secret…" my voice went softer at the last part, drawing both of their attention, before I whispered the rest. *"There's magic in the river."* Mathew's eyebrows shot up in surprise, and I winked at him before we both smiled.

"My name is Mathew," he started then, watching his feet as we continued at an easy pace. "I've never had a horse of my own before. I really like watching the polo games, though, and my father said I could start playing if I did well in my schooling and minded my nanny." I remained quiet as the lad discovered the comfort that could be provided by speaking to someone who could do nothing but listen.

"Good," I encouraged him, nodding when he glanced at me. "She'll like getting to know the sound of your voice. I talk to my horses every day."

He chuckled again. "Really?"

"Really. Riding a horse requires a lot of trust, on your part and hers." I shifted my gaze to the pasture where my own horses were standing, tails swishing, heads dipped toward the grass. The trees dotting the gentle hill they were gathered on were a little past full color, with a magnificent display of reds, yellows, and oranges floating down from the branches each time the wind picked up. The evergreen trees in the distance held true, matching the grass that never seemed to grow tired on our land.

The chestnut mare was with them, strolling on a lazy walk toward a patch of roughage that must've looked especially appetizing. She stopped when she found what she was looking for and started to graze.

"That's the horse you were riding when you won," Mathew piped up as he noticed her, a new excitement in his voice. I nodded, feeling a sense of pride. She deserved to be recognized for the win as much as I did. I noted the way seeing her brought out the passion for the game he'd been speaking about before. Maybe that was the key to getting him focused.

"After we've gotten you more comfortable on your own horse, we can go for a ride together." I didn't know how long that would take, but it was a promise I was willing to honor if it kept him motivated. Some of the best lessons I ever learned were on a quiet ride with Dad along one of the many trails that stretched out across our land. I would never forget how nice it felt to get that time, just the two of us and our horses, leaving everything else behind for a while.

We walked Mathew's mare until our time was up and his father's man was there to collect him. I'd never been in the position of giving lessons before, but I already had a list of the things I wanted to teach him forming in my head. As I walked the mare into the low stone building that was her new home, I decided that our next meeting would begin and end with him learning how to care for his horse. He likely would always have enough money and staff to handle that for him, but that wasn't the way I did things, so I would teach him what I knew. That's what his father was paying for, after all.

I worked silently as I untacked the mare, admiring her as I ran the brush along her coat. A hand came to retrieve Mathew's new saddle and bridle to put away. When we were alone again, I moved to unhook her from the ties so I could return her to her stall. "I think he's a good lad. Inexperi-enced, no doubt, but willing to learn," I told her. "Everybody has to start somewhere. He's lucky he gets such an advantage with you, though." She blinked her deep brown eyes, and I stroked her neck before I walked her into the stall and slid the door shut.

By the time I finished with the rest of my chores for the night, I barely had enough light to make it up the hill to my own house, let alone Finna's cottage. I'd made plans to be there for supper, but I'd forgotten to tell Nan. I braced myself as I stepped up the path along the ivy-coated wall and across the cobblestones to the door that led to the kitchen. It squealed loudly at the hinges as I opened it, as it always did. The chatter of my family was unaffected by the intrusive noise.

William was already seated at the table, along with my sister Lucy. They appeared to be having a heated conversation about whichever vegetable Lucy didn't feel like eating that night. Nan was arguing along with them as she placed two bowls on the table; Anne was coming around the counter with two more in her hands. She was the only one who noticed me. We exchanged a look, and she gave me a shrug. We both knew better than to get in the middle of this one. I rubbed my hands along the seams of my breeches as I prepared to interrupt Nan and tell her my news.

Before I could, though, Lucy bounced from her chair and switched her emotions from being on the verge of tears to excitement in a single breath. "You've a letter, Peter! Please open it and read it to us." She ran from the room, her heels pounding heavily on the floor, pausing, and then retracing her steps as she returned with an envelope in her hand. "Please, please, *please?*" she begged as she handed it to me. I took the letter and turned it over, scanning the delicate, curving letters of a handwriting I didn't recognize. As soon as I read that it was addressed to a *Mr. Pete Walshe*, however, I couldn't help but roll my eyes as a grin spread across my lips.

"Luc, I'm afraid I'll have to proofread this one before I share it with anyone else." Her shoulders fell and her bottom lip went out, but no amount of begging could convince me to read a letter from Henry in front of my family without knowing what it said first. I gave her an apologetic look before Anne steered her back toward her seat at the table with a gentle hand on the back of her head. My food was already waiting, and Anne was the last to slide into her chair beside William. Nan was looking at me expectantly.

"Not hungry tonight, are we?" she asked, an edge to her voice that meant I needed to hurry up and sit down. She glanced up at me again after she helped Lucy put her napkin in her lap. I shifted my weight uneasily from one foot to the other and rubbed my thumb over the indentions marked in the red wax seal on the back of the envelope that felt heavy and expensive in my hands.

"I forgot to tell you I made other plans for tonight. I'm sorry." A whole string of excuses for why I'd been too busy to let her know earlier started running through my head. Maybe my lesson ran longer than I expected, or something had come up that Wally needed my help with, or one of the horses needed more tending to than normal. I didn't get the chance to use any of them, though. She just nodded and waved her tired fingers at me dismissively. I stared at her for a moment, letting my surprise settle, before I looked at Anne. She was wearing a tiny, knowing smirk as she took the first bite of her food.

I wasn't sure if I wanted to know what she'd been telling Nan or not. I knew better than to push the subject, so I thanked Nan for understanding and wished everyone a good evening before I excused myself to go change out of my clothes that smelled like horse and dirt and sweat.

CHAPTER TWO

Twilight had faded to night around me on my brisk walk to the cottage. I wasn't sure what was driving me more – the thought of the meal Finna had prepared, or the company I would find waiting for me – but I managed to keep my coughing to a minimum as I breathed in the cool evening air. Despite the stars overhead, it smelled like rain, so I'd worn my heavy cloak just in case. The past months had given me time to learn both paths to Finna's cottage as well as I remembered any from my childhood, but that didn't make it any less miserable walking them in the rain with no cover. I'd done it too many times and finally learned my lesson.

As I approached the tree-covered hill that her quaint home rested on, I saw the light spilling from the windows, and the welcoming path lined with lush flowers that led directly to her bright red door. The paint on it appeared a dark purple in the low light until it opened and reflected the candlelight from inside, before it shut again silently. I blinked at the figure that was approaching me, hands in their pockets, and all at once the nerves under my skin zinged to life as my heart leapt.

"Couldn't wait to meet me inside?" I asked as calmly as I could manage, a ridiculous grin already hurting my cheeks as my steps slowed. He chuckled and turned his head to peek at the window to the kitchen as his hands came from his pockets and slipped underneath my open cloak. He pulled me along with him on a few quick steps backward out of view of the window. Before I could stop my momentum, he pressed our lips together. I laughed against his mouth as I stumbled into him and kissed him back, my hands coming up to his arms. The tingle of fresh mint tickled my nose.

"Couldn't wait to do that," he murmured as he kissed me again, slower this time, and then he let me go and turned back toward the door. I drew in a slow breath to settle myself before I followed him, already sliding my arms out of my cloak so I could hang it up inside. Breck had been gone for nearly a week with the others again, working on his training and who knows what else. He rarely talked about what it was like in his world when we were together. I didn't know if it was because he wasn't allowed to, or because he didn't want to, but I couldn't deny my curiosity about the parts of his life I didn't get to see.

"Hello, love!" Finna was there to greet me in her sweet, raspy voice as soon as I stepped across the threshold, taking my cloak and accepting the kiss I placed on her cheek. I trailed Breck into the small kitchen and slid into the seat that had become my usual spot at her table. Breck did the same across from me. Our eyes met briefly across the short distance between us, and his gaze dipped to my mouth before sliding away.

Dirty bastard, I thought, and a smirk played across his

10

features before it faded again. We had discovered through experimentation that he could hear what I was thinking, even at a fair distance, if I made the conscious effort to think for him. *At* him, in a way. When he was gone with the others into his world, however, it didn't seem to work the same.

I realized I was staring at him only when Finna came with our food and set the bowls down in front of us. It was possible, I decided, that meeting him here for the first time after an extended absence wasn't the best idea. Maybe it was my own fault for allowing myself to anticipate seeing him so eagerly, but I had to guess that anyone who had feelings like mine behaved the same way. When William returned from his business trips, Anne's gaze always held a special tenderness toward him for the first day or two. I imagined that the same had been true with my mammy and dad, though I couldn't remember first-hand.

"How've the lessons with wee Mathew been going?" Finna returned with her own bowl and settled into her chair at the end of the table. I regarded the food in front of me for the first time as I picked up my spoon. The thick potato soup was steaming and hearty, perfect for a late autumn night. Mine was topped with crumbles of crispy bacon, as was Finna's.

"Em," I started, thinking of the right words as I stirred the soup, letting it cool before I took a bite. "It's been a learning experience for both of us."

Finna laughed sweetly and nodded. "I would imagine. Breck was mighty willful at that age." He gave her a cautious glance and then looked at me as he blew carefully on a spoonful of his supper. I grinned back at him, raising an eyebrow. "It turned out to be the first blossoming of his fiercely independent side, but at the time I worried he would never come 'round." Finna's bracelets landed noisily on the table as she rested her hand on his forearm, giving it a loving squeeze. "Lucky for both of us he's turned out for the better, hmm?" Her words encouraged a warmth to spread across my chest. I nodded and continued with my meal, considering what her inclusion of me in that statement meant.

A new courtship, if not previously arranged, was typically approved by both sets of parents before it was allowed to continue to something more serious. It often came as more of a business transaction between fathers than anything else, especially if there was a great deal of money, property, and inheritance involved. Henry had been equally as nervous for this meeting between his da and Sarah's as he had been for the night their engagement became official.

My situation with Breck was so far from typical that I couldn't even begin to wrap my head around any formalities, or lack of them. Neither of us had our fathers around to speak of such things. And even if we did, I couldn't imagine the courage I would've needed to bring me to my dad's study to tell him that I had intentions of courting a... stars above, which would be easier to stomach first, that I had intentions with a fairy, or with a man? My father was one of the most patient, understanding people I'd ever known, but where had he stood on these matters?

As for Breck, Finna was the closest thing he had to a mother, and she hadn't been shy from the start that she was accepting of our friendship, then more. Fallon and the others had remained cautious, understandably, although it vexed Breck to no end. There had been no more incidents with Orin or any other member of the Unseelie. Truthfully, things had been better than I'd expected. We had both been busier than ever, with me handling the aftermath of our winning polo season, and him preparing for his ceremony before Eabha. Our time together had become precious and meaningful in a way I'd never experienced before. That was the fire beneath my unabating thoughts of us and what the future held.

I was pulled from them when I felt Breck's cool magic reaching out. It slipped around my ankles and wrists like a whisper, making me shiver just slightly. I swallowed and my eyes met his blue ones across the table. We'd also agreed that he wouldn't pry into my thoughts unless I welcomed him in, which was why he searched my face then, silently asking if I was alright. I didn't know what he could sense, exactly, but he claimed that he could feel my emotions too; see my energy. I nodded to let him know I was fine, flashing another grin before I breathed in deeply and coughed into the crook of my elbow, temporarily relieving the tightness in my lungs and the thoughts in my head at the same time.

Our conversation was light until we finished our soup, and then Finna announced that she'd made a fruit cobbler. She served it to us with a healthy dollop of freshly whipped sweet cream. I could've cried.

When I was done with mine, Breck offered me the rest of his. I only asked if he was sure once before I slid the bowl toward myself and enjoyed every remaining speck. Only after I'd finished did I realize that I'd eaten it with his spoon instead of my own. The intimacy of that, as I dragged the gently curved metal surface down my tongue and past my lips, colored my cheeks. My mouth had been on him in much more intimate ways, but this was different somehow. Even William and Anne didn't share cutlery. It was too familiar for proper etiquette. But I'd never been very good with all that etiquette stuff, had I?

When we retired to the sitting room for tea around the hearth, I stopped short before I sat on the sofa. "Ah, I've something to show you," I told Breck as I went for my cloak hanging by the door. He was already seated with his legs crossed beneath him when I returned. I handed him the envelope with the red wax seal as I fit myself into the cozy spot he'd left for me. He read the front carefully, his brows coming together as he turned it over and pulled the thick parchment from inside. "Read it aloud," I encouraged him. He wet his lips as he unfolded the letter, turning it the right way. His eyes quickly scanned the words on the paper before he took a breath and began reading.

"Our Dearest Pete." He paused for effect, which made me stifle a quiet laugh. "We hope this letter finds you well. As you might've noticed by now, we have decided to extend our stay by the coast for a presently undetermined length of time."

Breck looked at me then, his hands and the letter dropping gently down to his lap. He knew I missed Henry. His concern showed on his face.

"Go on," I urged, tilting my head toward the letter. He appeared uncertain but lifted it again and returned to the flawless script. I'd seen my best friend's handwriting enough times to know that Sarah had clearly been writing as Henry told her what to put down.

Breck continued. "That being said, we wish to request a favor. We would be much obliged if you would kindly fetch our horses for us and deliver them to the estate so that we may enjoy them, and also relieve you of your duties as temporary caregiver, for which we are endlessly grateful."

"My, they want you to bring his whole team all that way?" Finna joined us, carrying a tray with our tea. I took both of our cups and sipped from mine, waiting for the rest of the letter. She set the tray down and climbed into the chair by the low fire, brushing her thick hair over her shoulder.

"We ask that you do not delay, as we are very much looking forward to your arrival, upon which we hope you will stay for as long as you are able. In addition," Breck paused again, a faint grin appearing on his mouth, "we request that you bring along a guest of your choosing. Preferably someone to help with the horses and keep you fine company on your journey. Warmest Regards, Mr. and Mrs. Henry O'Connor III."

Finna giggled from her place by the hearth as she sipped her tea. "I like that Henry of yours," she mused, nodding approvingly, her lips pursed. Breck read the letter again, silently this time, and then folded it up and put it back into the envelope.

"That's a full two-day journey, at least," he said, handing it to me. I exchanged it for his cup of tea and got up, returning it to the pocket of my cloak so I wouldn't forget it. "It won't be easy."

"No," I agreed. "I think he's right that I need to bring someone who can help." I sat down beside him again, my confidence wavering slightly, but I decided to keep the act going. "I'm just not sure who would make the best fit for the job."

Breck drank from his cup, a twinkle in his eye. He was going to make me work for it, then.

"I can't imagine you'll want Thomas to go with you," Finna piped up. She sounded serious, but when I looked at her, she gave me a sly wink before her face fell back into the role she was playing. I'd come to learn that Finna was incredibly quick. She made a thoughtful sound and tapped her fingertips against her lips lightly, pretending to run through other, more suitable options in her head.

"Certainly not Thomas, no." Was it too forward to ask Breck to come with me? I'd been as surprised by their letter as anyone. Henry was meddling even from the faraway seclusion of his honeymoon, but I had to appreciate his efforts. He knew I hadn't been on a proper holiday in years. The thought of getting that time away was tempting enough, but the thought of taking it with Breck was something else entirely. "I'd considered the stable hands, but I fear they would prefer to stick around for their paychecks, rather than take a jaunt to the seaside with me. Can't blame them for that."

"You know I'd volunteer, love, but I'm no good with horses," Finna said earnestly. "Let's think, shall we? Who do we know that can ride, wouldn't be inconvenienced by time away from their responsibilities, and could possibly even enjoy a few days of recreation with you?" She feigned a struggle of thought, her eyes narrowing, and then we all fell apart into quiet laughter, the farce over. Breck shook his head with another grin, then he looked at me.

"You're sure I'm the most qualified choice? I'm just the miller," he said humbly.

You're far more than that, I thought before I could stop myself. I swallowed and nodded, looking down at my tea and then at the glow of the fire across the room. To Henry and Sarah, yes, he was the miller who lived just across the river. But to me, he hadn't been "just the miller" for quite some time.

"You won't have to worry about anything around here. I'd be happy to look after the mill while you're gone," Finna offered excitedly.

"I don't think we'll be away longer than a few days," I said, reassuring both of them that I didn't plan to drag this out for an unreasonable amount of time. I hadn't even made any plans for my own affairs yet. Someone would have to look after my horses, and then there was the matter of my lessons with the young lad. How would I go about pausing them when we'd only really just started? Would that reflect poorly on myself, or on William? Would he even be accepting of me making the trip? If he had business to attend, he wouldn't be happy if I went too, leaving Anne and Lucy and Nan alone.

"Thank you, Finna." Breck said this in a way that was almost more for me than for her, a comforting gesture to go along with the way the back of his forefinger was stroking gently against the outside of my thigh, his hand tucked in the small space between us on the sofa. Our eyes met briefly, and I knew the nod he gave me had double meaning. It meant yes, he would go with me. It also meant that everything would work out fine. I sighed out a breath, trying to let go of my worry. Breck took one last sip of his tea before he unfolded his legs and stood up. "Supper was delicious. Now I'm ready to go and sleep for as long as possible."

"You're always so tired when you return, Breck. Don't they ever let you rest?" Finna was on her feet now, as well. They worked together to collect the empty teacups onto the tray, and I got up as Breck carried them to the kitchen for her. She and I said our goodbye silently, her sweet smile appearing after I kissed her cheek.

"Sometimes, if I've behaved myself," he told her with a playful smirk when he came back. She scoffed at his joke and tilted her cheek up to accept his kiss, too. She squeezed his arms above his elbows, as she always did, before she let go and followed us to the door. I grabbed my cloak off the hook and shrugged it on before we stepped out into the night air that had grown even colder since I'd arrived.

"I'm going to tell Fallon she's being too hard on you. What good will you be if you're run ragged?"

"I'm plenty good, thanks," Breck retorted on a laugh. "You know I've never been able to sleep well anyway." I'd learned this to be true. I almost never saw him asleep, and if I did, it was impossible not to wake him. Even silence seemed to cause him to stir.

"Aye, I remember. I would awake in the middle of the night to find you running about outside in the nip, playing like it was already morning! Nothing could convince you to come back in to bed, so I'd just leave you be." She laughed warmly at the memories as Breck put his hand on my back and urged me down the path toward the road.

"Pleasant night, Finna," he called over his shoulder. I couldn't help but laugh, too, and I could just barely see him roll his eyes with a sheepish grin in the moonlight. I waited until Finna closed the door behind us before I spoke, our footsteps falling into synch on the tamped dirt.

"Tell me, have you outgrown this, or do you still indulge in your naked nighttime romps?" I teased, bumping my shoulder into his.

"Well, you're there for all of them these days, so you tell me," he crooned. My cheeks went scarlet in the dark. I pressed my lips together to hide my smile.

"Not outside, though," I came back with, quietly, after I'd regained my composure.

"I wouldn't take you for a man who likes to rut around in the grass."

My grin faltered as thoughts of Jamie came crashing into my mind like a broken dish, sudden and loud, with pieces scattered everywhere. I'd found myself thinking about him less over the last months. My head and my heart had begun to fill with new memories, but sometimes the old ones would sneak in without warning. I was taken back to the few times we found ourselves in that very position; his back against a tree as we kissed, his hand down my trousers once at a party at Henry's. We'd escaped the festivities and hid behind one of the outbuildings. We were far too drunk to make anything of our efforts, but that didn't stop us from trying valiantly, until I'd told him he was tugging me raw and we had to give up.

"I'm not opposed to the idea," I told him finally, my face still warm.

"You're only saying that because you missed me." I felt his hand brush the back of mine as our arms moved at our sides. Then, for only a moment, he hooked one of his fingers around mine, squeezing gently before he let go. The affection in this small gesture sent a thrill down my spine. Even though it was dark, we weren't alone on our walk. Other cottages dotted the landscape along the road, and nearly all of them still had candlelight glowing in a window or two. A protective dog barked from inside one of them, further proving the fact that we could be seen by anyone.

"I did miss you," I admitted. "I hope I didn't put you on the spot too much with the letter. I was so excited to hear from Henry, and then the thought of, well, you know. A trip, just the two of us. I don't know." I pushed my fingers back through my hair and held the back of my neck, sighing out another calming breath and a few coughs.

"It's nearly too good to be true." After a pause, Breck added, "Does Sarah know?"

"I... I don't know," I repeated, shrugging my shoulders as I glanced at him. "Henry has never told another person after all these years. Even at times when it would've been so easy for it to slip out, he's always kept it to himself. But I don't see how she could've written that note with him and not understood the meaning behind it. She's as clever as she is beautiful." Those were Henry's words, not mine, but they did help prove my point.

"Then surely they wouldn't have sent it to you if it was an issue between them."

"I suppose not," I agreed, my pulse thumping at the thought. Was it even possible to get so lucky that my best friend's bride would be accepting of me, too?

"In any case, we can deliver the horses to them and come straight home if that's what you decide. Nothing says we must stay. Even if Henry insists, if you don't feel comfortable, you can blame it on me and say I've got to return to the mill."

I looked at him again, longer this time. At his tousled, dark blond hair. The strong line of his jaw. The thin band of silver that hugged the edge of his nose, and the others along his ear. Selfless, kind, *and* attractive, he was. Only because we'd reached a more secluded part of the road did I risk grabbing him by the inside of his elbow so I could lean closer to his ear and whisper, *"I've half a mind to take you in the grass right now."*

Breck's lips curved into a smirk as he glanced down at his feet before he looked ahead again, avoiding my heavy gaze. *"As much as I would enjoy that, I truly am tired,"* he whispered back. *"But I promise that you can take me however you want me when I've had some sleep."*

CHAPTER THREE

The next morning, I began setting the groundwork for my trip to see Henry. I took my time, eating breakfast with Lucy, waiting until I knew I could find William in the study. After a knock on the heavy door, he called me in. I closed it behind me and stepped forward to set a plate down with jam-coated toast in the only spot on his desk that wasn't covered with loose parchment or books. His eyes flicked to the plate, then to me, and then back to whatever he was reading in front of him.

"What do you want?" he asked shortly. Off to a good start.

"It's about the letter I received from Henry. He's requested that I bring his team to the estate. They're staying longer than they thought they would, and they want the horses there."

"He could've sent his own people to retrieve them, if he wants them so urgently."

"But I'm the one who has been looking after them all these weeks. I should be the one to deliver them so I can give any necessary updates he'll need to know."

William finally looked up from his paper with a critical eye. "And what updates are there to deliver? Have any of them been stricken lame or ill since he saw them last?" We both knew he would've already known about it if they were. I bit back an impatient sigh. "Besides, you've other responsibilities here. What would I tell Mr. Galligher about his son's lessons?"

"I've already got that sorted," I lied. "All of it." He blinked at this and looked back down at his paper. When I didn't move, he sighed for the both of us and looked at me again.

"How long will you be gone? I've got business travel in two weeks that I cannot miss. Anne should not be left by herself—"

"I'll be back before you leave, I swear it." I tried to mask the relief and excitement in my voice, but my grin probably gave me away. "Thank you," I added before I left, leaving no room for him to change his mind or add stipulations to the deal. I pulled the door behind me until it clicked and then took off for the stables, feeling light on my feet and one big step closer to this unexpected respite.

* * *

"But I hate children." Thomas scrunched his face as he adjusted the girth on his saddle.

"You don't *hate* children, you just never spend any time with them," I tried to reason, coming around his horse to stand next to him as he worked. He shook his head.

"No, I definitely do. Have you met any of my cousins? They're horrible little creatures. They're loud, they smell. I could go on."

I brought my hand up to rub my forehead. I already knew

that Thomas didn't like children. If Thomas didn't like some-thing, he made sure everyone knew about it. Unfortunately, he was my best chance at covering Mathew's lessons for a week. I didn't want to cancel them altogether and risk upset-ting Mr. Galligher or losing his business, especially since I'd told William that it was all worked out.

"What will Henry say if you're the reason I can't bring his team up to him? You know he'll never let you hear the end of it."

Thomas finished with his saddle and rolled his eyes dramatically as he turned to look at me. "Yes, along with about a million other things." He stepped around and reached to untie his horse, leading her out of the stables toward the mounting block. I followed behind them, rubbing my hands along the seams of my breeches and struggling to stay sure of myself.

"Mathew is a nice lad. He's just a sponge right now, taking whatever you'll give him. I was going to start showing him about the husbandry side of things. Feeding, cleaning, caring for equipment. You don't have to do anything special, just let him follow you around and answer his questions for an hour."

Thomas swung his leg over and slid into the saddle, adjusting his hips as he gave me a disapproving glare. His strong, straight nose was built for looking down at someone with, especially from the back of his horse. "I have no interest in doing this favor for you. I'll help look after your horses while you're gone, but the lessons can fall to someone else." With that, he clicked his tongue, telling his mare to move toward the trail at a trot. My mind spun as I tried desperately to think of something.

"Wait!" I called after him. "I'll tell Sarah what a help you were." Their trot slowed to a walk, but he didn't turn back. I took a few steps after them as I spoke, my voice growing louder than normal to cover the distance between us. "I'll tell her how you were more than happy to take over the lessons in my absence. I know she'll mention it to Emma Clare in her letters home. All the sisters find it very endearing when a man shows his ability to care for others, especially children." My efforts made me cough, but that quickly faded when Thomas turned his horse around.

He was silent until he stopped her directly in front of me, and then he seemed to weigh his response before he said it. "How do you know?" he asked skeptically.

"Henry told me," I said. And he had. "They all want big families. He said Sarah wants ten."

Thomas looked aghast. "*Ten* children? And here I thought *your* family had too many as it was." He looked away into the distance, as if he was considering what this meant for his own future. His horse swished her tail, waiting patiently. "I suppose I will need an heir someday," he added thoughtfully. I raised my eyebrows and nodded, indicating that he had a very good point. Finally, he took a deep breath and straightened his back. "Very well. I'll do this for you *only* if Emma Clare hears of it in the highest terms."

"You have my word, absolutely," I promised him, hand over my heart.

I didn't know what had shifted to inspire me to play matchmaker for two people who created such drama in my life, but truth be told, they were perfect for each other. Emma Clare wanted someone to dote on, and Thomas was desperate to be admired. After another short silence between us, Thomas nodded curtly and wheeled his horse around, starting for the trail again. I watched them go until they disappeared around a curve that dipped behind a hill, silently celebrating as I walked back toward the stables. If I'd known how to whistle a tune, I would have.

* * *

Wally was the easiest to talk to. Since I'd already gotten William's approval, there wasn't much he could say to stop me from going. He'd asked if I had anyone joining me to help with the horses, and I told him that I'd asked the miller specifically so I wouldn't take away any of the stable hands, which he appreciated. When he seemed satisfied that I was going to do this safely and responsibly, he took his cap off and rubbed his sleeve back and forth across his head a few times, the way someone might use a rag to shine a shoe, before he rolled his shoulders and flopped the cap back down.

"Which of your own horses will you take for the ride back?" he asked as he continued reassembling the bridle he'd taken apart to thoroughly clean and oil. I watched his fingers move, showing the skill of someone who had done the task hundreds of times. I knew how to do it, as well, but there was something about the way a person did things when they knew every step so intrinsically. He could've done it with his eyes closed.

"I thought I might take my gelding and the chestnut mare," I told him. The gelding had always been my best trail companion, and the chestnut mare would benefit from the exercise that went beyond what she would get in the paddock every day while I'd be gone.

Wally made a rough sound in the back of his throat as he nodded.

"I agree on the gelding. You'll have to leave the chestnut, though. I've several people lined up to come look at her over the next few days."

I was too distracted watching him work to really hear what he was saying. "What are they coming to look at her for?" I asked absently. His calloused fingers flipped the dark brown leather straps and shiny buckles around effortlessly, bringing them together without a second thought.

"To see if they want to make an offer on her," he said. My brows came together as my eyes shot up to look at him, the weight of his words finally settling in my mind.

"Make an offer on her?" I echoed, my tone growing serious.

"Aye. We've had several people inquiring after you won with her. One fella in particular is quite interested, he just wants to bring his rider along to give her a go before they make a final decision."

"Why didn't you tell me you were going to sell her?" Something like panic started to rise in me.

"I never intended to keep her forever." Wally held the bridle up to inspect it, making sure everything was secure and hanging the right way, before he got up from his stool at the worktable in the barn to return it and a few others to their respective owners' tack room pegs.

As he left, I found I couldn't move from my seat on the corner of the sturdy table made of thick, heavy wood. I'd watched Wally work from this same spot since I was short enough to need help climbing up. I suddenly found myself feeling like I knew John Wallace a little less than I thought I had. How could he sell her? She'd come so far from the thin, scared animal she'd been when she arrived over the summer. She was an excellent addition to my team. Foolishly, I'd thought that after our winning season, she would stay.

I turned my head to look out the wide double doors that were always open and provided a good view of the paddock my horses used. I couldn't see her out there with the others. Did Wally know the man who was interested in her? Did he know any of them? Would I ever see her again? After a moment, I realized that I didn't know if it would be better or worse if I did. How would I feel if I had to see her during a match, flying across the pitch with someone else on her back? I swallowed the lump that had formed in my throat and finally found the motivation to push off my wooden perch.

The rest of the day dragged on. The excitement I'd felt about my plans had quickly been tarnished by the news about the chestnut mare. She wasn't the first horse that had come in and out of my life, and I knew she wouldn't be the last, but there was something about her that made it more difficult than the others ever had been. Maybe it was because I'd spent so much time working with her. I'd put more time and effort into training her than I ever had with another horse. The truth was that I'd formed a strong bond with her. The thought of losing her was like losing a loved one, and I was no stranger to that, which made it all the more difficult to accept.

I wasn't doing a good job of hiding my emotions as I walked through the door that afternoon.

"Peter, what's the matter?"

I stopped on my way to the stairs and glanced over to see Anne in the sitting room, her thumb closed in a book, saving her spot. She had a knitted throw draped across her lap, low enough to reveal the bump beneath her dress that her other hand was resting on. William and the doctor were working in tandem to keep Anne at rest through her pregnancy, which translated to her being fussed at for doing anything above a slow walk from one room to the next. I could tell it was driving her mad, but I also knew how much this baby meant to her. She was doing her best to follow their directions.

"I'm fine," I told her. "Just a long day." I wanted to go up to my room and lie on my bed to stew in my feelings before supper, but instead I found myself moving to the chair opposite the one she was sitting in. I slumped into the seat and leaned against the back, which wasn't quite tall enough to support my neck, so for a moment I found myself staring at the ceiling. That didn't help me look fine at all, so I picked my head up again and met her analyzing eyes.

"You look like Lucy when she's been told no," she said, closing her book fully now and setting it on top of the stack beside her. A short, helpless laugh escaped me. "Same pouty lip, same hunched shoulders. I'd say it's more than a tiring day that's weighing you down."

"Glad to know I look like an eight-year-old girl when I'm upset," I retorted, which made her grin. I couldn't keep much from Anne. She had a way of working things out of me when I didn't even know there was something to be worked out. We'd been close since she nursed me through my illness, and that relationship had only grown after we learned why she was having so many issues starting their family. We'd had a long, emotional discussion about it one night when the awkwardness of avoiding it had become too much to handle any longer. I still had some secrets, but we now knew without a doubt that we both believed in fairies, that magic was real, and that her condition had never been her own fault.

"Would a turn about the garden and a stolen sweet before supper soothe you the way it does her?" she teased, bracing her hand on the arm of her chair as she pushed herself to her feet. I got up and went to help her, but she waved my hand away.

"Would you think less of me if I said yes?" I asked, and her smile grew as she tucked a stray curl of blonde hair behind her ear, turning to drop her throw onto the chair behind her.

"We'll just say it's what I needed if anyone asks. Wait here." I was left to stand in the sitting room for only a moment before she returned with a small, decorative box in her hands. Before I could ask what was inside, she was already out the front door and making her way around the back of the house to the garden, avoiding the windows of the kitchen or the study. I caught up to her and she looped her arm with mine, making it appear to any watchful eyes that I was supporting her as we slowed to a stroll.

"How are you?" It made me feel good that I had become something of a safe space for Anne during this time, just as she had been for me all those years. She and I both knew the truth about why she'd suffered so many losses. We both knew why this one was different. She didn't have to keep up the act of fearing another high-risk situation when it was just the two of us. There had been a shift in her. She was back to her old self, no longer worrying about what each day would bring. Anne drew in a deep breath and sighed it out dreamily.

"Wonderful. It's so different this time. It *feels* different." I didn't know what that meant, but she'd said it with such relief that I was glad to hear it. She looked up at me then.

"How are you? It's been strange to see so much of you lately. I hate to say it, but I know your world is a little lonely when your friends are away."

A self-conscious grin spread across my face. "I didn't know what to expect when Henry left. At first it felt awful, but then I realized that if I can survive him being gone completely, then it won't be so bad when he comes back, and I just get to see him less often than before."

"That's the spirit," Anne enthused quietly, making us both laugh. I hadn't told her that I was going to see him yet, but she jumped right on it with her next questions. "What did his letter say? When are they coming home? Have they been behaving themselves in that beach haven all alone?" Her tone was slightly suggestive, and I raised my eyebrows at her in mock surprise.

"That's a powerful accusation coming from someone who has been committed to finding herself in the family way since the moment she said her vows."

Anne squeaked, turning her face away from me since she didn't have a free hand to cover it with. "Peter! That's inappropriate," she said with a giggle. She huffed out a short breath to collect herself before she added, "It's been my dream to be a mammy since I was a little girl. I've no shame in having worked hard to make that happen with the man I love."

"Aye, the only shame belongs to those of us who had ears on those nights of *hard work*."

"That's enough of that," Anne said sharply, and I caught the blush on her face as she let go of my arm to sit on the bench we'd walked to at the far end of the garden. "Sit."

I did, settling onto the other half of the plain wooden bench that had seen better days. Anne turned the small box in her hands and opened the lid, finally revealing what was inside. Delicate pieces of parchment so thin you could see through them were bunched up around some curious confections. She reached in and carefully plucked one out with the tip of a finger and thumb.

"What's this?" I asked, holding my hand out for her to place it on my palm. It was cut into a perfect cube, smooth on all sides, so brown it was almost black, and topped with a sprinkle of chopped nuts.

"William said they're called chocolate caramels. He got them for me on his last trip." My gaze went back to the box as she reached in to grab one out for herself, and I couldn't help but notice the handwriting on the underside of the lid before she closed it. *Sweets for my sweet Anne*, it said. I looked away then, suddenly bashful from my innocent invasion on their private love note. Nobody but Anne ever saw that side of my brother. I cleared my throat as she set the box between us on the bench and brought her treat to her lips.

I did the same, noting the faint outline of melted chocolate left behind on my hand as I took a bite. The richness of the thick caramel made my mouth water instantly. I marveled at the way my toothmarks remained in the side as I chewed and chewed, savoring the delicacy. "*Mmmmh*," I said, not sure which emotion to show on my face in that moment, so I allowed several in quick succession.

"I said the same thing," Anne agreed when she'd finally swallowed.

"I'm going to have to ask Finna if she knows how to make something like this." I stuck the rest in my mouth and tried to remember everything about it so I could describe it in detail to her later. Anne's eyes lit up.

"I want to meet this Finna. She sounds like an incredible

woman from the way you describe her." The weight of her request didn't go unnoticed. She wanted to meet Finna because she'd decided that was the name of the lass I was quietly courting without the rest of our family knowing. That was part of the story that Anne didn't know. It felt wrong to go on letting her believe something that wasn't true, but it was easier. When I didn't answer, she picked up her box and scooched over so that she was close enough to talk just above a whisper. "Come now—"

"I'm going to visit Henry and Sarah at the estate," I blurted, changing the subject and trying to ignore the welling of nerves inside me. "That's what his letter was about. He wants me to bring up his horses."

"Oh." Anne blinked a few times at the abrupt shift in our conversation. "Well, that's grand. That's... when are you leaving?"

"I'm not sure yet. There's still a few things I need to settle before we go."

"We?" she asked, her interest piquing all over again. *Feck.*

"Em, yes. Breck is going with me. To help manage the horses."

"I see." She went to stand up, and this time she accepted my hand so that I could help her to her feet. The doctor had said she only had a few months left now before the baby arrived. She steadied herself briefly before she linked our arms again for the journey back to the house. "For a second, I thought you were going to tell me that this would be a little getaway to facilitate your courtship. How romantic that would be," she hinted lightly.

My attempt at a casual laugh came out more strangled and high-pitched than should be possible from a fella my age. Anne gave me an odd look. Before I had time to rectify the situation, the kitchen door whipped open loudly and William came racing across the yard.

"What's going on?! Why are you out here?" He looked between us several times, panicked.

"I asked Peter to bring me out for some fresh air. I needed a break from my novel." There was a fast transfer of guardianship as William took Anne by her other arm and supported her as if she could break at any moment. Anne sent one more glance at me over her shoulder as he guided her back to the house, grinning in a way that meant this conversation was far from over.

"Supper's ready," Nan called from the open doorway.

CHAPTER FOUR

Finna had never heard of chocolate caramels before, but she promised that she would look into it and see if she could learn how to make them for me. She'd been at the mill when I arrived the following afternoon so Breck and I could finalize our plans. Even though we'd agreed that we wouldn't be gone longer than a week, Finna had all but begged Breck to show her how to run things at the mill in his absence. I thought this was strange, considering that whenever he would leave with the others for days at a time, he just closed the shop. It was impossible to tell her no, though, so he'd done as she asked.

As it faded into evening, it was just the two of us sitting at his small table upstairs, finishing tea and the blackberry scones that Finna had brought. He reached to dip his pen into the squat jar of ink next to the parchment he was writing on. A few of the soft lights I'd grown accustomed to floated overhead, casting a gentle glow over his work with help from the candle on the tabletop.

"You taught her more just now than what one man might

hope to learn in a year. What else could you possibly have to say?" I asked, watching as he brought the metal tip to the paper and continued with the word he'd been in the middle of. He didn't look up as he answered.

"I'm just putting it all down here. Reminders for her. Practice for me."

I grinned at that and put the last bite of scone into my mouth, washing it down with my tea. He'd taken this task to heart. Not only were his words coming together easier, but his penmanship was nearing perfection. He dipped the pen again and finished his sentence with a flawless swoop of ink. "What will you do with your time when you've decided you don't need to practice anymore?"

He finally met my gaze then, a smirk playing across his lips. "You say that like I've got nothing else to do with myself." We both knew that was far from the truth. He was always doing something, and it was always something important. Helping someone. Learning. Training. Improving.

"You can be quite the dosser," I told him blandly. He set his pen down and stood from his chair, collecting the used dishes from the table and bringing them to his small sink to wash them, as if to prove me wrong as fast as possible. I reached across the table and used my fingertips to turn the paper toward me so I could read what he'd written. Even though it was beautifully scribed, it still didn't make much sense. Words like *hopper* and *bedstone* meant nothing to me. "How did *you* learn all of this?"

"The same way anyone else does, I suppose."

"You had an apprenticeship?" I turned in my chair to look at his back while he worked.

"Of sorts," he said, keeping the mystery firmly in place. He reached for a towel to dry his hands, resting his hip against the counter. "How does anyone learn anything?" Before I could respond, a burst of cold air in my face forced my eyes closed. When I opened them again, he was gone. A chill spread across my body as I stood up and looked toward the stairs. Then, I felt something soft hit my shoulder. The towel he'd been holding fell to the ground by my feet. I spun to find him lying on his side across the bed, head propped on his hand. "You watch, and you learn," he finished with a playful smile.

I sighed and gave him a stern look before I shook my head. "You spied on some poor miller from the shadows and stole his trade, is that what you're telling me?" I picked up the towel and threw it back at him. He chuckled as it hit him in the chest. I was still uneasy about this new skill he'd been perfecting.

"And just like you and your excellent hand-eye coordination skills, I practiced until I was good." He sat up with little effort and crossed his legs, tilting his head slightly with a thoughtful expression on his face. "Also, I'm not sure you can steal something that isn't tangible."

"Of course you can," I replied, kicking my shoes off and sitting on the thick rug in front of the bed, resting my head back against the mattress. "You steal my attention all the time. My focus. My thoughts."

Breck leaned forward and held the sides of my face in his hands, placing a gentle kiss on my forehead. I swallowed down the emotions that his sweet gesture stirred in me. "Fair enough," he said. Our eyes met briefly before he disappeared again, only this time he just ended up on his back on the bed.

"So, you're sure you know the way to the estate?" To say I had no clue how to get there was being generous. I'd never traveled outside the village without the guidance of someone who knew how to get us where we were going, and even then, those times had been few and far between.

"There are about ten different ways we could go, depending on how adventurous you wanted to be. But I think it's best to stick to the easiest route with the horses."

"I'll be fine if we stay within sight of a road the whole time, thanks," I said dryly. Breck laughed to himself, and I heard him shuffling around behind me.

"You mean you don't want to disappear into the forest together? We could get into all sorts of adventure that way." I could hear the mischief in his voice. I wasn't sure if I was more tempted or terrified by this thought. I had no doubt that Breck could get us where we needed to go, but I also didn't want to risk being too far away from... what? Other people? Civilization? Anywhere that might help ward off the magical unknown?

"I thought the Seelie frowned upon tricking humans," I said, grinning as I scratched at a smudge of dirt I hadn't noticed on my trousers until then.

"It's not tricking if you come willingly," he countered.

He had me there. I shifted up onto my knees and turned to rest my elbows on the mattress, a smart remark already brewing, but it was quickly forgotten. Breck was still on his back, but his clothes were gone. His hands were linked behind his head, eyes closed, one leg pulled up at the knee. I groaned and dropped my face to the bed.

"Speaking of coming willingly," I mumbled into his blankets.

"*Muinín na nDaoine Maith, Peadar,*" he said softly, not helping the situation. The lilt of his voice when he spoke in his native tongue did something to me that I couldn't explain in any other way than being an instant arousal. The addition of my name at the end was enough to send a quick shiver down my spine. "Trust the Good People," he repeated for me. I picked my head up to look at him, and he opened one eye, peeking back.

"I trust you," I told him.

"Then try to understand. Fairies like Orin don't live here. We work every day to make sure of it. But I'll keep you safe, no matter what happens." He moved one hand from behind his head and brought it to my cheek. I leaned into it without thinking as he studied my face. "Now," he began, sliding his touch to my chin, his thumb tracing my bottom lip, "shall we make good on my promise from the other night?"

"I can't," I managed, stealing a quick glance out the window above his bed to see how dark it had gotten. "I told Luc I'd read with her tonight." She'd cried when she found out I'd be gone for a few days. I hadn't expected that reaction, but Anne reassured me that she would be alright.

Breck hummed as a soft smile tempered the sultry look he'd been giving me. Reading a fairy tale with my little sister for the thousandth time was the last thing I wanted to do right then, when I had my own fairy tale ready and willing right in front of me, but the thought of upsetting Lucy more was enough to force me to my feet. I braced my weight on my hands as I leaned down to press my lips to his, savoring the goodnight kiss. As I pulled away, Breck reached up and hooked his hand around the back of my neck, bringing us together for another quick kiss, and another, and another, until I couldn't help but laugh at the smacking sound it made. "I'll see you in the morning," he grinned.

"In the morning," I agreed.

* * *

Despite my efforts, Lucy cried again when I started to tuck her in after we finished our fourth reading of the story she'd picked out. I wiped away her tears and told her I'd be back before she even had time to miss me.

As I laid in bed trying to fall asleep, I realized why she was so upset. The last time we'd been apart for so many days was when Dad had sent her and Nan away because of the illness. In her young mind, she'd left her family whole and returned to a broken mess. I honestly couldn't remember how much time passed from that day they took the carriage to when I saw Lucy again. The years and months since it all happened had done an excellent job of blurring the memories of that time – what few I had to begin with – into a hazy recollection at best.

I'd found this to be true with other things, as well. Details started to fade after a while. Emotions of certain situations that had once left such an impact didn't seem so intense. The hardest was accepting that I couldn't remember what my parents' voices sounded like anymore. I could no longer hear my sisters giggling together as they danced and played. Sometimes, I thought I could feel a whisper of them coming back to me, like an oddly familiar scent on a breeze that was gone before you could put a name to it. For one fleeting moment, I'd hear my brother's voice echo in the stables, or I'd catch Mammy calling me from the doorway as I left. But it never lasted long enough for me to truly *remember*.

The only comfort I had in this was the photograph of all of us together in William's study. Even though I couldn't hear them anymore, I could still see them any time I needed to. Matching auburn hair and green eyes had been turned to shades of gray and black by the print, emotions calmed as much as possible to avoid blurring our faces. It was undoubtedly the most valuable item in our home.

As far as I knew, there were no photos of Jamie.

The memories of him were all I had, and now that I'd been allowing them to surface less and less, he was starting to grow dim in my head like the rest of them. If I had known our final goodbye was the last like he had, I would've spent more time looking at him. At the face I'd secretly wanted to touch and kiss for so many years before I finally could.

A pang of guilt cramped in my chest. I let out a slow breath and coughed as I turned onto my side, pulling the blankets up over my head. Another reason I kept my memories of Jamie hidden more often was that I didn't want Breck to see them in my mind. I worried that it would upset him, even though he was rarely tilted by anything. It just didn't feel fair to him, though, that I would still think of Jamie despite our own growing relationship.

I'd told myself that I should be more open about it with him. After all, what I'd told him at the mill earlier that night was the truth. I did trust him. Not just because I knew he was unable to lie to me, but because he showed me every day that I could. He held his word when he told me he would do something. He made the effort to ease my anxious tendencies by keeping me informed about things that he knew made me worry.

Heat spread across my chest and up my neck as I thought of the way I'd been growing that trust in our more intimate moments, too. He didn't make me feel ashamed for anything. He made me feel wanted. The comfort I felt with him was slowly chipping away at the years of absolute silence I'd been forced to adopt before. I'd started to understand the tales told of humans abandoning their lives completely for one seductive fairy.

I couldn't stop the grin that tugged at my lips. I turned more and pressed my face into the cool fabric case on my pillow, muffling the coughs that escaped me. We were a few hours away from a trip that felt like a dream. Not moments, not an evening, but whole days together lie ahead of us. I was going to see more of the land that Breck held so close to his heart, and I was going to see my best friend. If someone had asked me to plan my ideal holiday, I'm sure I couldn't have thought of anything better. My last thought before I fell asleep was that I hoped the weather would cooperate for us.

CHAPTER FIVE

I was awake before the sun even hinted at coming up over the mountains. Anne had helped me pack the personal items I would need on our trip the day before, which I thanked her for several times over. She did it for William every time he left for business, so she was a self-proclaimed expert. The only difference was that he traveled with two bulky leather suitcases that sat neatly in the carriage. Everything I was taking had to fit in a few saddle bags that the horses would carry for us.

When she'd asked me what we would be doing once we arrived at the estate, I'd told her I had no idea, so she decided to pack my most functional clothing. I wasn't sure what that meant, exactly, but I was too afraid to mess up her impeccable folding job to risk a look. I decided I would just find out when I arrived.

On top of the clothes sat a supple, light-colored leather traveling case with a scrolling *W* embroidered on it. When I'd opened it to see what was inside, Anne had explained that she'd given it to William as a gift, but the razors, fine combs, and other delicate grooming tools inside were no longer helpful in managing my brother's thick beard and mustache. It was better suited to someone like me, she'd said, which made me chuckle. I vehemently rejected the trend of wearing facial hair.

I'd slung my bags over my shoulders, wanting to test the weight and balance of them for myself as I carried them to the stables in the low light before dawn. A swirl of anticipation moved in my stomach as I followed the worn dirt path from the house. I briefly considered going back to ask Nan for some breakfast, but as my eyes landed on a familiar figure, I decided my hunger could wait. Instead, I had to put all my energy into keeping a neutral face, because I knew Wally or anyone else could be up and about, despite the early hour.

Breck was casually sliding a brush along my gelding's coat, preparing him for the saddle. I should've known he would beat me there and be halfway ready to leave by the time I arrived.

"Did you get enough sleep?" I asked him, my voice a little rough still from being unused.

He replied only with a small grin, successfully avoiding a direct answer to my question.

"I was too excited to sleep much," I admitted, suddenly overwhelmed with the urge to touch him. It wasn't safe here, though, so I settled for a friendly pat on the shoulder as I went around my horse and into the stables. I passed by the gelding's half-door, which was where Breck had hung the saddle bags I'd given him to pack with his own things for the journey. Curiosity got the better of me and I backed up a few steps, lifting the flap of one bag to see what was inside.

It was empty. My brows furrowed as I undid the buckle of the other bag, opening it too.

Nothing.

You forgot to pack your bags, I thought for him. I wondered if my confusion also traveled through this line of communication we shared, or if he only got the words.

"I didn't forget," he said as he came around the corner, his bare feet quiet on the smooth stone where my boots clicked and echoed with each step.

"But they're empty." I held one bag open and gestured to it with my other hand.

"Finna said to leave room for when we stop by on our way." My stomach grumbled at his words. I hadn't even thought about what we would be eating on the road. Hopefully it was food she'd be sending with us. "Besides," he started then, looking down at the same shirt and trousers he always wore before he stepped closer to me, our eyes locking as his magic crept around me, "I've already got everything I need."

I couldn't do anything to stop the blush that warmed my body as he turned to step back out into the crisp morning air. I managed to avoid coughing as I took a breath, clearing my head so I could focus.

The next stall belonged to my big bay mare, but before I could stop myself, I looked across the aisle to the chestnut. Her neck was stretched out over the door, her head turned just enough so that she could watch me. I crossed the short distance and carefully reached up to run the short hair of her forelock through my fingers, which was finally getting some length back after our season ended. I pressed my lips together, fighting a frown.

Was I ever going to see her again? Wally seemed

44

convinced that someone was going to buy her within the next few days, which meant I wouldn't be there when it happened. Maybe that was for the best. I wasn't sure I could handle watching her leave. I slid my hand down her face and went to collect a bridle and rope for the bay mare so I could lead her out for a quick grooming.

* * *

Sunlight was just peeking over the mountains as our party of eight made its way up the hill toward the house and the road beyond it. I'd already said my farewells to my family the night before since we were leaving so early, but to my surprise, Anne opened the kitchen door as we approached and stepped out, wrapping her shawl tightly around her shoulders. She peered up at us from underneath her bonnet as we slowed the horses to a stop. The leather bags attached to the saddles added to the typical shifting and jingling of tack that I always found so comforting.

"Anne?" I asked carefully, unable to read the expression on her face.

"I just wanted to remind you lads to take care. This is a big undertaking," she said, raising her eyebrows as she gestured to Henry's team with a tip of her head. They stood patiently, waiting as well-trained horses did. I wasn't worried about them at all, aside from making sure they got enough water and rest along the way. I glanced at Breck. If anything, we would be the ones who might do a little misbehaving, unbeknownst to her. He must've felt something from me, because his eyes flashed in my direction and he shifted in his saddle.

"No need to worry, Mrs. Walshe," he said then, giving her

one of his genuine smiles. "I grew up exploring all over the route we'll be taking, and you know Peter is a grand horseman. We'll look after one another." Our eyes met again, and then I looked down at Anne, nodding.

Her gaze shifted between us several times as she seemed to consider his words. The last time the three of us had been together, I was hiding in Breck's upstairs after she'd almost discovered us.

"Yes," she agreed finally, her curious expression softening. "Well, try to have some fun. What I'd give for a holiday at the beach," she said, grinning then. "To be young and carefree once more," she added wistfully, looking between the two of us again.

"Maybe after the baby comes, you and William can take a proper trip as a family," I suggested.

"Perhaps." She slipped one arm out from under the thick shawl, and I reached down for her to grab my hand and give it a squeeze. "Don't you worry about us here, either, alright? I know my husband already gave you a guilty conscience over leaving us for so long. You deserve this. Enjoy it." She let go of my hand and tucked her arm away again, taking two steps backward toward the house. We started to move the horses again, daylight growing by the minute, when Anne gasped. "Oh!"

"What is it?" I looked back at her, stopping my mare again.

"When you return, we're having a dinner. Nan and I have already started planning it. You'll invite Finna so we can finally meet her." Dread washed over me. I swallowed hard. "You're welcome to join us, too, Breck," she added, giving him a hopeful look. His eyebrows raised slowly, a smirk growing on his face as he gave a simple nod.

"We can talk about this when I get back," I managed, my voice strained. Anne grinned in a self-satisfied way as she turned on the cobblestones, and I urged my horse along, more ready than ever to leave the house and everyone in it behind for a little while.

I could just *feel* the questions he wanted to ask as we turned onto the road, Henry's horses following along dutifully. They were used to traveling this way to and from our matches, so they easily fell into a comfortable pace behind us. The bags they carried held supplies we might need to care for them along the way, including grooming tools and extra ropes. Our personal bags were settled just behind our saddles, topped with bed rolls that I'd been shocked to see Breck securing just before we set off. I'd envisioned this trip being spent riding by day and sleeping comfortably in a rented room at night. Apparently Breck had different plans.

"Go ahead and say it before you split in two from holding back," I said finally, bracing myself for this conversation. I knew he was going to make fun of me.

"What do you mean?" he asked casually. I noted the smirk he wore. We rode beside each other, so I could see the comfortable way he sat in his saddle. I tried to relax, too, easing the tension of my straight posture. I was accustomed to being on horseback for hours at a time, but I was always moving, swinging a mallet or doing drills. Our pace now was rather monotonous. I knew I would feel it the next day if I didn't try to keep myself out of one position.

"I know you want to ask why she's inviting Finna to the dinner."

"I already know why," he responded with an easy confidence. Of course. Her thoughts.

"Is she already planning our wedding, too?" I asked, coughing. He chuckled.

"Only parts of it. She's very preoccupied with the courtship and why you have been keeping it a secret for so long."

"It hasn't been that long," I complained. Then I scrunched my face and shot him a look. "But it's not even *real*. I don't know how to tell her that it's not Finna." Maybe I could start with the fact that she was probably hundreds or even thousands of years old.

"You could tell her it's me," he offered, and I couldn't stop my laugh. I felt bad for it instantly.

"I... you know I can't." My voice went quiet as I answered. Then more words came that I couldn't stop, either. "But I wish I could." His head turned to me fully, but I kept my eyes fixed on the road.

"Do you?"

As we approached the bridge, I let myself focus on the tunnel of trees I loved so much. The leaves had changed colors here, too, and the horses' hooves shuffled and crunched through the fallen ones until we met the worn stones that crossed the river. Then, the jumbled clip-clops of their steps, mixed with the running water below gave me another few moments to get enough confidence to give him my answer. We both looked over at the mill instinctively, as one does when they pass by a familiar place.

"I wish I could tell everyone," I said finally. Then my eyes flew wide. "But I'm not making the wish. I just. I—"

"I understand." His expression was gentle again, arched brows raised slightly. "I wish we could tell your family. I know it's difficult for you to keep the truth from them."

Something occurred to me then that I'd never thought

about before. "Can you tell what they would think? If they knew...?"

"I can only hear what people are thinking in the moment. I can't search their minds to find anything I want. That would be dangerous."

I let some silence stretch between us as we took the road that led toward the village and then beyond, in the direction of Finna's cottage. Remembering our first morning out together, when we'd hiked into the mountains, I knew that Breck enjoyed welcoming the early hours in with some quiet moments. And it was a nice morning for it. The weather was mild, clouds light with no threat of rain, though a fine mist did hang low around the river. I was glad to have the rising sun to our backs this time, rather than shining directly into our eyes, but that might've had more to do with the wicked hangover I'd had than anything else.

After we'd ridden in silence for a while, I couldn't help myself any longer. "What are you thinking about?"

His calm grin remained in place as he looked down and back up again. I could tell he was considering deflecting with a question of his own, or not saying anything at all, since that was sometimes easier than his forced truth. But finally, he said, "I'm thinking about my ceremony."

I'm sure he could feel the surprise spill from me. We hardly ever talked about these things. Not to say that he would then, either, but it was rare that he would even bring up that part of his life in our conversations. From the beginning, it was always his preference to talk about me instead.

"Are you nervous?" I asked. From what little information I'd gathered, mostly from Finna, his ceremony before Eabha would be his official acceptance into the Seelie high court. It wasn't something that you were born into. You had to be selected. It helped to guarantee that only the right fairies were chosen to protect the land, their people, and the humans.

"Not nervous. Just…" he drew in a deep breath and let it out slowly. I watched his throat as it worked down a swallow. "Winter solstice is fast approaching." That's when he'd told me his birthday was.

"Does it always happen on the day you were born? Or just someday after you come of age?"

"Traditionally, it happens on the day. But since we don't know for sure when I was born, that's just the best guess."

I could see he didn't enjoy talking about this, but I was so curious that I couldn't stop.

"Will the others be there?"

"Everyone is invited. It's similar to Lughnasa. Only bigger." He said this with a low level of distaste in his voice. I'd enjoyed myself that night, but I hadn't been the one sitting amongst the most powerful Seelie with endless responsibilities weighing on my shoulders.

A grin spread on my lips as I tried to imagine the scene. "You'll wear a crown?" He gave me a withering glare. That was a yes. The memory of him wearing the harvest wreath in his tousled hair, cheeks and nose dusted with shimmering freckles, was enough to warm my face. Other places, too.

"It's serious, Peter." His voice was quiet. He truly was worried about it. I forced away my thoughts and the teasing curve on my mouth.

"I know." After a pause, I added, "Are you sure you want to do it?"

His eyes dipped briefly, but he didn't respond. His silence was an answer, though I didn't know what the words were that he didn't want to say. Did he even have a choice in the matter? Why was Breck destined for this role? In my world, there were only two ways a man could rise to the top – wealth and a family name. If you were a nobody who came from nothing, you were lucky to find work, and even luckier if that job paid enough to support a spouse and children. On the rare occasion, it might be overheard that "new money" had entered the scene, but that did not guarantee that they'd be welcomed.

Maybe Breck's connection with Fallon and the others was enough to earn him the right to a spot on the high court. It seemed unlikely to me that an orphan found in the forest would magically be the right fit for such a role, but then again, maybe it had everything to do with his training. He had learned from the best since he was a lad. He'd clearly worked hard to earn their trust and acceptance, and Eabha must've agreed if he was still on course to have his ceremony in a little over a month.

It was another difference between his world and mine, I decided. His people could move up in the world without a title or an inheritance; my people could not. I wasn't ashamed to admit which one I preferred.

CHAPTER SIX

The horses slowed to a stop under our direction outside the cottage as the sun finally broke through behind us. I hoped that they would busy themselves with the patches of grass nearer to the trees we secured them to rather than the tasty-looking flowers and shrubs that decorated Finna's front garden.

"Come in, fellas!" she called as we approached, her voice carrying from the open kitchen window.

"Mornin', Finna," I called back as Breck let us in the door. She came around the corner with a bright smile, arms stretched wide. We leaned in at the same time to plant a kiss on each of her cheeks, eliciting a giggle from the tiny woman.

"Now. Aren't we just excited as we can be?" As we pulled apart, I noticed the way her eyes seemed to look not at us, but *around* us. At the energy we brought with us. "Come, I've packed some things for you to take along." A few steps into the kitchen later, my eyes went wide at what we found waiting for us on her table. There had to be at least twenty packages of thick parchment, wrapped neatly and tied up with twine.

"Finna," Breck started in protest, but she waved her hand at him, bracelets tinkling wildly on her wrist.

"Hush. You can eat what you like on the road and share anything left over when you arrive. It's polite to bring favors when you're visiting, especially if they're hosting you for several nights." I hadn't thought of this. I knew Henry wouldn't care what I brought, if anything, but I wanted Sarah to have a good opinion of me. I'd be seeing a lot more of her now, after all.

"Thank you," I told her, reaching for two of the packages that were nearly the same shape and size. I picked them up and brought one to my nose, inhaling deeply as I tried to catch a whiff of what was inside. My lungs ached in return. I couldn't smell anything. "How will we know what they all are?"

Breck picked up another and angled it for me to see. "It's written on them," he said with a faint smirk. I looked at his, and then the two I was holding. Sure enough, Finna's delicate handwriting was there, labeling each item in detail. Breck bumped his elbow against my arm playfully and set his bundle of hard cheese down. "Is there anything we can eat now? Peter is starving in silence."

"Of course! Sit, sit." Finna whirled, her skirts fanning out as she hurried around to her press. "You've time for tea?" she asked. Our eyes met and Breck nodded. There was always time for tea.

"I'll put it on," he offered, standing back up from the chair he'd just settled on seconds before. Watching the two of them work together in the kitchen always left me feeling a little helpless. Breck claimed that he only knew what he did out of necessity. Finna had taught him well, preparing him to go out into the world on his own, as young fairies did. But I knew that he secretly enjoyed it.

The nights I spent with him almost always resulted in me waking up alone. Sometimes, he would tell me that he'd leave for training before first light. Other times, he had to go because the river was calling to him. Usually, he just couldn't sleep, so he would get up and get started with his day. Once, however, I'd woken to him at the stove, silently preparing tea for us by the light of a candle. I watched as he took extra care to remove the leaves from one of his mint plants, rolling them between his slender fingers, his rings clicking together softly as they met on each pass, before he placed them in the water to steep. For him, the steps to make the tea were as important as drinking it. He put thought into the process; a serenity that I swear you could taste.

Finna's kitchen had many things, but fresh mint leaves were not one of them. Instead, Breck opened a cannister of dried leaves to use as Finna placed thick slices of dry, dense bread on plates for us. She served it with soft butter and jam and urged Breck to eat while she finished the tea. Since there was little room left on the table, we held the plates as we ate, catching any crumbs that fell. By the end of my piece, I was glad to have tea to wash it all down.

My anticipation and nerves were making it hard to sit still. I glanced out the window at the horses as I stood up from my chair. Finna began loading our goods into a basket to carry outside as she and Breck discussed the places he planned for us to stop along the way. Some of the other villages and landmarks sounded vaguely familiar, but I had already decided that I would leave all of that up to him. I was just hoping for an uneventful journey that would deliver us to a relaxing visit with my best friend and his bride.

"Elina is going to make sure Fallon keeps her promise," Finna said as she hoisted the basket up by its braided handle, her voice straining slightly at the weight.

"What promise?" I asked, opening the door and stepping out of her way.

"She's not to bother either one of you until you return home. No matter what happens." The horses turned their attention to us as we made our way across the garden. Finna set the basket down by my gelding and puffed out a sigh of relief as she straightened her back, eyeing the animals cautiously. Breck came around her and started picking the bundles of parchment up to place them carefully in his empty saddle bags. Finna turned and brushed her hair away from her face, giving me another smile and beckoning me for a hug. She embraced me tightly. *"Take good care of my Breckabhainn,"* she whispered against my ear.

Before I could respond, she let me go and turned to give an even bigger hug to Breck. She squeezed his chest until he made a helpless little noise, his body's response to the last bit of air leaving his lungs. I couldn't help but chuckle as he smoothed his hands over the front of his shirt when she released him.

"You know she'll still reach me if she needs me," he said after a deep breath.

"She better not! And if she does, she'll be right to fear what's coming," she warned. My eyebrows went up as Breck and I shared another glance, both of us surprised at how serious she sounded about it. He finished loading the last few packages into the bags at the horses' hindquarters as I went to untie my mare. I put my foot in the stirrup and swung my leg over, trying hard to avoid catching my boot on the extra items attached to the back of the saddle. The last thing I needed was to injure myself before we ever really left. As I wondered what we would do if something *did* happen to us on the way, Finna waved us a final farewell. The moment her cottage disappeared behind a curve in the road, Breck sighed.

"Sorry about her," he muttered.

"What did she mean by that? No matter what happens?" I pressed.

"Nothing bad is going to happen," he reassured me.

I'd told him that I trusted him, and I meant it, so I just nodded and looked ahead. The road beyond the cottage was uncharted territory for me. I swept my gaze across the valley that opened on either side of us. The thinning trees gave way to an expanse of land that had no buildings, no walls. Just nature. The river was in the distance, carving through the rise and fall of the gentle hills. I drew in a slow breath and coughed roughly before I could raise my arm to cover it, disturbing the peace and a cluster of birds from the brush near the road. Aside from the tilt of one ear, my horse didn't respond at all.

My thoughts went to the chestnut mare. To the morning she tossed me, when she was barely rideable. I knew that she would've responded differently now to the rush of birds flapping away.

"What are you thinking about?" Breck asked, echoing my earlier question.

I felt the frown tug at the corners of my lips. "Wally is selling the chestnut mare," I told him.

"When?" The tone of his voice went sharper in his response, indicating his surprise.

I shrugged. "Today. Tomorrow. I'm not sure, but soon. He said there are a few people interested, so someone will make an offer good enough to make it quick." I was happy about that, at least. She was worth a lot. More than money could buy, in my opinion, but I knew Wally would get a generous price for her, too.

Breck didn't say anything right away, but I felt his magic slip around me, curling gracefully around my wrist and up, brushing at my cheek in an invisible, comforting stroke. Before it disappeared, I breathed his magic into my lungs, the chill of it an instant relief. I closed my eyes, holding the breath in for as long as I could before my body forced it out with several short coughs.

"Will you get another? You could afford a decent one with your winnings, couldn't you?"

A thought I was trying hard to ignore crept up my back. Each of Henry's horses behind us were worth more than what I'd earned during the last season. I would never be able to justify a horse from the breeder he used, even if we won a few more seasons in a row.

"Maybe Wally will find another diamond for me," I said, trying to keep the conversation light. I didn't want to talk about how I'd given most of my winnings to William to help support the family and the business as we continued to recover from what we'd lost during the illness. The truth was that I couldn't afford even a good horse with what I'd kept behind for personal spending. I didn't want for anything, but it was still difficult to know that without my family name and the resources our business provided, I wasn't worth much at all.

"He needs to be careful in these… business transactions," Breck cautioned. I could only imagine the things he'd learned about Wally at our matches. I'd always known he participated in some things that involved money touching lots of hands, but I didn't want to know the details. I was only concerned about the horses.

"Wally's mind must be a terrifying place," was all I could say.

Breck made a thoughtful noise. "Terrifying isn't the word I would use."

"Shady, then?" I guessed.

"Sticky," he decided finally. It made me laugh. That was probably true, with all the secret meetings and quiet deals. Wally was a good man, but he had his vices. Didn't we all, though? I looked at mine as he adjusted his shoulders slightly, arching his back.

"Getting sore already?" I wondered if his bare feet in the stirrups made much difference with his support in the saddle. I'd never ridden without my boots.

He grinned and turned to look at me, his eyes sliding from my face down to my hips. "Few have such flawless carriage." His gaze lingered at where I was planted in the saddle. "Even fewer have such impressive muscles." He let go of the reins with his hand nearest to me and gripped the outside of his thigh, jiggling what little he had there to move around. "You don't even have to hold on, do you?"

I snorted out a laugh and let the thin straps of leather rest across the back of my mare's neck. I wasn't sure what to do with my empty hands, so I rested them atop my legs, elbows slightly bent. "It's a bit more impressive when we're going faster," I told him. I couldn't exactly show off with two other horses tagging along.

"Oh, I can speak on that," he replied smoothly. The

cheeky bastard. "Though, you're still quite adequate when you're going slow."

I scoffed and picked up the reins again. "Adequate, huh? I'll have to work on that. Must not be getting enough practice."

* * *

We rode on as the sun continued to rise in the now-cloudless sky, warming our backs to the point that I wanted to remove my riding jacket before I started sweating. We steered the horses to the edge of the road; they took little time shuffling through the grass to the edge of the river. Breck landed with a slight wobble as he dismounted. As I pulled my jacket off my arms, I watched him move upstream from the horses and kneel by the water, cupping it in his hands and bringing it to his mouth.

"Alright there?" I asked as I tucked my shed garment under the strap of a saddle bag. I crouched beside him as he took another long pull from his hands. When they were empty, he rubbed them over his face and back through his hair, momentarily exposing his heavily freckled forehead. Scant blue flecks appeared across his nose and cheeks from the dampness, and something twisted inside me.

He stared out at the river and swallowed. "My lower back is... painful," he admitted quietly.

My lips pressed together as I tried to hide my grin. "Aye. We've been riding for several hours now." I moved closer to the water so I could get my own drink. I felt it go down, the chill racing toward my gut, and wiped my mouth on my sleeve. "Maybe we should rest for a while and eat something that Finna packed for us." Breck nodded but didn't move, so I got to my feet and went to my gelding to search through his bags.

A minute later I'd found cheese and some bread. Breck had managed to lie flat on the grass, his legs pulled up at the knees and his hands resting on his stomach. The poor lad. I would have to do a better job of making sure that we took breaks to give his body a chance to adjust. The horses had wandered a short distance and were grazing happily, so I went to join Breck and sat next to him.

He turned his head to look at me, his blue eyes bright in the sunlight. "Sorry," he said.

My brows pinched together as I started unwrapping the twine. "No need for that." I broke off a piece of the hard cheese and held it out for him. He groaned as he pushed himself into a sitting position. As he took a bite, I ripped off a hunk of bread for myself. "You know, you could probably remedy the pain with some regular lessons." I savored the grin that pulled from him. "And it just so happens that I know a fella who gives fantastic lessons. The best around."

"Do you, now?" Breck asked with a forced interest, playing along. "He must have a full schedule if he's the best."

"Quite full. But I'm sure he could make time for you." I chewed a bite of bread and finally tore my gaze from the side of his face to look out at the water that was silently slipping by. Jokes aside, having a few hours a week that I was guaranteed to see him would be grand. I'd do anything to be able to spend more time with him. Even half a day into our journey, I still couldn't believe that we'd been able to make the trip possible. It was even better knowing that he wouldn't be called away by Fallon for once.

Breck finished his cheese and lowered himself back into

the grass gingerly. I looked down at him as his eyes closed. "Does this fella also offer massages?"

I laughed and put my hand on his thigh, which was still angled up toward his bent knee. I rubbed it slowly, working the muscle there. "That could probably be arranged. Might cost extra, though."

Breck hummed and nodded as well as he could with his head against the ground. "If his hands are anything like yours, I'll gladly pay it."

I felt the heat start to creep up my neck at his words. The hand in question moved to the inside of his thigh then, sliding up and back along the seam that held his trousers together. Breck's leg relaxed under my touch, leaning out until it rested against my own thigh. He seemed otherwise unaffected, but the way my pulse quickened made me swallow hard. My eyes were drawn down as my hand approached where the seam ended at the top.

I hesitated. We were exposed, out in the open, in the middle of the day. Anyone could be traveling along the road just like we were. Anyone could see us. There wasn't even a tree or a tall shrub to hide us from view. Inside my head was a swirl of confliction.

I felt Breck's hand on mine then. He brushed my knuckles with his fingertips and then wrapped his fingers around my wrist, bringing my hand to his lips so he could kiss the back of it. "It's okay," he said gently. With some effort and another grunt, he managed to get to his feet.

I watched him as he made his way back to where the horses were waiting. I let out a heavy breath and shook my head a little to clear my mind, turning to pick up the remnants of our impromptu picnic before I stood up. I tried to smooth the scrambled mess in my head so I could form a clear thought for him. An apology. An explanation. I didn't want him to think it had anything to do with him, because it didn't.

"Breck—" I started, taking long strides to catch up. Before I could reach him, he was back in the saddle, a pinched look on his face as he tried to find a more comfortable position. My gelding stepped sideways with his front leg to brace the movement on his back.

"I'll be happy to find a soft place to lie down tonight," he said, giving me a smile that looked more like a wince. The battle of my emotions raged on, but in the end, I just returned his pained grin.

"Me, too."

CHAPTER SEVEN

The road had taken us through two smaller villages, and then a third that was split in half by a wide part of the river. The bridge connecting the two sides stretched impressively across the water, dwarfing the one we had at home. Breck rode ahead to make sure that we didn't take up the entire street with our team as we passed drivers with carts and pedestrians. Most appeared to be men dressed in decent clothes on their way to the pubs for the evening. Hats and thick moustaches were abundant.

I could tell by the way the villagers ignored us, or offered curt greetings rather than suspicious glances, that people traveling through must've been common. That meant it would be easy to find an inn with stables for the night.

I was about to ask Breck if he knew where the inn was when he turned off the main stretch of road, onto a narrower one that was walled in with terraced brick houses. The light from the windows allowed me a brief glance into some of the homes as we passed by. I wondered what life was like for them. What kinds of families lived here, so close together? Had the illness come for them, too? A group of children stopped briefly to watch us as we rode by, interrupting whatever game they had been playing. I thought of Lucy and hoped that she wasn't giving them too much trouble back home.

The road curved at the end and sloped away from the houses, and I had to pull my mare to a stop so she wouldn't follow Breck off the path into the trees.

"Where are you going?" I asked, glancing back over my shoulder.

"Finding a place for us to sleep," he called back.

I was speechless. What about the inn? A place to get a drink? A bed? When he didn't stop, I urged my horse forward down the hill after him, Henry's two still close behind. I scanned our surroundings. The oranges and yellows of the leaves above us caught the faltering light. More were scattered on the ground. The sweet, musky smell of them being pressed into the dirt by the horses' hooves met my nose as we continued along the unmarked trail.

After ducking under several low branches, we came to a large one that the horses could barely pass under, so we were forced to dismount. I felt the faint ache in my own hips then, so I knew Breck must've been in agony. The only indication was the muffled sound he made as his foot met the ground. He brought the leather straps over the gelding's head and walked him to another branch, looping them into a knot to secure him in place. I found another sturdy one to tie my mare to, curiosity clouding my confusion over what exactly Breck was getting us into.

When I turned, he was looking at me expectantly, his hand stretched out in my direction. I slid mine into his, lacing our fingers together as my cheeks warmed. The last time we'd been in this situation, he was about to show me something unforgettable. I got the feeling it was happening again.

"*Do you trust me?*" he whispered, a soft grin on his lips. I nodded. "*Close your eyes.*" I did.

He kept me close, putting his free hand on my cap when we had to avoid another branch. There was a slight incline, and I was proud of myself for not tripping over anything or being completely out of breath by the time we stopped walking. It helped that Breck's magic had washed over me like a winter breeze, filling my lungs and cooling my skin until the hair on my arms stood up.

When Breck didn't say anything, I cleared my throat and asked, "Can I look now?"

"*Mhmm,*" he confirmed airily.

When my eyes opened, I had to blink at the harsh light.

The sunset was reflecting off a lake in front of us, bright gold that melted into a rippling honey along the surface. Mountains and clouds framed the scene with soft pinks and purples. The air I'd managed to hold onto left me in a breath of awe. A small light zipping by caught my attention. I turned to look at the space we'd stopped in. It was a clearing by the edge of the water, framed by the autumn-hued trees. More swoops of light passed over us. Fairies. That meant...

"Still want to go back to the inn?"

My eyes shot to his. Freckles sparkled like tiny silver and blue gems across the middle of his face. He brought our joined hands up to kiss the back of mine again, giving it a gentle squeeze. I felt it like a wave through my whole body.

"*Here's grand,*" I breathed, still overwhelmed by this place. By him.

"Let's gather the horses, then." He turned to start back toward wherever we'd left them.

"Wait," I told him. There was an urgency in my voice that I hadn't expected. He hadn't either, because he looked back at me with a wrinkle between his brows. "Just... wait," I repeated. I wanted to look at him. I wanted to soak in the beauty of his features. I wanted to live in this world of his so I could see him like this forever. I brought the hand he wasn't holding up and brushed my thumb across his cheek. He was made of magic, and I never wanted to let him go.

I don't know how long he let me stare at him. Time felt a little blurry as we stood there by the lake. The sun slid behind the distant mountains. The warm colors of the trees faded to a deep blue. Bugs took up their nighttime singing, and the temperature dropped. For some reason, of all the things I wanted to say to him, the first words out of my mouth were, "Do you know how to start a fire?"

Breck nodded. "But I need two hands for it."

Regretfully, I let him go. We collected the horses before it got too dark to see and brought them to the clearing. I helped find sticks while Breck unpacked some of our things. Before long, he had a fire going, and we sat around it with packages of food between us. We ate the rest of the bread and cheese from earlier before we opened a few more, including one that Finna had labeled *For Peter*. I unwrapped it carefully, tossing the twine into the flames by my feet. I was hoping for dessert. As I peeled back the edge of the parchment, something rolled onto the ground with a dull thud.

"What the—" I picked up the apple and managed to keep my jaw from going slack in surprise. Another one remained on my lap, nestled between my outstretched legs. Breck chuckled as he took another bite of his scone. He was on his back again, head resting on one of the saddle bags he'd removed to serve as a pillow. "How?" The food bundle had been perfectly square.

His brow arched as a smirk formed on his mouth. "Magic," he said simply.

"Is it safe to eat?" I asked, studying the fruit in my hand. It looked normal enough.

"You might want to brush the dirt off first," he suggested with another little laugh.

I narrowed my eyes at him. "That sounds more like you avoiding the question than a yes."

"It's safe to eat."

I wiped it on my shirt like he'd advised and sunk my teeth into the side with a juicy pop. It was sweet. We ate in a comfortable silence, the small fire providing just enough warmth and ambiance to make me feel more tired by the minute. My eyes kept drifting between the mesmerizing light of the flames and the equally intoxicating effect they were having on Breck's cheeks. His lids were growing heavy, too. I finished my apple and rubbed my hands on my trousers before I shifted to match his position on my own sleep sack. I adjusted the bag behind my head and stared up at the leaves and branches above, which were dark except for the faint glow from the fairies hiding in them.

My thoughts started to wander. "Breck?"

"*Hmm?*" he drawled sleepily.

"Are we staying like this all night? In the… in your world?" I didn't know if that was a good way to word it. He didn't respond right away, and for a moment I thought he'd fallen asleep.

"It's our world. You're just seeing it the way I do." There was a pause, and then he added, "Is that alright?"

"Yes," I said right away. "It's wonderful."

Wonderful? I rolled my eyes at myself. But it was.

I turned onto my side so I could see him. His eyes were closed, his chest moving evenly. I soaked in this rare moment. It was strange to see his expressive eyebrows and lips so relaxed. Maybe those riding lessons really would be beneficial if they could help him sleep.

* * *

Morning came quickly. My legs were stiff and my back was sore. I didn't know if traveling all day or sleeping on the ground was more to blame. I tried to stretch out what I could as I sat up to the unfamiliar place we'd spent the night. The lake wasn't quite as stunning as it had been at sunset, but the tranquility of it all had me blinking out at the water as my haze of sleep faded. I rubbed a hand over my face and turned to count the horses. They were all there.

My attention fell to the spot Breck had slept in. His bed roll was already packed away. It was back on the gelding's saddle, along with the bags he'd removed the night before. I wondered how long he'd been awake as I forced myself to my feet. The fire had smoldered to a thin whisp of smoke overnight, which I realized when a shiver hit me. This one wasn't from magic, though. Just the cool air.

Where are you? I thought for him. He was usually quick to say something when he realized I was awake, but everything around me was quiet except for a few birds in the trees. I glanced up and squinted at the leaves. I couldn't see the fairies anymore. Did they hide during the day, or had the magic faded from around us while I slept?

After I'd found a spot to relieve myself, I walked carefully to the edge of the water. It looked calm enough to walk across, except for a few places that rippled from the slight breeze that was blowing. I crossed my arms over my chest and studied the clouds. They looked innocent in the moment, but I knew better than to ever assume a rainstorm wasn't possible.

In an attempt to quell my rising concern over the fact that I was still by myself, I went to check on the horses. I ran my hand down my mare's leg and she dutifully bent it for me so I could check her hoof. I repeated the process with the other horses, stopping to grab a pick from the saddle bag so I could remove a few stones I found.

I led them in groups of two to the edge of the lake so they could drink. The youngest of Henry's horses took the opportunity to splash in until she was chest deep. I let go just in time to avoid being pulled in with her. A bath sounded nice to wash away the dirt from the road, but not in water that cold. Surely there would be a tub to use when we reached the estate. According to Breck, that wouldn't be for another full day's worth of riding, though.

The young mare took a few steps deeper into the water and further out of my reach. Henry's horses were trained to respond to different cues than my own. I was momentarily glad that I was alone as I made a few obnoxious kissing sounds with my lips to get her to turn in the right direction. I stretched out to grab the rope as she came back to me and had it in my fingers when something caused her to startle.

She jerked her head back, and with it went the rest of her, front legs flailing up out of the water. The icy splash landed directly on the front of my trousers, soaking me to the skin in all the worst places. I yelped and cursed louder than I meant to as both horses spooked away from the water to rejoin the others by the trees. I turned to the sound of laughter and found Breck collecting them before they could go too far.

"Good morning," he said, the humor still in his voice.

"Is it?" I asked, unable to mask my annoyance. I wiped pointlessly at my wet clothes.

"Let me help you," Breck offered as he finished securing the horses. I huffed out a deep sigh and coughed a few times. It would probably take a couple more to dislodge my bollocks from wherever they'd retreated to inside my body. My teeth threatened to chatter as his magic swept around my ankles and rushed to my midsection, the dampness in my clothes drawn away in an instant.

"Thanks," I mumbled in relief. I rubbed my fingers on the front of my trousers again, just to confirm that they were dry. Breck started gathering the things that remained on the ground where I'd slept. "Where did you go?" I used the side of my boot to kick some dirt over the collection of burned sticks to smother any flame that might've still been hiding within them.

"The village." His response was simple, but it held weight. Someone had needed his help.

"Is everything alright?" I watched as he expertly rolled my bed and attached it behind the saddle.

"It is now." His tone was serious. "I'm sorry you woke up alone."

I laughed bitterly. "Aye. Leave me alone for too long and you see what trouble I can get into." I gestured to my crotch with a sweeping motion for emphasis. His gaze lingered where I'd inadvertently directed him to look as he checked the saddle bags, an alluring smirk settling on his features.

"*Sea, mo ghrá,*" he said gently. My pulse spiked, even though I didn't know what his words meant. "Next time I'll be more helpful when you've some trouble there. But we really should be on our way. Are you ready?"

I was only able to nod in response. We escorted the horses through the trees, ducking again under the same low branches we'd avoided the evening before, until we reached the road. I was hopeful that the walk would give me time to clear my head, but instead I spent the whole time staring at Breck's back as I followed him. Even after a long day of travel and a night of sleeping on the unforgiving ground, he was only as disheveled as he normally was. His hair was never styled with wax or oil, and his clothes were never pressed, but somehow, he always looked... perfect.

I, on the other hand, likely looked as if I'd rolled down a steep hill after our night outside. My worn cap was good at hiding my loose curls when I couldn't manage them, but even that could only help so much. Luckily, my riding jacket did a decent job of covering up the wrinkles that had formed in my shirt. I glanced down at my navy waistcoat and then at my newly dry trousers, and Breck's words came back to me in a rush just in time for us to mount up.

I forced myself to look away from him as he moved gracefully into the saddle on my gelding's back. I put my left foot in the stirrup, and with a slight bounce I pulled up, sending my right leg over my bay mare. I lowered myself carefully to the smooth leather seat, trying to avoid any unwanted friction. I wasn't sure which was worse, the tightness between my legs or the relentless thoughts of how badly I wanted him.

If I wasn't careful, I knew those thoughts would reach Breck in a flood of emotion. I wasn't ashamed of my feelings for him. I worried constantly, though, that I would come on too strong. He hadn't said that he loved me back. I took a breath as deep as I could without my lungs reacting and let it out slowly. My eyes closed briefly as the air left my chest.

In an effort to disguise my true thoughts, I started letting images of other things play across my mind. Almost immediately, it was the chestnut mare. My heart sank. Was she already gone? I opened my eyes to find Breck staring at me, his arched eyebrows high, showing his concern. I sent the thought to him. His expression softened.

"Try not to worry about her. You trained her well, and that opened a future for her that never would've existed without you." That was probably true.

"Goodbye is hard for me," I said before I could realize how heavy it was.

"You've gone through immeasurable amounts of it." He paused for a moment as we rode beside each other, the horses lazily following the dusty road we'd come back to. "It's why they cried over you leaving. Lucy and Anne."

"Anne?" When had Anne cried?

Breck nodded. "She'd been crying before she came out to say her farewells yesterday morning," he explained. "She worries about you more than you realize." His tone was somber.

I was silent for a long moment, considering my next question. "Can you tell me?"

"What she was thinking?" he asked, cautious.

"I can't remember much about what happened then. Almost nothing. And now, the things I used to be able to remember are starting to disappear, too." I shrugged one shoulder. "I never wanted to upset her by asking too many questions. But she was the last one to see them, I think. Mammy and Dad, my siblings, and…" I stopped.

"And Jamie," he added.

"And Jamie," I agreed, barely above a whisper. I never knew how she got his letter. Had she found it somewhere, or had he given it to her directly? I'd always thought Jamie snuck in my window to see me that last time. Climbing up to my window would've been incredibly difficult, but what if he'd tried to come see me and Anne refused to let him in? Maybe it had been his only option. I quickly spiraled on thoughts of everything he went through. Everything he did for me in those last few days of his life. My emotions grew thick in my throat until Breck finally spoke.

"She was thinking the same thing she thought about when she came looking for you at the mill, that morning after Lughnasa." He seemed to hesitate.

"Yes?" I prompted. His mouth opened, and then he sighed, pushing a hand back through his hair. What could it be that he was struggling so much to say? "Breck, what is it? You can tell me."

"I *have* to tell you," he corrected, an edge to his voice. It wasn't anger, though.

"Nevermind," I said quickly. "I don't want to know." He visibly relaxed, but it did nothing to soothe my own worries. What could it possibly be to get a reaction like that from him? "I'm sorry I asked."

CHAPTER EIGHT

We stopped more often to rest that second day, taking the time to enjoy everything Finna sent. Only a few packages of food remained by the time we ate an early supper just outside another village along the river. We sat beneath two massive ash trees that had already lost most of their colorful leaves, creating a natural blanket to sit on. We each leaned against one, the deep vertical ridges of the bark not particularly comfortable against our tired backs, but it was better than nothing.

"It looks like Finna planned for your request last night," Breck said as he read what she'd written on the bundle he was holding. The twine came untied easily and he set it beside his hip. "It says to open *very* carefully in big letters." I chewed a bite of my slightly stale piece of bread and watched as he unfolded the thick parchment. A surprised laugh barked out of me as the neck of a bottle emerged.

"She packed *wine?*" I leaned forward to take it as he held it out for me.

"It's quite good. She makes it herself," he explained as he settled back against his trunk.

"Aye, she told me about it." I studied the bottle and the cork at the top. "Shall we?" I asked, meeting his gaze across the distance between us. He just grinned. I examined the cork again, trying to decide the best method to get it out. If there was a stick the right size, I could poke it down into the bottle. "She didn't happen to pack a corkscrew in there, did she?" I wondered absently as I scanned the ground for something that might work.

"No need," he replied. "You might want to move it, though."

I looked at him again and then down at the dark green bottle I'd nestled securely between my upper thighs. I decided handing it back to him was the safest option. Within seconds, the cork popped against the pad of his thumb. When he returned it to me, the glass was as cold as the water from the river. I removed the stopper, took a tentative smell, and put it to my lips.

"How does she make everything so feckin' *good*?" He took the bottle from me again for his own taste. He didn't need to answer that. "I know, I know. Magic."

"She's also had lots of time to perfect her hobbies," Breck added, taking another quick sip before he gave the bottle back. I'd never seen him willingly drink so much of anything, aside from tea. He'd probably been drinking it since he was a lad. The thought – mixed with the wine – brought a warmth to my chest.

"How old do you think she is, truly?" My voice was low, as if she might hear us.

Breck laughed and rolled his eyes up toward the nearly bare branches hanging over us, his head resting back against the rough bark. "I really don't know," he confessed. I took another long pull and noted the way his legs weren't crossed like usual. They were stretched out like mine, ankles stacked, our feet resting beside each other's knees.

"But if you just had to guess," I goaded, and then let it rest. "She doesn't even look that much older than me. I thought she could be William's age when I first met her."

"And she's looked exactly the same since the day I met her," he said, taking the bottle when I held it out for him. Our fingers brushed in the process. I noticed the faint grin it caused on his mouth before it formed around the lip of our shared refreshment.

We plowed through it faster than either of us realized as we sat and talked, and soon I drained the last drop with my head tilted all the way back. I went so far that the bottle clanked with a hollow echo against the tree behind me.

Breck let out a hearty giggle, and a laugh of air sprayed from me, creating another amusing sound as my breath blew across the narrow opening. I picked my head back up to face him and noticed the way his cheeks held more color than I was used to. I swallowed and set the bottle down by my leg, not worried that it fell over since it was empty.

"Beautiful," I said before I could stop myself. Breck's grin grew, and he turned his head away. I bumped my boot gently against his thigh with a tilt of my foot. "I mean it."

"You've had too much wine," he told me, though he was still smiling.

"I've had just enough to be honest." It was a dangerous place for me to be most of the time, with so many secrets to hold. But with Breck, I didn't have to hide.

"That could still get you in trouble," he said lightly as he turned to collect the scattered aftermath of our meal. Rather than crumpling the parchment up into little balls as I had done with some of the others on our previous stops, he gently smoothed and folded each piece against the top of his thigh. I watched his hands as he worked to create a small stack of the papers, before he collected the discarded lengths of twine and stood up to place all of it in the empty saddle bag. "Good thing we'll arrive in the morning, now that we ate everything we packed."

As much as I was looking forward to seeing Henry, the fact that our time together just the two of us was coming to an end made my chest burn a little. Having a taste of what it was like only made me long for more.

"Thank you," I started, drawing his attention.

"What for?" he asked as he slid the leather strap back through the fastening on the bag and reached to start unbuckling one of the bed rolls. My eyes fell to watch his calves flex as he lifted onto his toes to reach the far tie. He was more muscular than he gave himself credit for.

"For agreeing to come with me," I answered, recognizing that without the drink in my system, I would've started to feel embarrassed about sharing my feelings. "I was worried you'd say no. Or you'd just feel obligated because I needed your help. You know, fairy things. You didn't, did you?"

Breck's hands slowed on his task as he turned to look at me then, and the expression on his face was hard to read. He pulled the roll of thick fabric down and set it by the tree he'd been propped up on, then stepped over and sat next to me, our shoulders touching. I turned my head slightly and watched as he pulled his legs up and crossed them, leaning back against the trunk like before.

The truth we'd refused to talk about hung heavily between us in that moment. Even if Breck did love me, the magic that festered in my lungs and kept me alive would also keep us apart.

From the time I was little, it had been drilled into my head that when you grew up, you'd find someone, and you'd marry them to show your commitment and faithfulness. That learned behavior had begun as a whisper, then a murmur, and now it was fully shouting in the back of my mind. I wanted to devote myself to him and him alone in a way that everyone would know it. But it was impossible.

A wave of something came over me then, warming my skin in a hurry, and I swallowed hard. As I tried to decide if it was from my emotions or from the wine, Breck picked up one of the ash tree's discarded yellowish-brown leaves by the stem and twirled it between his thumb and finger. The way the pointed shape of it blurred on each spin reminded me of the tiny golden wings of the fairies we'd seen in the trees the night before. They were beautiful, too.

Slowly, I realized that Breck still hadn't responded to my question. Maybe he did feel obligated to help me. Maybe he'd decided somewhere along the way that he didn't want to be on this trip together, after all. He wasn't watching the leaf whirling back and forth between his fingertips. Instead, his eyes were cast down and unfocused, indicating that he was in his head even more than I was. My heart sank.

I pulled one of my legs up at the knee, my boot dragging through the leaves, so I could get to my feet and unpack my things for the night. I hadn't noticed until then, from our place under the thick branches, that we'd soon be in the dark.

Before I could stand, though, Breck was gripping my thigh, holding me in place. I didn't have time to express my confusion before he'd turned to face me on his knees and put one leg over both of mine. My hands remained atop the dirt and leaves as his moved carefully to the sides of my neck. They were so cold against my skin that his touch almost burned as the chill swept through my whole body.

When our eyes met, my breath caught in my throat. I choked on a cough. A breeze stirred the air around us, tossing his hair to the side for a moment and ruffling his shirt, but all I could see was the look on his face. His freckles twinkled like stars on a cloudless night, matching the intensely blue color of his eyes as he stared at me. I coughed again and breathed in deeply, knowing his magic would help ease the pain in my chest. It was practically pouring from him, as the rapids did over the rocks outside the mill back home, though it could only be felt and not seen.

I started to say something, but before the words could come, his lips were on mine. My eyelids clamped shut. I hardly felt the way his kiss pressed my head back into the unyielding ridges of the bark, or the way my skin had broken out into tiny bumps from the cold.

"There is nowhere I would rather be than wherever you are," he whispered against my mouth.

My body shook as he kissed me again. I finally remembered my hands and brought them up to his back, pressing with my fingers to hold him closer. His hips settled against mine, lighting me up all over again.

"Breck, I—" I wanted to tell him more. More about how I felt. More about what I wanted. What I hoped he wanted, too. But his delicate fingertips were against my lips before I could say any of it.

"I had an argument with Fallon before we left," he confessed quietly, watching my mouth as if all he could think about was kissing me again. I wished that he would. "I cannot seem to convince her that you will not distract me from my responsibilities, even though I've continued to prove otherwise." His eyebrows pinched together as his fingers stroked lightly at my chin and jaw. "The only reason I was able to come with you is because Finna got involved. I don't know what I'd do without her."

Breck's thoughts were hard to keep up with as he said them. He spoke quietly, but also quickly, and some of the words didn't make sense to me as they seemed to tumble from his mouth in whichever language was easiest for him to process them in. He was breathing hard, and the look of worry on his face continued to grow. I wasn't sure what my own features looked like, other than the fact that I was certain my lips were turning blue. I brought my quivering hand to the side of his face, brushing his hair back with my fingers as the wind had done, and his eyes finally found mine again in a snap of attention.

"Oh," he said in surprise as what his magic was doing to me finally seemed to register. I felt it slip away instantly. My muscles relaxed with a final shiver.

"Breck—" I tried again, my voice unsteady.

"I'm going to ask Eabha—"

A crack of thunder directly over our heads made both of us jump. It startled the horses, too, and both of us scrambled to our feet to get to them before they hurt themselves tugging on their restraints. Moments later, the rain came. The naked branches above did nothing to keep the fat, cold drops from finding their way to us.

"We can't stay here," Breck called to me. Right on time to help emphasize why, a flash of lightning streaked across the dark clouds. Naturally, we'd managed to pick the two tallest trees within sight to rest under.

"Shite!" was all I could think to yell back as we rushed to secure our things and untie the horses so we could get to some kind of proper shelter. A normal rain shower would've been one thing, but I couldn't believe we'd somehow missed the weather brewing into something much stronger. I threw another glance at Breck as we both pulled ourselves into our saddles. Did his magic have something to do with the sudden change?

I didn't have time to give it more thought. The only thing I needed to focus on was getting the horses out of the storm. The village was small, so the odds of finding a true livery stable weren't good, but I was hopeful that someone would be willing to shelter us until the worst of it was over. Each pelting raindrop chipped away at the buzz I'd been feeling, though I could tell that my control in the saddle was a little off. I coughed out the deep breath I took to help clear my head as the horses' hoofbeats transitioned from the swishy, wet grass to the hard dirt of the road that would be mud before much longer.

After a hurried survey of the options spread out across the valley, a bolt of light so bright that everything went silver and white made the decision easy for me. I cut my mare back into the grass. My gelding and Henry's horses followed closely behind. It was far from ideal to be moving so fast with the horses tied as they were, but the situation called for it.

My stomach dipped as I realized the break in the low wall I was aiming for wasn't actually an opening, but a spot where the rocks had fallen into a pile and were obscured by over-grown grass. With no time to change direction, we vaulted the stones and cleared them without issue. I whipped my head around in time to see Breck flying over them effortlessly on my gelding's back. I decided that was an image I'd tuck away to fantasize about later as I turned my attention back toward my target.

The house was tiny and plain, not much smaller than Finna's cottage, but certainly less decorated. Only a few flowers were alive in the bed next to the front door, which held mere streaks of the red paint it was once covered with. Nearby stood a barn, larger than the cottage itself and constructed with more of the jagged, stacked stones the walls were made of. A thatched roof in need of repair topped it off. With no time to second-guess myself, I was out of the saddle and racing toward the shabby door before my mare had come to a full stop.

The door opened a crack after I'd knocked a few times, and I was greeted by a woman with a bundle in her arms. Two more sets of eyes peered up at me after pushing the woman's skirts aside.

"I apologize—" I hadn't realized I was so out of breath until I started to speak, and I coughed a few times into my sleeve. "I apologize for disturbing you, but I was wondering if we might be able to shelter our horses in your barn until the storm passes?"

"We?" she asked quietly. The door opened a little more, just enough for her to see the horses and Breck, who had dismounted and was holding the team with his back to us, shirt shoulders translucent.

"My companion and I are just passing through. We won't cause you any trouble, we just need a place to—" Thunder cut off my words. The children shrieked and the baby in her arms started to cry. She shushed and held the littlest one close to her chest and nodded curtly, shutting me out with the storm.

The barn had no doors, just an opening that was barely tall enough for the horses to pass under with their heads held high. We crowded into the small space with little concern for what we'd find inside. It was dark enough that I nearly ran into the back wall, if it hadn't been for the bucket I kicked over in my haste, making me trip and spooking the horses away from the clattering noise it made.

"Peter?" Breck asked from somewhere behind me, worry in his voice.

"Fine, I'm fine, sorry," I reassured him, pushing away from the wall. The horses shuffled with uncertainty in the dark, their hooves scraping and picking against the compact ground beneath us. I used my hands to gently touch their necks and shoulders as I squeezed between them. The last thing I needed was a broken toe from getting stepped on.

For the second time that day, Breck's magic pulled the moisture from my clothes, leaving me with only the memory of the sodden adventure we'd just had. I reached up to remove my cap, grateful that it had decided to stay on my head, and shivered as I ran my fingers through my hair. My hand came to rest on the back of my neck, and when our eyes finally met in the low light, his slow smirk made me laugh.

"Glad you're still in good spirits after all that," I said, leaning against the inside edge of the doorway and peering out into the rain. I dropped my hand from my neck to cross my arms over my chest. A long, deep rumble set a vibration to the world around us.

"It doesn't bother me." Breck's hand came to the worn, wooden frame of the doorway as he looked up into the sky. A few of his shimmering freckles remained on his drying cheeks, and I realized then why he'd been turned away while I spoke to the woman in the house.

"Aye, and neither does sleeping on the dirt floor of some shitty auld barn, I'm sure," I mumbled, my face twisting a little in aversion as I looked around, though I still couldn't see much. It was probably better that I couldn't. It smelled horrible.

"You can use both the bed rolls if it makes you feel better," he teased, though I knew he meant it.

"No, no, I'll just close my eyes and dream of your bed back home instead."

"My bed?" Breck chuckled. "Why mine?"

"Because," I dragged out, giving him my best attempt at a seductive look. "My bed wouldn't also have you in it."

He arched a brow in response, tempting me in so many ways that I wasn't sure how I ever managed to leave him sprawled out on his bed the night before we left. How could I have wasted the opportunity to have my hands on him, my lips on his lips, my mouth on his—

"*The woman is coming*," Breck whispered. I blinked and leaned a little further out to find her approaching through the rain, holding her thin shawl up over her head with both hands.

"Thank you again for allowing us to get out of the weather," I said to her. She stopped just outside the doorway, carefully avoiding the puddle there. Her feet were bare under the hem of her skirts. For a moment, I was worried she'd changed her mind about letting us stay.

"Are ye hungry?" she asked.

CHAPTER NINE

We followed her the short distance back to the house. I could hear Nan's voice scolding me already about remembering my manners, especially with a lady I didn't know, but the smell of food and the warmth coming from the fire were enough to convince some of my worries away.

While I stood awkwardly by the door, fretting over my muddy boots, Breck had already made his way across the cozy room and was crouched in front of the stone hearth, subtly wiping his face with the sleeve of his shirt to dry his cheeks and nose. I couldn't help but feel a pang of something in my chest as I watched him. A mix of admiration and protectiveness, I decided. I hated that he had to take such care to hide something about himself that was so beautiful, but he did it effortlessly.

"It's not much, but it'll make ye warm," the woman spoke again, her voice a little weary. She'd placed two bowls for us on a table that looked like it might collapse if she added the weight of a third.

"That's very kind. We didn't expect weather like this. It

took us by surprise," Breck told her as he approached the table and sat gingerly on one of the chairs. I did the same. Mine made a slow sound of distress.

"Weather's unpredictable this time of year. This one spun up outta nowhere." She wrung her hands in her smock and sat in a rocking chair by the fire. It was the only piece of furniture in the place that appeared to be worth anything, with intricate details carved into the solid wood.

I picked up my spoon and stirred the contents of the bowl slowly, trying to identify what was inside before I took a bite. It appeared to be cabbage and a few hunks of potato in a clear broth, or possibly water. I brought the spoon to my mouth. Just water. But she was right, it was warm.

"My dear Albie has taken our last hog to sell at the big market a few villages over. Said he won't return until he's gotten what she's worth, so I'm not sure I'll ever see him again," she said with a faint, tired smile.

I laughed despite myself, glancing at Breck to find his focus on something above my head. I turned and looked up to find the two older children peeking down at us. Their tiny hands clutched the edge of the loft they were in, and they giggled when they noticed me looking.

"Off to bed with ye now!" their mother scolded. They disappeared with another fit of laughter. "Three little girls are a blessing and a curse," she added, not quite under her breath.

Breck and the woman, whose name we never learned, made more small talk until the rain had slowed outside and our bowls were refilled and emptied again. I didn't want to accept any more, especially after learning what little they had to spare, but she insisted. Her husband, Albert, made his money cutting and selling turf. He'd lost his father and his two brothers during the illness, plus many of their loyal customers. Without the help he needed, they'd fallen on hard times like so many others and were still struggling to recover.

"I try to help him when I can, but the last two summers I've had a new babe or one on the way," she explained as she peered at the littlest of her daughters, who was asleep in a basket by the fire, still bundled securely in her blankets. I couldn't help but think of Anne. Soon, she would be gazing upon her own child in this way, with the tender eyes of a watchful mother.

"I lost family, too," I told her, finally finding my voice in the conversation.

"Aye," she nodded sadly, her eyes still on the baby. "It's a mark on every heart."

Breck's attention had turned skyward again, the mischievous look on his face all too familiar. I peered above my head to see stubby fingers hanging over the edge of the loft as they had been before. The girls couldn't seem to get enough of the sly attention he was giving them. I understood exactly how they felt. There was just something about him that could draw you in, completely unaware, until you eventually realized you'd been staring the whole time.

"Does anyone here fancy a bedtime story?" Breck asked easily, turning to the woman. Her attention shot up to the place where her daughters were still not sleeping. A flash of exasperation faded to surrender as she waved her hand, giving them all the permission they so badly wanted. The girls giggled again and made their way down the rickety ladder, their bare feet and hands expertly forming to each rung until they reached the floor. They both bounced the few steps over to the bed along the wall where their parents likely slept and settled on their bellies.

Breck stood from his chair and moved it closer to them, straddling it backwards with his arms crossed atop the back-rest. "Now, let me see," he started, narrowing his eyes and tapping his fingertips lightly against his lips in deep thought. My heart twinged at the sight, knowing it was Finna he was copying. "Ah! I've got it. You like stories about animals," he said, pointing to the younger of the two. "And you like tales of fairies and magical creatures," he concluded, flashing his eyebrows at the older one. The girls exchanged a look of genuine surprise.

"How did ye know?" the oldest daughter asked with a hint of wonder, rather than the skepticism any adult would've met him with.

Breck gave me the briefest glance, his grin growing. "I'm right, aren't I?" he prompted, his tone gentle. The girls both nodded feverishly. The younger one pushed her messy hair away from her face with her tiny hand, her brown eyes focused on him entirely. I remembered that look from when Lucy was her age. The awe and excitement of hearing a story, be it a new one or an old favorite, never seemed to fade.

Breck went on to recite the tale he'd told me that day on the mountain, about the river and the animals who were being treated poorly by the humans. How the fairies took coins from the men and laced them with magic before they tossed them in the river, hoping to bring wellness to the animals who drank from the river forever more. His version for a young audience was slightly more animated, the inflec-tions in his voice making the children visibly react several times. Their mammy listened contently from her place by the fire, eyes closed and chair swaying forward and back, a peaceful grin on her lips.

I couldn't help but wonder what she thought about the story. Did she believe tales such as these to be true? Or did she simply enjoy listening to a sad narrative turned happy by whatever means necessary? Hearing it again myself, with the knowledge I had gained, felt very different than the first time.

As I fully expected, the girls wanted to hear the story again the moment he'd finished telling it.

"Can you really see the gold in the river?" the oldest asked excitedly.

"You can ask my friend for yourself," Breck reassured her. My face went warm when all of their eyes landed on me at once. I cleared my throat and nodded earnestly.

"It's true. I've seen it." I delved into my own storytelling skills, feeling rusty after only a few nights of being away from Lucy and her fairy tales. Granted, I was usually reading from a book, not coming up with anything on my own. "The gold sits at the bottom of the pond, high in the mountains near my village." The girls' eyes went wide yet again. I couldn't help but miss when Luc would react in such a way during her bedtime retellings. "In the morning, you might notice how our horses show the effects in their shiny coats and bright eyes."

In reality, they'd probably emerge from the barn caked in mud and grass, their fur matted together and desperate for a bath and brush. But the girls didn't seem to care about that. The younger daughter squealed with delight after hearing my confirmation that the story was true.

"May we ride them tomorrow?" the eldest begged.

"Nora," her mother warned. "These gentlemen will be on their way far too early for that."

The little lass deflated before our eyes, but Breck and I understood the meaning behind her words. We were strangers to them, and getting too familiar while her husband was away didn't sit well with any of us. We thanked her for the meal and for allowing us to warm up inside before we wished them a pleasant night and returned to our horses.

The team had settled in our absence, several of them sleeping with heads dipped and one hind leg cocked. As much as I wasn't looking forward to spending the night in this place, I was exhausted. The drizzle of rain that remained outside wasn't enough to keep us there, but the massive puddles and muck everywhere else would make it nearly impossible to find a dry place to lie down on our temporary beds. Breck and I worked together to unpack the bed rolls.

"Look up there." I turned and blinked in the low light, following his directions.

"A loft?" I asked, trying not to sound too hopeful.

There was a flash of lightning that lit up the small over-head space, but then it didn't fade. The dim glow was Breck's doing. The fairy light floated past my shoulder and settled high in the corner. I tried to avoid looking at anything below me as I tossed my roll up onto the platform. There was a crate by the wall to put one foot on; the rest was upper body strength and good luck as I shimmied my way up. I kept my head low to avoid the roof. This was nothing like the hay loft in our barn back home, which was big enough to stand up and walk around in.

I unrolled my bundle as hurriedly as I could. "This would've been easier if I did it before I got up here," I mumbled, mostly to myself. After shuffling around awkwardly on my hands and knees, patting and straightening the mat bit by bit, I finally had it flattened down enough to add the second one. I took it from Breck and he helped me, reaching up to smooth one side as I did the other, most of my body pressed back against the uneven stones of the far wall.

The loft was so narrow that the rolls of fabric overlapped almost completely. I remained where I was as Breck stepped up onto the crate and joined me with little effort. I huffed out a contemptuous breath as he stretched out on his stomach, reaching for the two saddle bags he'd set up there, too. He put one into place for me and brought the other under his head.

"What?" he asked innocently, referring to my scoff that turned into a bit of a coughing fit, made worse by the centuries of dust we'd stirred up. I carefully positioned myself on the mats beside him. They were a whisper of comfort between our tired bodies and the hard, wooden slats holding us off the ground. At least we weren't sleeping directly on the compacted pig shite below.

I groaned a little as I readjusted onto my side, facing him. The glow of the fairy light was less than a candle, but still bright enough to discern the way Breck was looking at me. His eyes caught the gleam coming from the corner, his face relaxed with only a hint of a grin lingering on his features. I hated that my hands were so dirty as I brought one up to brush his hair aside. The lingering effects of the wine, the sweet way he'd had with the girls, and our proximity were stirring within me.

"I've never wanted to kiss someone so badly in a pigsty before," I told him quietly. A soft giggle escaped him as he turned onto his side as well, mirroring me. There was barely enough room between us to take a deep breath without our chests touching. One of his knees bumped mine.

"So, you've wanted to kiss someone in a pigsty, just not this much?" he teased back.

"Exactly," I murmured against his mouth as I closed the gap between us. His hand came to the side of my face as I deepened the kiss. "But I realize now that the smell doesn't exactly lend itself to a romantic moment."

"This is true." Breck's thumb stroked along my cheekbone. "Though, I'm not sure how much of it is the animals, and how much is just... us."

"I'm trying not to think about it," I admitted with a laugh. "I'm already preparing for what Henry will say when he sees me." The grooming tools in my bag were calling my name. Chanting it, really.

"He's your best friend. He won't care."

Breck used his hips and shoulders to shift his weight over so that he was facing away from me. My arm instinctively wrapped around him, locking him in the most secure embrace.

"Can't have you falling and getting hurt," I reasoned as I tucked my face against his hair and the back of his neck. He was right about both things. We really did smell quite bad, but I also didn't mind too much. I was just glad to be there with him. He relaxed, flush against me from our shoulders to our feet. I still had my tall boots on, but I felt as one of his legs tucked back between mine, the top of his bare foot hooking around my calf.

"I'm sorry about earlier," he spoke into the quiet that had settled around us. "The storm."

I did a poor job at hiding my surprise. "That was you?"

"I let my emotions get the best of me." The memory of the engorged river outside the mill came to mind immediately, as well as when it had run dry after his meeting with the Unseelie.

"But this wasn't like the other times. That was the river. This was…" I trailed off, uncertain of how much I should say. I felt his body tense against mine.

"I think it's because of my training. My magic is growing. I'm trying to keep up with it, but I don't understand all of it yet." I hugged him tighter against my chest when he paused. "I don't understand how to control all of it, anyway. Fallon says that's normal. I'm still young. It'll take time." His shoulders moved in a small shrug. "It just feels like so much sometimes."

The swell in my heart for him felt untimely, but there was nothing I could do to stop it. He had opened up to me, without any prompting on my part, and it felt as close to those three little words as he'd ever been.

"That's alright," I said finally, realizing that it was probably a good time to say something comforting. "Nobody expects you to be perfect. I'll bet even Fallon made mistakes when she was a young fairy."

Breck let out a huff of a laugh and adjusted against me, settling in more. "I doubt it."

I kissed his shoulder and closed my eyes, trying to think of sleep and not of where we were. I listened to the fading rain, the horses breathing softly below us, and told myself that I owed Finna the biggest thank you for helping make this trip possible when I saw her again.

CHAPTER TEN

The dull ache in every part of my body wasn't enough to prevent me from sitting up and smacking my forehead against a low beam of the roof early the next morning.

"*Feck*," I cursed under my breath and brought my hand up to press away the pain. I cautiously looked at my fingers. No blood. Supported on my other elbow, I quickly surveyed the space below me. It was empty. Worry tightened my chest as I shuffled toward the end of the loft, remembering to keep my head ducked this time. I slid down onto the crate with both feet and bounded toward the doorway. If Breck had been called away by the river, nobody would've been awake to stop the horses from wandering out. We'd left them untied overnight.

The first thing I saw were several of the saddles hung together over the stone wall. I let out a sigh of relief and coughed into the crook of my elbow as the rest of the scene unfolded. The horses – one, two, three, four, five, I counted – were busy grazing on the few available patches of grass in a field of mostly mud. The sixth, my gelding, was standing nearest to the barn, his tail lashing once in the dim early light. Breck held his reins in one hand, and with the other, he rhythmically brushed the dirt and dried sweat from the horse's flank with one of the tools we'd brought along.

"Alright there?" Breck asked in a hushed tone as he glanced at me over the gelding's back end.

I grunted as I fingered the sleep out of the corner of my eye. I wasn't entirely sure of the answer. My head was throbbing slightly where I'd bumped it. The rest of me was tired, dirty, and smelling downright offensive. On an average day, I would've considered that far from alright. Given the circumstances, however, it was probably the best I could've hoped for.

"How long have you been up?" I stepped closer to them so I could run a hand down the gelding's neck. He turned his head toward me for a scratch between the eyes. There was no evidence of the downpour left on his coat. It had been groomed to a smooth shine. I leaned to peek at the rest of the team. They all looked the same, with clean legs, untangled manes, and glossy sides. I knew all that work would've taken hours. I gave Breck a flat look, and he challenged it with a small smirk.

"A while," he answered simply, like it'd been no trouble at all. I shook my head at him, unable to stop the grin that fought its way onto my lips. He knew I wouldn't have wanted to deliver Henry's horses to him looking like a pack of wild animals.

"Thank you." I felt my emotions begin to slide in a soft direction, but the wink he gave me quickly tilted them the opposite way. I cleared my throat and turned my attention to the nearby house. I wondered if the little girls were awake to see the horses looking polished as I'd promised. The sun wasn't up yet, but I knew nothing could deter an excited child.

"They've been watching," Breck confirmed. "Mammy won't let them out, but they're not planning on giving up their begging any time soon." He said the last bit with a chuckle as he crouched to brush gently at the gelding's legs, removing the caked dirt away with care. Clearly, he'd been listening to their thoughts as he worked. "They did set out a basket with a few pieces of bread for us, if you're hungry."

I was, grippingly so, but I decided it was more important to help Breck get the horses ready for the last stretch of our journey. While he finished with them, I checked the saddles. They would need to be properly aired out and conditioned when we arrived at the estate, but our only choice was to put them back on and hope for clear skies. Together, we saddled the team. I retrieved the bags and bed rolls from the loft so we could pack them away. The comfortable silence between us made me grin to myself.

When we were nearly finished, Breck came next to me and unbuckled one of the bags. He reached inside and dug out a piece of the parchment Finna's goods had been wrapped in.

"Is there any twine in there?" he asked as he smoothed it out against his thigh. It was one of the pieces he'd folded up neatly, rather than one of my crumpled ones. I felt down into the corners of the bag until my fingertips touched a length of the rough string. I pulled it out for him to take. "Hold this. Both hands." I held them together as he laid the parchment flat across them, before he slid his hand fully into his pocket. My eyes grew as he pulled out a generous number of coins. He carefully placed them into my cupped palms, pressing the parchment down against my fingers. He used the twine to secure the gathered edges with a careful knot and lopsided bow.

We looked up at the same time and he smiled gently.

He took the weighty bundle from me, my hands bouncing up slightly before they parted. I watched as he walked toward the front door of the house. He bent at the knees and waist next to the little woven basket they'd set out and stood a moment later, returning with only two pieces of bread. He held one out for me to take.

"Ready to see Henry?" he asked with an excitement that was infectious. My heart sped up with anticipation. I nodded as I took his offering. He stuck his piece in his mouth, gripping it in his teeth, and flashed his eyebrows at me before he stuck his foot into the stirrup and hoisted himself into the gelding's saddle.

I blinked rapidly a few times and closed my mouth. It had fallen open at some point. Even in the midst of his casual generosity, he was thinking of me. I copied him with my piece of bread, freeing my hands so I could hold on and swing my leg over my mare's back.

As we set off, we passed by the front window the wee girls had been watching from. The younger one waved at us excitedly. Breck waved back at her with a waggle of fingers on his raised hand. I held my bread up and nodded to show my appreciation. The oldest daughter turned her head and said something with a big smile, probably letting her mammy know we'd taken it.

As a breeze blew across the stretch of flat ground we were crossing, I realized for the first time how cool the air had turned overnight, likely pulled along behind the storm. A shiver went through me despite my riding jacket.

"Are you cold up there?" I called out to Breck, who had

ridden ahead after spotting the true opening in the wall that we'd needed yesterday. Surely that breeze had reached him through his thin shirt and cuffed trousers. He turned to look at me over his shoulder and slowed his horses down until I caught up to him.

"Why, are you offering to warm me up?" he asked when I was close enough for him to croon.

I snorted out a laugh and shook my head. He took another bite of his bread and chewed it slowly as he breeched the wall first, leading us onto the road that was littered with puddles and sunken carriage tracks. The horses might not stay quite as clean as Breck had managed to get them, but they'd still look a whole lot better than they did before. I sobered quickly as my mind replayed everything he'd done.

"Thank you. For the horses. It'll mean a lot to Henry. It meant a lot to me." Before he could try to reason away my praise, I added more. "And what you did back there, for that family? For the little girls? That was…" I didn't know how to finish.

"They needed it." That and a simple shrug were his only response on the matter. I turned the piece of bread over between my fingers. I didn't know a lot about anything when it came to baking, but the lingering taste in my mouth and short rise told me the ingredients used weren't as fresh as they could've been. I pictured Finna's bread, light and airy, and even the bread my Nan loved to bake. The woman was just trying to feed her family with whatever she could. My hunger and the respect I had for her to share what little she had with two strangers helped me finish the last of my breakfast as we made good time toward the coast.

CHAPTER ELEVEN

"Henry will be so glad to see his team," I thought out loud as we crested a small incline. When I'd been too weak to get out of bed for all those months during my recovery, the only thing I could think about was getting well enough to see my horses. They were like my family. They even knew my secrets from the whispered confessions I'd revealed to them when it was too much to keep to myself any longer. So I knew Henry must've been missing his, too. I was feeling the excitement for him.

"I can imagine." Breck had fallen back so that we were riding alongside one another again. I stole a quick glance in his direction, confirming that his absent focus had settled somewhere in the middle distance. Thanks to the wine and the chaos of the thunderstorm, I'd almost forgotten our conversation under the ash trees the evening before. His emotions, whatever they were about, had been strong enough to conjure the weather. Fallon was the only other one I'd seen do that before. But since she was the one training him, it made sense that it would be part of what he was learning. Wasn't I doing the same thing with Mathew? I could only teach him well on the things I knew well myself.

Before I could think of something else to say to bring Breck around from wherever he'd gone in his thoughts, he pushed his fingers into his hair and rubbed a few circles with the heel of his hand against his temple before he looked at me.

"Do you want to see something?"

My curiosity piqued instantly. His face was almost pained, as if this was something he needed to do to get some relief.

"Alright," I told him, my voice a little uncertain, which I tried to cover up with an encouraging nod.

Breck turned the gelding off the road in the opposite direction of the river. The rest of the horses and I followed. My confidence in their ability to detect and alert danger kept me calm as their hooves swished through the damp grass under us, which quickly gave way to a more craggy, uneven hillside. I angled my hips and tightened the muscles in my stomach and legs to stay in the saddle as the horses maneuvered their way to the top. Only one of them had a moment of unsure footing as a small rock came loose.

On the other side, the trees grew thicker, though many of them were also bald or nearly so this time of year. There was enough space between them to ride through comfortably as we continued down the slope toward a stand of stocky evergreens. I slowed my mare when Breck did the same. He turned at the waist and held his hand out. A thrill went through me as I reached to take it, knowing what was about to happen.

My eyelids fell shut as I felt his magic wrap around the wrist of the hand he was holding, before it washed up my arm, across my chest, and out to my fingers and toes. I took a deep breath, treating my lungs to the crisp, minty air that would disappear long before I wanted it to.

The horses started to move, presumably under his command, and when I opened my eyes, we were just emerging from the wall of deep green yew needles into a clearing. The lush grass was littered with the tiniest wild-flowers of yellows, whites, and purples. It was as if spring-time had been trapped within the trees. I looked up, unable to avoid the centerpiece of this eden. The short trunk of the tree before us exploded upward with a thousand branches. Golden flicks of light were busy weaving in and out of them. Fairies. But what caused me to bring my free hand up to cover my mouth in surprise were the pieces of cloth and ribbon wrapped amongst the boughs.

"*The Wishing Tree,*" I whispered against my palm.

Breck squeezed my hand and let go so he could dismount. The horses were already grazing, wasting absolutely no time to have a taste of the magic themselves. I slid from the saddle but remained close to my mare. I felt overwhelmingly out of place.

"Am I allowed to be here?" I asked in a hushed tone, working the reigns in my hands to calm my nerves. Breck looked at me then, a burst of glitter across his cheeks and nose catching the sunlight. My knees went a little wobbly at the sight. He arched an eyebrow and nodded.

"Aye. You know the story. These ribbons are like the ones Anne and Jamie used," he explained. I could tell he was trying to be gentle as he picked his words. "Humans have come to Wishing Trees like this one for centuries to make their greatest desires heard." He was underneath the low branches now, back bent slightly and eyes closed as he rested both hands against the trunk. Slowly, he shifted down to his knees. Then he turned to me again, holding out his hand. "Come and listen."

A few coughs escaped me as I looped the leather straps back over my mare's neck. I had only taken a few steps when two golden lights floated down from the branches and circled me, lazily at first, as if they were observing me the same way I was observing them, but then faster as they zipped away. My brows bunched together, but Breck only grinned.

"They're not used to humans being able to see them here."

When I reached the tree, Breck instructed me to kneel as he was with one hand against the bark. I tried my best to avoid the longest ribbons above our heads. It felt disrespectful for me to touch another man's wishes, even if they were only scraps of fabric to me. He took my other hand after I'd settled onto my knees, lacing our fingers together, his thumb rubbing gently against mine. He nodded once and closed his eyes, so I did the same. I had no idea what he was about to show me, but I trusted him.

The sounds started quietly, almost like whispers of the chimes hanging outside Finna's cottage back home. As they grew louder, new noises joined in. It reminded me of the low, polite chatter amongst guests at a party. None of the voices were discernable, though. At least not to me. The chimes and sounds of pleasant music increased, joined by the resonations of our favorite pub on a busy night, all clanking glasses and hearty laughter. Hoofbeats against hard ground filled out any remaining spaces.

Every bit of it swirled in my head, nearly making me dizzy, when suddenly the noises evened out and were replaced by things I could see, but not clearly. It was flashes of color and whirls of memories I'd forgotten about over the years. I saw the faces of my siblings, of my parents, of the family I still had. There were my horses, my friends, opponents on the pitch, people from the village. Jamie. *Jamie.* Henry and Sarah at their wedding. Finna, Fallon, all the others. The chestnut mare. Anne holding a baby with William at her side.

The kaleidoscope came to a crashing halt on one final image. I could hear the tinkling chimes, or maybe they were tiny bells. I could feel the sun on my back, grass tickling my skin, a gentle breeze in my hair, and beneath me was Breck, his freckles glittering unabashedly in the afternoon light. I could see the ones scattered across his chest and shoulders, too, because his clothes were gone. So were mine. *Peter,* he said, though his lips didn't move. He just gazed up at me with soft eyes and the smirk I couldn't ever get enough of. *Peter,* it came again, thick and dreamy against the sounds of the fairies.

Say it, I told him. *Tell me you love me. Please. Just tell me. Tell me.*

"Peter. Peter!"

I gasped and my eyes flew open. I coughed hard once and a few more times after I took another deep breath, letting go of Breck's hand and landing on my arse away from the tree.

"What was *that?!*" I wheezed, still panting. I coughed again and realized my heart was ready to thump right out of my chest with how hard and fast it was beating. Breck moved closer to me on his hands and knees, cradling my head as he leaned it back atop his thighs. I looked down at myself as I reclined and discovered what was likely the reason for my palpitations. I swiftly pressed my legs together, bent at the knees, to try and hide my massive erection between them. I stifled a groan at the movement.

"It's the magic. The Tree. It can look into your memories, at what makes you the happiest. It can see your greatest wishes." He paused, still holding the side of my head on his lap with one hand while the other rubbed gently over my heart. I knew he was only trying to help, but my body was on fire, lit from within, and his delicate fingers tracing across my chest was the last thing I needed.

"Even without the ribbon?" I shifted my hips to the side, one leg higher than the other, to try and mask my situation better.

"The ribbon is used so your wish can be chosen. The Tree already knows what it is. Wishes are made of magic, after all." He paused only long enough to move his hand from my chest to my hair, brushing it back from my forehead in slow strokes. I squeezed my eyes shut. If I didn't stop him soon, I'd be lucky if I made it back to my feet without my biggest wish being a clean pair of trousers to put on. "What did you see?" he asked, genuine curiosity coating his words.

"Em," I managed, my voice high and a little strangled. *Fantastic.* "I... I saw lots of things. I saw Anne with her baby. She and William looked so happy. I saw Henry and Sarah happy, too. At their wedding." I could feel my arousal starting to fade, but Breck wouldn't let it go.

"What about yourself? Don't you have any wishes to make you happy?"

"Couldn't you see them?" My response was a little rougher than I meant it to be.

"I told you I wouldn't unless you said so," he replied, his voice falling slightly. His hand stopped moving against my hair then, so I took the opportunity to sit up. I twisted to face him.

"I just thought it was probably like last time. When you and Elena showed me the wishes on the ribbons. You could see it then, right?"

He nodded and pushed himself to his feet in one easy motion before he reached for my hand. I took it and let him help me up. Before he could let go, I pulled him to me and brought my other hand to the side of his neck. We searched each other's eyes before I touched my forehead to his.

"I only asked because—"

"I know," I cut him off gently. "You just want to help. I didn't mean for it to come out the way it did." I let go of his hand and slid my arms around his shoulders, gripping my own elbows as my face tucked against his neck. "*You make me happy*," I whispered. Those last images played in my mind again as I pressed my lips to the collarbone that was exposed by the cut of his shirt, only to be interrupted by Breck's shoulder scrunching up as a single squeak of a laugh escaped him.

"Sorry. It tickles."

"What does?"

"The hairs," he said with another giggle, pushing at me with the lightest touch on my hips.

I groaned loudly and brought both hands up to cover the stubble on my jaw, feeling the untended growth after our days of travel. With a dramatic frown, I kept my hands in place and stalked back toward the horses.

"Get me to a basin and mirror before I cry!" I called to him.

CHAPTER TWELVE

Only another hour passed before the stacked stone wall along the road grew slightly taller and more structured, until finally we stopped in front of an impressive iron gate that was sitting open in two identical halves. Each side was supported by an equally impressive, ivy-coated stone pillar that reached higher than Finna's cottage. Nerves began to chew at my stomach. I lifted my cap to run my fingers through my hair, one last attempt to look somewhat presentable to our hosts.

The road beyond the gate was smooth and flat at first, carefully tended to match the pristine grass lining both sides. It soon became more of an uphill slope, however, as we followed the bend around a slight break in the rolling coastal mountains that separated us from the sea.

One more curve and we were exposed to the breeze blowing off the water. The new sticky, salty smell of it sent me coughing into my jacket sleeve. When I was finally able to lower my arm and open my eyes, I lost my breath for an entirely new reason.

High walls made of sandy-gray cut stones stretched up from the rocky outcrop. In each corner, a tower soared into the sky, surely giving a seaward vantage point that was rivaled by few other places. Narrow slats in the stone were the only breaks in the fortified exterior. Between us and the enormous structure was a solid bridge that spanned a gap in the rugged landscape. One wrong step would send you tumbling to the coastline far below.

"It's a feckin' *castle*," I blurted.

"Aye," Breck chuckled, encouraging the gelding forward.

I tapped the heels of my boots against my mare's flanks to get her moving, as well. I blinked a few times, making certain that what I was seeing was real. All I could think was how much Lucy would love it. It screamed *fairy tale*.

The horses' hooves clopped across the stones of the bridge. I risked a peek over the edge. How many men had met their fate on those jagged rocks when this place wasn't just a home? We stopped again at the gatehouse as we were approached by a well-dressed man who very formally requested to know our business at the residence, his nose turned up as he took in our appearance – and likely our odor. I explained who we were, and though it didn't cause him to relax in the slightest, he let us through without any more questions.

The courtyard beyond the wall was a decorative mix of manicured grass and crushed stone, which arced around in a wide circle toward what could only be the keep of the castle. I spotted the slanted roof of stables to our left, with many available stalls waiting to be filled. Several other small structures and doorways lined the interior walls. A woman was busy carrying a basket full of linens, while an older man tended to shrubbery that formed part of the walking garden in the middle of the circle. A statuesque bird bath in the very center completed the look.

A young lad came racing over to us, his boots crunching in the pebbles. He greeted us quickly before he took the reins from us after we'd dismounted. I felt the urge to follow him across the yard to inspect the stables for myself, but I didn't get the chance to act on it. The sound of wood hitting stone drew our attention back to the keep. The heavy door had been thrown open, allowing two figures to emerge.

A grin instantly broke across my face as Henry spread his arms wide and approached me with quick strides, his own crooked smile an instant comfort. He was just as I remembered him, his red hair neatly cut and styled, wearing yet another pompous outfit that I was sure he hated. We embraced, his arms squeezing me tight before he delivered a few slaps on my back. When we pulled apart, he grabbed my shoulders, and I shook my head in disbelief at the only difference I could find.

"You traitor, you've grown a beard," I teased. It was thick and even more orange than his hair.

"Traitor!?" he echoed in question, inspecting my own chin in an exaggerated way. "Looks to me like you're well on your way there, boyo!"

"Not by choice, believe me," I ground out. Henry gave the rest of me a once-over then, his eyebrows pinching together.

"Aye, you smell like we'll be needin' to write your eulogy. I hope you left the animals to me," he said with a wink. "Ah, we'll get you both cleaned up quicker'n two shakes of a lamb's tail." At that, he abandoned me to shake Breck's hand. I turned my attention to the other familiar face waiting on the cobblestone steps. Sarah extended her hand, the one still brandishing her stunning ring, and I held her fingers delicately while I touched my lips to the soft skin there.

"I do apologize for our appearance. We had to settle for less-than-ideal sleeping arrangements last night thanks to an untimely storm."

"The baths will be drawn at once," she said mildly, a soft grin on her features. "I'm just glad you've finally arrived. My beloved has spoken of nothing else since we mailed your letter. I trust that your trip was made uneventful by your choice of companion."

It wasn't a question. We both looked to where Henry was holding Breck's right shoulder hostage while they spoke. He'd hidden the points of his ears, but the rings in them were still in place, as well as the one at the edge of his nose. I cleared my throat and let go of her fingers as I turned back to face her. A subtle, knowing look was all she gave me before she went down the remaining step and sidled up beside Henry, her skirts dragging over the small stones at our feet.

She knows, I thought. Breck looked up at me from their exchanged pleasantries, a silent acknowledgement, before his attention returned to Henry's questions about the horses.

"They didn't give you any trouble now, did they? I know that wee mare can be a right madwoman," he said with a laugh, though I knew he really wanted to hear the truth.

Sarah put a delicate hand on his chest.

"Why don't we let them settle for a bit before you start in with the questions, hm? They've come a long way. We can all gather as soon as supper is ready. Then you can talk the night away, if you wish."

"Of course, of course." Henry placed his palm over hers.

Hand-in-hand, they welcomed us into the keep. I

expected the furnishings to be expensive but antiquated, considering how old the place was. Instead, the only old things I could see were the paintings on the walls. Everything else was a modern, lavish display of wealth and success, from the foreign rugs up to the impressive light fixture hanging above our heads.

"That's our newest gasolier. It's a twin to the one over the table in the formal dining room. You'll love seeing the way it lights up the space at night," Sarah said proudly as they continued toward the staircase at the end of the entry hallway. With a smile, she added, "I'll give you the grand tour later." I blinked up at the intricate piping and decorative, white globes of it. I'd never seen gas lights used inside before.

We ascended the wide steps two by two, Henry and Sarah ahead of us. I looked to my right and found Breck with his head bent back as he studied the curved, thick wooden beams supporting the floor above. His hand was sliding up the polished banister, fingers moving gracefully along the smooth surface. His gaze shifted and he noticed me staring, which he answered with a smirk. I pressed my lips together to hide my grin, returning my focus to my feet so I didn't trip. I couldn't wait to hear what he thought about this place.

"We've had these two rooms made up for you. This one here, and the next." Sarah gestured to the two doors as she spoke about them. "Your personal items have already been delivered. If there's anything you need, you'll let the staff know. Please make yourselves comfortable. We'll see you for supper." The three of us watched Sarah retreat to the top of the stairs and gather her skirts before she seemed to float back down to the main floor.

I waited to speak until the sound of her shoes tapping against the stone was gone.

"A castle, though?" I mocked, my voice pinched with disdain. "Really?"

Henry cackled and reached to flick my cap off my head, but I pressed my hand to it just fast enough to keep it from falling to the ground. With my arm up, he took a quick shot and slapped my stomach hard with the back of his hand. I stifled a groan and reached for him, using my height to my advantage as I wrapped my arm tight around the back of his neck so that his nose was pressed into my underarm. He let out a muffled scream before I let him go.

"Feck me," he panted, gasping for clean air. "Go get in that bath, or I'll throw you in meself!" He clapped my shoulder and followed Sarah's footsteps with much less elegance, leaving the two of us alone to settle. When I spun around, I found that Breck had already disappeared inside the far door. I reached for the handle of the other one and pushed it open.

I had never seen so much pink in my whole life. Pink on the walls. Pink on the rugs. Massive pink flowers on the duvet, which was fluffed to a perfect dome atop the bed. Even the artwork was flowers with golden frames. A delicate white dressing table with a mirror sat along one wall, and next to it was a basin with another mirror. My leather grooming kit was there waiting for me. On the wall behind me, the wardrobe already had my few outfits hanging neatly in a row.

A click caught my attention, and Breck's head poked around a door on the third wall that wasn't the one I'd come through. We'd been placed in adjoining rooms.

"That's convenient," he said before he realized what he was looking at, his eyebrows arching in surprise at the décor.

"I feel as though they're trying to tell me something." I

removed my cap and tossed it down onto the vanity, my hands going directly for the rolled leather kit. I was truly scared to look at my own reflection. Breck came into the room and shut the door behind him as I reached for the porcelain pitcher of hot water waiting for me.

"They do have four daughters," he reasoned. "I expect these rooms were made up for them."

"What color is yours, then?" I looked at him suspiciously.

He gave an innocent shrug. "Dark green."

I rolled my eyes and poured until the basin was halfway full, already savoring the warmth of the steam rolling up from it. I took a deep breath and coughed it out before I stooped in front of the mirror.

I *looked* dirty. The curls in my hair had flattened into frizzy waves. Bags under my eyes held the truth of how well I'd slept the past two nights. The faint scar on my temple stood pink against the rest of my skin, which I could hardly see thanks to the coating of dust that had settled on me from the road and the loft in the pig barn. And the hair. I rubbed at my chin from one side to the other, the dark stubble making a scratchy sound in return.

"I think it suits you," Breck said cheerily over my shoulder.

I glared at him in the reflection.

"It doesn't," I told him flatly. I cupped my hands into the water, which immediately clouded with tendrils of brown, and leaned to splash it onto my face. I repeated this twice before I removed the shaving stick from its place and let it glide over my jaw and neck several times. Breck was still watching, having settled against the dressing table, one arm bracing his weight with his fingers curled around the carved edge of the tabletop. "What is it?" I asked, not pausing to look at him.

"I've never seen this before."

I dampened the brush and began to work it against my cheek to form a lather, tucking my lips in between my teeth as the bristles circled under my nose and over my mouth.

"Anne let me borrow it. She bought it as a gift for William."

"No, I mean... this," he corrected, gesturing to me with the tilt of his chin.

My brows ducked in confusion. "You mean shaving?"

He nodded, his eyes still focused on me, as if he really was trying to learn everything he could about this menial task I'd done thousands of times. I paused my lathering and finally looked at him. "Don't tell me you've never shaved before."

"I've never," he answered.

I straightened then, turning to him fully. He hadn't even the faintest of a shadow on his jaw. I gave this thought time to bloom in my mind. He didn't have a mirror at the mill. I'd never seen the tools there either, though I'd never gone looking for them. My gaze moved from his face to his chest as I tried to picture it underneath his shirt. Did he have hair there? Was there any that trailed down his stomach, along the same path that I'd kissed and tasted in the dark? My eyes settled only for a moment on the front of his trousers before they shot back to his face.

"I—?" I stopped myself. Breck's smirk grew. I was glad he couldn't see the self-conscious blush that sprung onto my cheeks underneath the frothy shaving soap still waiting there. How had I never thought about the fact that he didn't have a trace of hair *there*? I certainly did.

"Finna says it comes later for fairies." He looked down but

kept grinning. "I don't think Carrick was able to grow his beard until he was in his late fifties."

"Oh," was all I said, forcing myself not to think about the hair on Carrick's body, either. I coughed, returning to my reflection before the soap started to drip onto my clothes. To save me even further, there were three sharp knocks on the door before it cracked open. A young woman dipped herself at the knees with a polite nod.

"Sirs, the bath is ready for one of you now." Her voice was soft but commanding.

"Go ahead," I waved a hand at Breck as I reached for the razor to finish the job I'd started. It was different from the one I used at home, so I knew I needed to be extra careful on the first few passes to determine how it felt in my hand. Breck pushed off the table, following the maidservant back out the door. Our gaze met in the reflection one last time as he pulled it shut behind him, that playful twinkle in his eye.

I closed mine and let out a quiet moan, free hand braced on the edge of the basin.

Focus, I told myself. *There'll be plenty of time to think about him later.*

* * *

The bath was yet another surprise. Rather than being in the kitchen as I was used to, or even on the main floor, there was an entire room dedicated to it on the same hallway as our rooms in the opposite direction from the staircase. I'd followed the maidservant in and discovered that it was a large space, draped with all sorts of fine curtains hanging from the ceiling, soft rugs, and a large stone hearth built out from the wall, home to a presently roaring fire.

She pushed one of the drapes back to reveal a tub much bigger than I'd ever seen before, let alone sat in. The shiny copper lining reflected the glow of the fire. It was early afternoon, but that time of year the sun disappeared so early that it left little natural light in this room that faced the sea.

"Salts, sir?" the young woman asked.

"Sorry?"

"Salts?" she repeated, standing at the edge of the tub with a small cannister in one hand, a deep spoon in the other. It was something to put into the water, apparently.

"Em, I suppose?" I answered, my shoulders bunching toward my ears. She scooped into the container and began to sprinkle these salts across the surface of the water. It didn't appear to change anything.

"Oils, sir?" was her next question as she now reached for a thin glass jar with a cork. The liquid inside looked yellow in color. I paused in taking off my boots to nod loosely at her.

"Aye, sure," I confirmed. She tipped the bottle and out came the oils, thick and syrupy. I was beginning to think they might be cooking me in this pot. "Will the herbs and spices be next?" I queried airily. The young woman tucked her head toward her shoulder to hide her smile as she placed the jar back where she'd found it on a shelf cluttered with other soaps, bottles, brushes, and more. She then hiked her sleeve clear up her arm before she stuck it deep into the water, past her elbow, after which she began to swirl the water side to side.

By the time she was finished, I'd removed my other boot and waistcoat, halfway done with the buttons down my shirt, my back turned to her politely.

"Will you require my assistance with bathing, sir?"

I nearly choked on a cough. I hadn't needed help bathing since...

"No. No, that won't be necessary, thank you."

"Enjoy your bath, sir. I'll be just outside if you need anything at all." She curtsied to me again and then pulled the curtains across to give me the privacy I was waiting for. I removed the rest of my clothes and tossed them against the wall in a pile. Her stirring of my brine had left the room fragrant in a way I couldn't quite describe. All I knew was that it smelled better than pig shite and horse sweat.

I put one foot in tentatively, trying to determine if the smooth, reflective lining was as slippery as it looked. The rush of warmth covering me as I sat down made me cough again, but my tired body reveled in it. With my knees bent only slightly, the water came all the way up to my shoulders. I marveled at this for longer than I should have. A bench alongside the tub held more scented items, including a bar of soap that looked particularly nice. I grabbed it with wet fingers and started to scrub it along my chest and arms. There was no mistaking the scent of this one.

I wet my hair and added soap to it, as well, using my fingernails against my scalp. I felt the heat soaking into my sore muscles. I decided that it wasn't a terrible idea to let the soap linger in my wet curls for a moment. I sunk up to my neck, leaned my head back against the gently curved edge of the tub, and closed my eyes. *Only for a moment*, I thought, comforted by the sweet-smelling mint.

CHAPTER THIRTEEN

The table was set for four at supper, though it could've been set for four times as many, at least. The family used what was previously called the Great Hall as their formal dining room. After Sarah's father had taken ownership – though it had been in her family for many generations – the entire inside of the castle had been slowly renovated. He was the first one to have the money to do anything respectable with it, she'd said.

The gasolier was hissing low and steady above our heads, impressive as she'd promised it would be. Another hearth, this one made of white marble, warmed our end of the room and added to the ambiance. Henry sat in the chair at the head of the table, Sarah at his side. I was opposite her with Breck next to me. We'd been served pastries stuffed with goat cheese and olives, then a creamy leek and potato soup. We all trained our attention on our plates as the cloches were raised, revealing the third course.

A mix of emotions flooded me. My mouth immediately watered at the smell of garlic and rosemary. I swallowed and shifted my gaze to Breck, who was looking down at the roasted lamb in front of him with a neutral expression.

I'm so sorry, I thought for him. *Let me ask for something else.*

His blue eyes met mine and he grinned, shaking his head as subtly as he could. I hadn't even thought to let someone know about Breck's meal preferences. He reached for another piece of bread.

"I can't believe you convinced Thomas to take over the lessons. Oh, to see the look on his face." Henry laughed and shook his head as he worked his cutlery.

"*Well,*" I started, dragging it out. "I might've said something about word getting back to a certain someone about his charitable undertaking."

Henry chewed and raised his eyebrows at Sarah, who was just setting down her glass of honey wine. They were still working through all of what they'd brought along with them. I was glad to help with the glass I'd been offered.

"I think we all know that my youngest sister needs no extra encouragement when it comes to ventures of the heart," she said, her lips quirked up at the corners. "Peter, you know that better than anyone here, I daresay." We all shared a subdued laugh at that.

I studied the pads of my fingers as I cut at my piece of meat. They were still wrinkled and swollen. I'd fallen asleep in the tub, only to be roused when the young maid came in to check on me. She'd apparently called to me several times from behind the curtain before I answered. When I finally did, the water was cold, I was cold, and I was nearly late to supper.

We discussed everything Henry could think of that he might've missed at home, talking our way through three more courses of roasted vegetable salad, a selection of various fruits and cheeses, and finally dessert: crumbly, buttery shortbread fingers with tea. I was glad these were served on a tray, so nobody noticed how many I took. I was even more glad that Breck was able to eat as the other dishes were served.

Sarah excused herself when the meal was over, encouraging the rest of us to retire to the sitting room, as it was more intimate and comfortable. We obliged, but as we passed through the hallway, Breck also left us in favor of his bed. I brought the rest of my wine along and Henry poured himself a Scotch. I watched my friend drop heavily onto a low-back sofa opposite the chair I'd taken, the deep golden color of his drink catching the light of the fire as it sloshed in his thick, short glass.

We sat in silence for a short time, listening to the logs crackling and the distant waves crashing upon the rocks below, the cool late evening breeze ruffling the curtains at the window behind me.

"It's even better than I thought it'd be," he said finally, entranced by the flames.

"Being married?" I took a final pull of my wine, leaning to set the empty glass by my feet.

"The sex, of course." Henry waggled his eyebrows at me. I rolled my eyes with a grin. "But that too, aye. A small price to pay." He chuckled and swirled his glass before he took another sip. I knew he was only joking. I'd never seen so many soft looks and gentle smiles from him as I'd seen that day. He was madly in love with his lady.

"Is that the reason you've stayed away so long? Too busy between the sheets to return home?"

I watched Henry's cocksure attitude slip into something more serious.

"We're trying, you know. It's what she wants. To return home with even more happy news." He paused and pushed himself to his feet with a bit of a grunt, moving to top off his nightcap. The decanter he poured from must've cost more than my riding boots.

"Is it what you want, too?" I sat forward in my chair, resting my elbows on my knees.

"Isn't that love?" he asked with a smile over his shoulder. "She wants children. I want whatever she wants." He found his seat again. "Of course it's what I want. I only hope what any man does, that I can provide for me family." He tipped his head back, making a face as the whisky went down. "Well, that and hoping that they look more like their mammy than their auld man."

"We can all hope for that," I said with false sincerity, earning myself a small, tasseled pillow to the face. "Hey!" I laughed shortly and picked it up from the floor, throwing it back at him. He caught it and put it where he'd found it beside him on the sofa with a heavy pat.

"And what about you?" The mood of the room went somber again. "Are things…?"

I let the silence hang between us again briefly.

"You told Sarah." I wasn't mad, not even close. I just needed to know.

Henry sighed heavily.

"It was such an honest mistake, Pete, I mean it. We were… well, we were *together*, our very first night here, and we were both a little sloshed, and Sarah said something about you not dancing with any of the eligible ladies at the reception. And —" he stopped, his face scrunching slowly with obvious remorse.

"And?" I encouraged him, feeling my heartbeat rising into my throat.

"And I might've said that it's because you only like to dance with the fellas." I thought he was done, but then he added, "And I said it with some, ah, emphasis with me hips. If you know what I mean."

My head dropped into my hands, my fingers tightening in my hair.

"Feck me, Henry." I said on an exhale.

"I *know*. I know. Like I said, the drink, the vulnerable position, and in the moment she only laughed. But the next morning it came up over breakfast. I couldn't take it back."

"It doesn't bother her? That I'm... that we...?" I picked my head up, glancing toward the stairs where I'd last seen Breck.

"No! I mean, I think she was a wee bit surprised at first. But I told her if she had a problem with it, then she had an even bigger problem with me. That whole part of inviting him was her idea. She's the biggest romantic I ever met."

A slow sigh escaped me, ending in a single cough.

"Is she going to tell anyone else? The staff, do they know?"

Henry stared at me for a long moment, his mouth twisting into a slight frown as he leaned toward me, his elbows on his knees to match my own. His voice was low when he spoke. For once, he was completely serious.

"Have you ever thought about it not being a secret anymore?"

An incredulous huff of air escaped me. Had I ever thought about it?

"Only every day of my life." It sounded more bitter than I meant it to.

"I could never imagine having to hide me feelings for

Sarah. It was hard enough for all those months of courtship, doing it," he paused to emphasize with his fingers, "the "proper way" with no public displays of our affection, no time alone. It nearly drove me mad. To go on doing that for as long as you have, with no end in sight? It's not healthy."

"I haven't got a choice." It felt so final. I knew I should've stopped there, but my confession rolled off my tongue so easily. "The difficult part isn't finding time alone. We manage that just fine. It's the rest. It's the sneaking around. The hiding. The making plans to meet at night because it's all we're allowed, and then dragging my sorry arse to the stables in the morning with only a few hours of sleep because I don't want to choose between him and my work." My voice broke on *him* and I had to stop, my throat burning with emotion. I rubbed my hands down my face, leaning back against the chair to get more air into my lungs that were starting to hurt.

"Don't hide." Henry's voice was pleading. "While you're here. Don't hide it. Promise me."

"Henry..."

"I mean it. If the staff have anything to say, they'll have to say it to me. To Sarah." He reached to tap the side of my knee with his hand. "No brother of mine will hide his true feelings in me own home."

How could that possibly feel? To steal a kiss the way Dad always did when he was greeting Mammy in the morning. To sit next to one another at dinner and let my leg touch his the way I wanted it to, rather than just feeling the simmering heat between us. To show everyone else the truth.

"Thank you."

CHAPTER FOURTEEN

It felt strange to climb the stairs and navigate the hallway
without a chamberstick to help me see through the dark,
especially in a place so unfamiliar. It wasn't necessary,
though, with the gas lanterns burning at evenly spaced
points along the wall. I found my door with little trouble and
pushed it open. A fire had been set in the small hearth for
me. My bed had been turned down, with the bedclothes
folded in the most deliciously inviting way.

Falling asleep in the bath had been an act of pure exhaus-
tion. Falling asleep in this bed, I could already tell, would be
the result of pure comfort.

I stripped my clothes and threw myself onto the bed.

The frame of it was taller than my own at home, and
much taller than Breck's. My knees were bent at the edge of
the mattress, leaving my feet to dangle. Even when I pointed
my toes, they didn't touch the floor. I turned my hands over
and rubbed them against the sheets. Soft, but not quite like
the ones at the mill.

I pulled my legs up and shuffled toward the headboard,

ostentatious and white, nearly high enough to reach the beams of the ceiling. There was a shorter footboard to match. I tucked up under the covers and settled onto my back, my head sinking into the thick down pillow underneath it. I closed my eyes and released a long, slow sound of contentment.

"I think I preferred the loft," his voice came, alluring and calm, after a soft click.

I snorted a laugh.

"Don't even joke about such things. This bed is incredible. Even with all the hideous flowers."

Breck chuckled and peeled the blankets back just enough to slip underneath them. I wrapped my arm around his shoulders as he pressed himself against my side, his leg finding its way between mine. I feigned surprise with a little gasp, my eyes still closed.

"Sir. Where are your clothes?"

"In my room," he all but purred as he pressed his lips to my jaw, which was perfectly smooth now, save for the one spot I'd nicked myself. The rhythm of my pulse responded immediately. My other hand found his lower back, traveling effortlessly over the curve of his arse and back again.

"Aren't you worried someone might hear us?" I was mostly joking, especially after what Henry had just finished telling me, but old habits were hard to let go of. We weren't in the safety of the mill here. Breck's delicate kisses trailed down my neck, one after another, as he shifted onto his knees. He placed a final kiss at the center of my chest before he sat up, moving his leg from between mine to bend beside my hip.

I forced my eyes open, heavy as they were with lust and fatigue. The fire had his fair skin flushed a warm, peachy color in the places that weren't cast in shadow. His hair hung down across his forehead, nearly into his eyes, which were bright and following the lazy path his hands were tracing down my chest and stomach.

"They would have to quiet themselves to hear us," he finally answered with a telling quirk of his mouth. The thought of my best friend in such a similar position only a few rooms away made my body clench. He was serious when he spoke of his favorite part of being married, then. I couldn't stop the laugh that escaped me.

"Stars above. It's probably a wonder this place doesn't reek of copulation."

"Oh, it does," Breck confirmed as he slid his palms from below my navel to the back of my shoulders, leaning down to kiss me as his fingers locked together behind my neck. "I think it's only right that we contribute."

I hooked my arm around his waist and turned us over, the bedclothes twisting with our tangled legs. Breck pushed up onto his elbow beneath me, bumping his shoulder against my nose as I attempted to place a kiss there. I recovered with a nuzzle against the crook of his neck, my hands against his sides, as he flopped back against the pillow with a tiny jar in his hands.

"This was the only personal item you packed, isn't it?" I asked with a ridiculous grin. "Dirty bastard." Breck giggled and handed me the jar. I sat back as he turned effortlessly onto his stomach, working his way up onto his knees, legs spread, hips angled.

"Finna," was all he said as he wrapped his arms around one of the pillows, resting his cheek against it. I unscrewed the lid and slid two fingertips across the surface of the viscous liquid inside. Breck took the jar back from me and dipped his own fingers, rubbing them in a circular way against his palm before he reached back between his legs.

His slick hand gripping my erection sent a shiver through me that made me cough. I truly didn't know how long I would last after so many weeks without him. That moment was even more proof.

One hand found his hip as the other touched him, gently at first, with one finger and then another. Right away he was breathing heavier, intimate little noises escaping him that spoke directly to my body. My middle finger curled inside him, searching for the spot I knew he liked. Only a few strokes later I was confident I'd found it when he gasped, his hips jerking.

"*Kiss me,*" he breathed.

Breck was on his back in seconds, my mouth against his. I could already feel that familiar warmth coiling within me. Breck adjusted his hips with a moan. I sat up, careful not to grip myself too tightly at the risk of losing it all right then.

"*Please, Peter,*" he whispered.

Heat flashed across my chest and down to my core, making me throb. *I should've taken care of things in the bath before*, I thought too loudly.

"Wait," he said, and I stopped. I raised my eyes to meet his, regret washing over my whole body as I realized that he'd heard it.

"I only meant—" I started, trying to explain myself. "I meant to take the edge off."

"I know." His voice was thick and beautiful. Understanding. "Lie here. Switch with me."

We swapped positions, both of us carefully avoiding any unnecessary touches. With my head back on the cloud of a pillow, we rewound time. Breck was snuggled close to my side again. His leg found its way between mine. The only difference was the hard curve of his arousal pressed against my hip as he kissed my jaw.

"Tell me the moment when to stop. Before you can't keep it back any longer."

I swallowed hard and nodded, watching his hand slide down from my chest to take ahold of me. That feeling started to build again as soon as his grip started moving. My entire body was humming with the press of his lips on my neck, his hips rocking gently against my thigh. The sensation grew until that liquid white heat burned so bright that I almost couldn't look away.

"Stop," I groaned, and he did. My chest was begging for a cough, but I panted through it as the pool of my near-release seeped back into the cracks and crevices within me. Breck's hand remained perfectly still, as did the rest of him, until I told him it was alright.

We repeated this process twice more, each time getting more difficult to stop than the last. Breck's thumb passed smoothly across the very tip of me, collecting what I'd had no control over releasing and eliciting a moan from me that I couldn't hold back, either. I felt his lips curve against my collarbone. And then his breath against my ear.

"This time I won't stop."

Pleasure ripped through me like lightning, striking all the right places at once. I pulsed in his hand over and over, my heart pounding, my vision not quite clear after I'd stopped squeezing my eyes shut from the intensity of it all. The coughs couldn't be held back this time. Breck sat up, bracing himself on one hand by the pillow. He waited patiently for my lungs to relax before he gave me a long, sensuous kiss.

"I cannot possibly deserve you," I said weakly, my chest still rising and falling hard.

"You deserve far more." He reached up to brush a damp piece of hair from my forehead. "Now, let's clean you up so you can get some real sleep. Tomorrow, I want to feel the ocean on my skin."

CHAPTER FIFTEEN

The maidservant woke me the next morning for breakfast. She'd knocked three times and come right inside my room, providing me with a fresh pitcher of water by the washbasin before pushing open the window to allow the crisp breeze in. All of this was done before I'd even managed to pick my head up off the pillow.

I slowly pushed myself into a sitting position, the sheets and blankets pooling at my waist. I felt as though I'd been wrung out like a wet rag in the most satisfying way possible. After rubbing the sleep from my eyes with both hands, I stumble-walked my way to the window and placed my hands on the sill, thankful that it came up above my waist. Not that anyone would've been able to look in on me.

The side of the castle plunged directly down a rugged cliff, ending in a chaotic mix of rocks, waves, and seafoam. I instinctively took a step back, looking instead at the water that stretched out into nothing, just a simple line where the sky met the sea. The only break was where the coastline wrapped around, forming a small cove. The land there looked more forgiving; the waves were calmer and lapped against a stretch of sand instead of stone. A fine place to put your feet in the water. Breck's words the night before had me hustling toward the basin to get ready.

I discovered that I was the last one awake only as I wandered into the smaller, more intimate family dining room where breakfast had been laid out.

"Not dead, just sleeping," Henry teased as I sat down in my chair. I held back the face I wanted to make at him for Sarah's sake. Henry's plate showed the remnants of a full breakfast, complete with sausage ends, scrambles of eggs, and the juice of tomatoes. Breck's plate contained only a half-eaten slice of toast with jam.

"Good morning," he said quietly after sipping from his tea. I shifted my puffy eyes up to his with a tired grin. His legs were crossed beneath him in the chair. I spread my leg to bump it against his knee.

"Morning," I returned.

I filled my plate with some random things from the bowls and dishes laid out in front of us. Toast with a thick marmalade, cut fruit, one piece of sausage. I was served some tea and promptly added two overflowing spoonfuls of honey.

"I'd like to see the stables this morning, if that's alright." It was the truth, but I also wanted to check on my horses.

"Aye, I'd love you to see them. Not quite what we've got at home, but impressive yet." Henry sat back in his chair as his plate was taken away, wiping his mouth with the corner of a starched linen napkin. "We can take a tour of the grounds together once you've eaten. Afterwards, my dear wife and I will take the horses out. I trust you'll both find something to fill your time while we're gone."

I refused to look at him. I knew the sly, crooked grin I'd find if I did.

* * *

Henry was right. The stables had been one of the first places to see a renovation under Sarah's father, which meant that they'd been updated nearly twenty years before. They were nice, but not brand new like so much of the place was. The *castle*. I still couldn't get over it.

As we all crunched our way across the rocks in the yard, several of the horses' ears pricked up. For the first time in my life, the thought of riding didn't excite me. I approached my mare, stroking her long nose as she pushed into my palm. I spotted a full bucket of clear water hanging on a peg for her, as well as fresh bedding and hay in the rack along the wall.

"Have they had any grain?" I asked the same young stable hand from the day before, who was standing at attention nearby, his cap gripped tightly in his hands behind his back.

"Sir, Mr. O'Connor gav'us strict instructions ta'wait for guidance on feedin' yer animals." His accent was much thicker than even Henry's, but I nodded, having caught most of it. I told him what they both needed, calculating in my head how much to give them for the morning and evening feedings. Their diets changed some during the off season, but I also wanted to make sure they had enough after two days on the road. The lad nodded and off he went to fetch the buckets.

I could tell the horses had been groomed again, with very little loose hair clinging to their coats. The saddles and tack had also been conditioned. I could see and smell the shine of the oil on them, even from a distance. There really wasn't any work left for me to do.

"They'll be turned out midmorning and brought in later," Henry said, gripping my shoulder and giving it a good shake. "I know this is hard for you to hear. But just relax, boyo. You're on holiday."

We were taken on a guided tour of the yard, which Sarah called the bailey. She pointed out the former blacksmith shop, the bakery, and the old mill, which had been run using wind and manpower rather than water. Henry opened the door for Breck to see the inside. I watched him inspect things closely, his hands coming from his pockets as he crouched to get a better look at the stones used to grind the meal into flour.

"A smaller operation than what you run at home, no doubt," Henry said, giving him a compliment that didn't sound at all like a compliment in the way only he could.

It made Breck smile modestly. "It would've been enough for the people who lived and worked here. Maybe a little extra to sell on market days."

Next, we were taken to the gatehouse, which Henry said was the easiest way to access one of the towers from outside the keep itself. We went single file down a tight passageway made entirely of grouted stone, narrow gaps every so often serving as the only source of light or fresh air. Henry passionately told us that's where they would've shot the arrows from if the castle was ever under attack. We eventually reached a staircase that twisted around on itself, with shallow steps also made of stone winding all the way up.

The small, empty room at the top was stale and dusty. I immediately started coughing. Sarah tried the handle of the door that would take us out onto the wall, but it wouldn't budge. All three of us went to offer our assistance. None of us got the chance. Clad in her skirts and jewels, she jammed her shoulder against the ancient wood, forcing it open. She smoothed her hands down her dress and led the way outside. Henry looked over his shoulder at us and jounced his eyebrows several times. Breck and I had to duck our heads under the doorway.

Wind whipped at our clothes and hair as we all stepped over the threshold. I squinted into the overcast morning light as Sarah pointed out the road where it came around the break in the hills, explaining that this had been one of the most well-protected strongholds of its time, impossible to be taken by surprise.

"I heard a story about a castle like this once." Breck was looking out over the water below, his hands resting casually on the rough stones that'd been picked away by rain and wind for centuries. "A fairy tale, really." Something tightened in my chest as I studied the reaction of our hosts.

"Oh, please tell us if you remember it. I haven't heard a good fairy tale since I was a girl."

He paused, collecting his thoughts. "The story goes that there was a castle high on a rock, where the land met the sea. The king of this castle knew he had something special, for it was naturally protected, with mountains on one side and the ocean on all the others. What he didn't know was that far below the castle, in a cave hidden deep in the cliffs, lived a troll."

Sarah had leaned into Henry's side, both of them listening intently. She tucked a stray curl of strawberry blonde hair behind her ear before returning her hand to where it had been resting on Henry's arm. Their other hands were clasped, fingers laced together.

"This troll – like all trolls – was unfriendly toward humans. He hated them so much, including the ones who lived in the castle above his home. He'd seen how wasteful they were, having parties, drinking in excess, throwing out food that was perfectly good. Meanwhile, he was living off the random fish or seabird he could catch from time to time. He'd had enough. He decided to start stealing from them. So every night, after the castle had gone to sleep, he would climb the rocks, scale the wall, and enter the keep.

"He quickly learned where to find the storerooms, the kitchens, and anywhere else the humans kept their food. He would eat his fill and escape back down to his cave before morning. The king didn't know what to make of this. Every man, woman, and child were questioned as they tried to find out who was stealing."

Sarah cut in. "Why didn't the guards ever stop him?"

Breck quirked his mouth and shrugged. "Trolls cannot be seen by humans."

"Aye," Henry said, nodding sagely. "Of course."

I pressed my lips together to hide my grin.

"After this went on for several weeks, the king couldn't take it anymore. They'd run out of nearly everything, and soon they wouldn't be able to feed their people. The king took a walk deep into the woods and wished for a solution.

"Luckily for him, a fairy had been nearby picking wild blackberries to make a pie. She heard his pleas for help. She knew of the troll who lived in the cliffs, and she also knew that his favorite thing to eat was a plump mountain goat. The fairy decided to brave the strong winds and journeyed down to visit with the troll. At first, he could not be reasoned with. But soon, with the temptation of a regular meal proving too good to pass up, the troll agreed to stop stealing from the humans in the castle if they agreed to leave a mountain goat for him to eat.

"The next day, the fairy requested an audience with the king. The guards normally turned away anyone who the king was not expecting. But after they told the king her story, he ordered them to let her in at once. You see, no one else knew about his walk into the woods. No one else knew what he'd wished for. The king listened in disbelief as the fairy explained what had been happening at the castle, and why the troll was stealing all their food. He laughed her away, telling her she was foolish if she thought he would make a deal with a troll on his own land.

"The king did not follow the fairy's instructions to leave a mountain goat out for the troll. So the troll continued to come, climbing the rocks, scaling the wall, and entering the keep night after night. Finally, when there was nothing left to eat but crumbs, the king had no choice. He sent his best huntsman to collect the biggest mountain goat he could find.

"The hunter returned with his prize. He was shocked when the king ordered him to toss it down to the cliffs, but he did as he was asked. The king waited up that night in his bedchamber, listening. He never heard a sound. In the morning, he was pleased to discover that the castle had not been visited by the troll that night. Right away, he sent out more men to hunt for the mountain goats. He'd also learned how precious their food was. The parties came less often, and their goods were no longer wasted. The troll never went back to the castle again."

Sarah and Henry broke into quiet applause when Breck finished his story. He grinned down at his feet and pushed away from the wall, his hands sinking into his pockets.

"That was lovely, Breck. Just lovely. I didn't know we had

such a storyteller in our midst." Sarah fixed her hair again, battling the wind, and Henry finally noticed.

We all went winding back down the staircase, my lungs arguing with the dust motes we encountered along the way. As we exited the gatehouse, I asked Henry the best path to reach the water, if there was one.

"Go back across the bridge. Before the road disappears around the hills, take the little trail down. It's the safest way we've found." After Sarah had left us for the stables, Henry stepped closer to me and lowered his voice. "We've managed it with a drink or two in us several times, so you shouldn't have any trouble." His mouth fell open as he gave me a wink. He started away from us walking backwards, raising his arms as he had a sudden realization. "Actually, it might even be better that way. Take a bottle with you. Take two!" With that, he turned and jogged after his bride.

"Sometimes I wonder how we're friends," I muttered to Breck.

He laughed. "How could you not be? He's your perfect balance."

We decided to try the trail without the wine, at least for that first trip. I let Breck lead the way. He found the path easily after we'd crossed the bridge. I kept stealing glances out at the water as the breeze grew stronger, the saltiness of it already leaving a texture to my hair and face.

When we reached the bottom, I caught Breck's arm before he stepped onto the sand. I used him for support as I removed my boots and socks. I knew I'd probably regret it, since the sand also looked to be full of pebbles and other hard objects washed ashore. I stuffed my socks inside the boots and set them on a rock before I took a breath and put one foot onto the beach we'd traveled so far to stand on.

It wasn't so bad. I only winced a few times as we crept closer to the water, my feet sinking a bit with each step. We were almost there when my heel found a very sharp rock hidden beneath the sand. My arms flailed a little as I cursed under my breath and sidestepped to find a smoother spot. Breck reached for me, grabbing my hand with a chuckle. I gave him an embarrassed grin, and he returned it with his own before our eyes fell to our hands at the same time.

My brain said let go. My nerves said let go.

My heart said don't. Henry said don't. So I didn't.

I slid my fingers between his, our palms flush. I squeezed once. He looked at me then, confused. He tilted his head just slightly. A question.

"It's alright," I told him, my voice straining against the relentless breeze we'd found. The line of concern between his brows softened. He squeezed back. And then he smiled a most genuine smile, sending a warmth through me that even the near-winter wind couldn't blow away.

The water was a different story. I let Breck drag me along, expecting him to stop at the edge. Instead, he splashed right in, leaving me no option but to follow.

"*Hah!*" I yelped. The temperature sucked the air from my lungs. "*Feck*, that's cold." He finally released me, going deep enough that the waves splashed above his knees, wetting his clothes. And he just kept going. "Breck!" I rushed to roll up the bottoms of my trouser legs, the water washing over my hands and ankles as the waves rolled in. My toes were already frozen. I shook and squeezed my fingers as I stood up, fighting the cold away, but I forgot all about them when my eyes landed back on my companion.

He was in up to his hips, standing with his arms stretched wide against the wind. His loose sleeves and shirt tail were fluttering violently, exposing the skin of his lower back to me. He said something, but I couldn't hear the words.

"What?" I called back. He didn't respond, so I cupped my hands at my mouth and tried again. And then he turned. And my heart seized. And he was the most beautiful creature I'd ever seen.

The wind continued to kick up his shirt, showing off his stomach now as he waded through the water back toward me. The waves of his hair were also blown about, taking me back to that morning on the mountain when I'd had my first real look at him. His sharp jaw. His full mouth. And those freckles. The spray of the ocean had brought them to life. They sparkled in the sunlight breaking through the clouds, further enhanced by the roundness of his cheeks as he smiled.

He emerged from the water with his trousers clinging to his legs, leaving nothing to the imagination. I had to peel my eyes away from them as he stopped in front of me, dripping.

"I said—"

I grabbed his face and kissed him before he could say anything more. I felt him tense at first with surprise, but then he relaxed into me, his arms coming up around my neck and shoulders. I deepened the kiss, one arm sliding down to wrap around his lower back to leave no space between us. He moaned softly against my mouth. I felt the water slide against my shins, then slightly higher, and finally we broke apart as a wave pushed Breck into me. We both looked down in surprise at how high it had come up our legs.

"Sorry," Breck said with a little laugh before he kissed me again. I wanted to tell him that I would gladly drown if it meant I'd die with his lips pressed to mine.

We settled for walking along the edge of the water, where

the sand was smooth and fully saturated. Only the occasional rock or piece of driftwood created a break in the waves as they pulled back out into the sea. The only thing I could think about was his hand in mine.

"I thought you could only control the river," I said mildly.

"The river is my responsibility. I have a connection to it. But my magic cannot tell the difference." As he said this, I felt the familiar chill of it wrapping around my legs, pulling the water from my clothes.

"The river, the sea, the rain… could you move water inside of a glass or something, too?"

Breck chuckled at that. "It's possible. But it's much easier for me to move the water that's still connected to nature." He was still ankle-deep in it as we walked.

"Does it make you feel something? Touching the water?"

"Murray says he feels like something is missing when he's away from the ocean. Like a part of him has been left behind. Sometimes I think I feel that way about the river." He kicked his toes against a new wave, making a tiny splash. "I'm not sure how I can explain the way it feels. It's…" He took a deep breath and let it out slowly. *"Abhaile. Tá sé cosúil le baile.* It feels like home."

"That's a good feeling." The sound of those unfamiliar words on his tongue churned something so pleasant inside me. I changed the subject. "That story about the castle. Was it true? Did a troll really live here?" I glanced up at the cliffside wearily. I couldn't see any caves.

"No," he said with a smirk, dragging the word out. "Trolls only live in Nordic countries, of course." Our stretch of beach had turned into more rocks, so we swapped hands and started back the other way. "But the story is true, I think. True enough, anyway. All castles have at least a little bit of magic in their history. And trolls are very mean."

"And kings are quite gluttonous," I added with a grin. He grinned back.

"And fairies do love blackberries." Breck patted his stomach for emphasis.

"And I love you." The words came so easily, but my body reacted in a rush. A bloom of emotions brought heat to my chest and neck. "I'm so happy you're here with me."

Breck brought our joined hands up to place a kiss on the back of mine.

"*Sea, mo ghrá.* I'm happy, too."

I hid my wounded pride over my one-sided confession and simply savored his touch.

CHAPTER SIXTEEN

Breck and I were invited to sit for tea while we waited for our hosts to return. Instead of being ushered to another sitting room, or simply returning to the family dining room, the maid asked where we'd like to be served. We exchanged a glance. Sarah hadn't given us a tour of the inside yet. I shrugged. Breck thought for a moment, and then seemed to have an idea.

"Is there a library?"

"But of course, sir. This way."

In my head, I was picturing something similar to William's study at home. A few bookshelves, some chairs, maybe a desk. When the double doors were pushed open, however, I quickly realized that I was wrong. As it turns out, staying at a remote castle at the edge of the world calls for many, many books. Two walls were lined with shelves that had no spaces left to fill. The third wall was left empty only because it opened to a balcony that was large enough to hold a table and two chairs. Inside were two more chairs with seats long enough to prop your feet on. A modest writing desk sat in one corner.

"Out on the balcony would be grand," I said, just stating my opinion.

It was taken as an order. "Right away, sir."

I started for the door made of windows. Breck immediately went for the books. He bent his neck to the side to read the titles, his fingertips walking lightly along the spines as he went.

"I was thinking." His voice was barely above a whisper. I could hear the mischief in it. "Finna told me once that long ago, castles like this had fairies to look after them, serving the kings and queens and their families for generations. It was a most special honor."

"Are there any here now?" My gaze instinctively swept the room for a hint of gold.

"Only one," he answered with an arched brow.

I feigned a forgetful face and tapped the heel of my hand against my temple theatrically.

"*I meant any other fairies, obviously,*" I whispered at him.

"No, not anymore." He pulled a book out to look at the cover, flipping some pages before he put it back. "These fairies would write in books. Names and dates, favorite recipes, when children were born, things like that. A record of sorts. Lots of things could change from one generation to the next, but rarely would anyone ever get rid of a book. That's why they ended up with libraries like this." He pulled out another but put it back without opening it, his attention shifting to a lower shelf on the next bookcase.

Breck dropped to his hands and knees, leaning on his forearm as he got a closer look at the very bottom row. He crawled forward then, somehow as graceful on the ground as he was on his feet, and supported his weight on his arm again. The slight sway and angle of his hips made me instantly grateful for their need to place books so close to the ground. I coughed and tried to focus.

"I can feel it somewhere…" he muttered under his breath. I was about to ask if I could help when he used one finger to tilt a thin book out of place. "Found you." He crossed his legs beneath him as he sat up, opening the book on his lap. I looked on as he turned each page with care. He stopped once to slide his fingers gently across the paper.

"What is it?" I asked. It looked like a normal book to me. I tilted my head the other direction to see if anything stood out to me that way. It didn't. Breck's eyes lifted to the doors. He shut the book gently and stood up in one fluid movement, tucking it underneath his arm.

"I'll show you later," he promised as the maid entered with our tray of tea and biscuits.

* * *

I decided after supper that my holiday would include taking as many baths as I could possibly manage. The sand still caught between my toes from the morning had been a large deciding factor.

My hair was still damp as I eased open the door that connected our rooms. I ran my fingers through it, brushing it back from my face. Breck was in the middle of his bed, legs crossed, with the little book open on his lap again. I'd wanted to ask him more about what he'd found all day. Trying not to disturb him, I climbed onto the bed, bracing myself on a propped arm behind his back.

"It's so fascinating." He turned a page slowly, the paper

stiff and discolored with age. "If I'm reading it the right way, the fairies here were also a family. One generation after another caring for the castle and those who called it home." He turned to me, his eyes big and hopeful. "Can I show you now?"

We moved back against the headboard. I kept my arm around him as he relaxed into my side, legs pulled up at the knees, the book resting against his thighs. My eyelids closed as his magic wrapped around me like silk. For one, blissful moment, the ache in my chest disappeared. Then I opened my eyes.

Small marks on the paper caught the light of the fire. They shone like liquid gold as he turned to the next page. Every margin and blank space between the text was full of the little lines and swirls of this glowing, magical ink. Breck flipped back to the beginning. I almost stopped him, my brain telling me that any slight movement would surely make the wet ink run and smudge, but it didn't.

"Here at the start, it's written in some of the oldest fairy language ever recorded. I recognize it, but I only know a few words." There was a sense of wonder in his voice that I couldn't help but find endearing. "See there, how the style of the letters change? Another fairy wrote this part. It's so rare to see any of this written down anymore." As he continued to flip through the book, I watched the movement of his hands. I battled my urge to look at the way I knew his cheeks were glittering in the firelight.

And then he started to read.

I closed my eyes again and listened to the rise and fall of his voice. I let the unfamiliar words and inflections do their worst to me, my pulse quickening. His voice was like wine in my mouth, smooth and luscious. Even my most favorite dessert couldn't taste so good. I stuck the tip of my tongue out to wet my lips. Breck's quiet laugh was the only thing to put a pause on the spell I was silently slipping under.

"Here's a list of the things the king liked to e—Peter? Are you alright?" He sat up some next to me. I peeled my eyes open, forgetting about his freckles until I saw them. Oh, those freckles. My tongue was too heavy to speak at first.

"Don't you know what your words do to me?" I sounded a little dreamy. A little drunk.

"What do you mean?" His eyes searched mine, brows furrowed. I reached for his hand. I would just have to show him. I brought his fingers – somewhat roughly, by accident – against the bulge at the front of my trousers. His eyebrows shot up in surprise.

"Every time you speak fairy words, it's like this." I let go of him then, my mind finally clearing some. I thought he would move his hand away, too. Instead, he adjusted his grip on me, slowly stroking the outline of my erection through the fabric with the very tips of his fingers.

"Nobody ever told me that would happen," he said, his voice low. Our noses were nearly touching. My lips parted. His eyes closed.

It was my turn to make him feel as good as he'd made me feel the night before.

I pushed him onto his back, already settling between his spread legs as I slid his shirt up, exposing his stomach. His trousers still smelled like the ocean. Breck let out a breathy moan as I kissed the skin just above his waistband. As much as I didn't want to waste a second of seeing the sparkles across his cheeks, I closed my eyes and curled a finger underneath the band, tugging the front of his trousers lower so I could find even more sensitive skin to brush my lips across.

Breck's fingers combed through my hair to the back of my head as I traveled lower still, using my nose to trace along his hardening length beneath the fabric before I placed some kisses there, too. I used my hand next, palming the base of him as I tilted my head so I could see his face. He already wore a soft look of pleasure as he watched me, his chest rising and falling with more heavy breaths and quiet, amorous sounds. I knew I was in trouble when that lusty smirk broke through.

"*Déan deifir le do thoil, Peadar,*" he panted. "Enough teasing."

The use of my name was all it took. I leaned up over him on my hands and knees, kissing him deeply on the mouth. I felt his legs wrap around me, providing the perfect opportunity to roll my hips down against his. He moaned louder then, his head falling back against the pillow. If I waited long enough, he'd tell me exactly what he wanted. It came only a handful of neck kisses later.

"*Put your mouth on me.*"

Back down I went, touching and kissing all the while. I made it to his waistband, hooking my fingers in at both of his hipbones. Breck lifted his hips from the bed.

"You're making it too easy for me," I told him, working one side down, then the other, until I was a blink away from releasing him from the restraint of his trousers.

"I just—" He stopped cold. I looked up. "*No,*" he whispered harshly. Then he groaned it again through his clenched teeth. "No."

I sat up some, not expecting Breck to do the same. He

reached for my face, holding it in both hands as he kissed me hard, a last little desperate moan escaping him.

"Please forgive me," he begged, kissing me again.

When I opened my eyes, he was gone. I didn't turn my head to search for him. The emptiness of the room was palpable, his magic ripped away. All I could do for a long while was sit there on the wrinkled blankets, staring down at the book he left behind.

* * *

I spent the rest of the night trying to come up with a reasonable excuse for where he'd gone so suddenly. No letter could have come for him in the middle of the night. Work couldn't have come calling unexpectedly so far away, especially after we'd told them how our friend had taken over the mill while he was gone. Sarah had been particularly interested in that information. It seemed that all the women in my life wanted to know more about Finna and the wide array of things she was capable of.

In the end, as much as it pained me, I decided the only believable lie was to tell them we'd had an argument so bad that it caused him to leave. The thought of it being the truth turned my stomach as I told them over breakfast. I had no other choice when he hadn't returned by morning. Henry got heated as soon as the words left my mouth.

"One set of cross words and it's out the door, is it?" He huffed and let his fork clatter down onto his plate after taking a bite of eggs. He chewed twice and kept talking. "That's no way to handle things."

"It's fine." I tried to placate him by keeping my own voice calm. "We just needed some space to think, is all. We've never spent so much time together until now." My face went warm at the words. There was no turning back. The truth was out about us. I glanced at Sarah, hopeful that Henry was right about her.

She only looked concerned. "He'll come around soon enough, Peter. Not to worry. Whatever it was about, I'm sure there's a solution to be found."

I nodded to show my thanks for her supportive words as I picked at the food in front of me. Maybe this was something we really would have to discuss. I knew he had no choice but to go when he was called away. Someone's life could depend on it. But then, what if it hadn't been the river? Was it Fallon instead, breaking her promise? Or worse, it could've been neither of those things.

My brows pinched together as I rubbed the corner of my toast through a smear of jam on the plate. That couldn't be true. Breck hadn't wanted to go. He'd sounded so remorseful, asking me to forgive him before he'd even gone. I thought of all the mornings I'd woken up alone. I recalled the days I spent missing him, the ache in my chest growing heavier, wondering if he was safe. If he missed me as much as I was missing him. Could I spend my life never knowing when he'd leave or return?

I was being silly. This was how it worked. We couldn't always be together. He had his job to do, just like me or anyone else. Anne waited patiently for William to return home from his work travels all the time. Certainly I was capable of doing the same.

Henry and I took our horses out after breakfast. It felt like old times, just the two of us on horseback, following a well-beaten trail with the river and mountains in the distance. Only the cool, sticky breeze on my face kept reminding me how far I was from home. We rode in silence until the sun had come all the way up, though it was mostly blocked by clouds.

"Will you tell me the whole truth now, boyo?"

My skin prickled with surprise. I couldn't hear any hint of humor in his voice.

"What do you mean by that?" I asked, trying to sound casual about it.

"The gatekeep didn't report any activity of people comin' or goin' last night. He's not one to sleep on the job." Henry slowed his horse to a stop, turning her to block me and my gelding from going any further. "And the horses. They're both still here. You're telling me your man just up and left on those bare feet of his and plans to walk all the way home?"

My brain couldn't formulate an excuse fast enough. All I could focus on was the nausea bubbling in my gut. Without a word, I dismounted and stumbled toward a tree I thought looked sturdy enough to hold my weight. I reached for it with both hands, resting my forehead against the bark, feeling the cold sweat that had broken out across my body. I knew when I felt Henry's hand on my shoulder that I couldn't keep my last secret from him any longer.

"He's magic," I choked out, my confession forcing unwanted tears to my eyes. I blinked them back and stood to face my friend, one hand still on the tree to support me. "Breck is a fairy. He's made of magic, and if I loved him any more, my heart would surely burst into a million little pieces."

Henry's mouth fell open, his eyes wide. I swallowed at the queasiness still fighting to send what little I'd managed to eat at breakfast back up. A range of emotions crossed his features before he finally gave me a look of resolve.

"So… he can fly?"

A sharp laugh burst out of me, thick with emotion. I shook my head.

"No, he can't fly. He just kind of… goes. He vanishes. And ends up where he needs to be." I shrugged and crossed my arms over my stomach, desperate for some mint tea.

Henry's crooked grin came back as if it had never left.

"Now that's the craic!"

Relief flooded me so fast that I had to sit down. Henry sat too, starting in with the first of a dozen questions he asked me there beside the trail. I watched the horses graze happily while I told him everything. And I do mean *everything*. I couldn't stand one more truth untold between us.

Henry finally hit me with a gentle punch against my arm so I'd look at him.

"I'm proud of you. For tellin' me all this. I know it wasn't easy. You went so pale there for a minute, I thought I'd have to catch you on the way down."

I chuckled and slid a hand along the back of my shoulder to my neck. "Thanks."

"And," he added, leaning in closer, "the lad's in *love*." He fluttered his eyelashes at me and clutched his hands together beneath his chin. "Now *I* get to make an embarrassing speech at *your* wedding!" He let out a *whoop* and leapt to his feet, brushing off the seat of his trousers.

"I don't know what you're talking about," I complained, following him to fetch the horses. "My speech was great." I might've included a funny story or two from our boyhood before I finished with a toast for the happy couple. It was all very proper, though. I'd been too nervous for it not to be. I stuck my foot in the stirrup and swung my leg over the saddle. Ruining the moment by reminding him that it would never be possible for us to marry didn't seem necessary.

Breck still hadn't returned when we made it back to the castle in time for an early dinner. I drank my tea in small sips, trying not to let my worry for him consume me entirely. Where had he gone?

CHAPTER SEVENTEEN

For the next two days, I roamed around the castle, trying to fill my time with relaxing things. I walked on the beach again, stopping to stare out at the waves. I went back to the library and searched the titles for something to read. None of them seemed interesting. Henry and I ventured up onto the wall so he could show me the view from the top of the tallest tower. It was incredible, but I couldn't bring myself to be as excited as I wanted to be for him. On the second night after Breck left, they even had the kitchen prepare an apple dessert just for me. Henry knew it was my favorite.

I made the decision to leave the next morning.

There had never been a plan set for exactly how long we would stay on at the estate. I only knew that I had to be home in time for William to leave on his trip, but that wasn't for another week or so. The more time that passed with Breck being gone, the more I felt like I was just imposing on their honeymoon. They were trying too hard to include me in things. It only made me feel more alone.

I'd let them know at supper how my plans had changed.

They were sad for me to leave so soon, but they understood. I'd left it up to Henry to share whatever information he felt he should with Sarah, so I really had no idea how much she knew about the situation. But she'd stopped me on my way to bed to let me know that the maid had collected my saddle bags to pack some things for my journey back home.

"It really has been wonderful having you here. I hope the... turn of events didn't completely hinder your enjoyment of being our guest." The sparkle of Henry's ring caught my eye as she dropped her hand from where she'd placed it on my arm. I'd learned this was gesture that ran deep in their family.

"I thank you again for your generous invitation. I've enjoyed myself very much, but my family and my work are waiting for me at home."

She tilted her head with a nod of understanding. "We will be along shortly. Within the next few weeks, I expect."

The conversation I had with Henry about what was keeping them so long flashed into the front of my mind. My traitorous eyes dipped to the place where her belly might already be cradling another future redheaded O'Connor. I felt my face go warm as she moved her hands up slightly to shield herself from my staring. I looked up to find a knowing grin on her features.

"Are you?" I asked, my voice thin with a sudden wave of emotion. My best friend, a father.

"Time will tell." That was all she said before she bid me a pleasant night.

In my bedroom, I found one saddle bag remaining, already packed with my clothes and other belongings. I sat gingerly on the edge of the mattress, my gaze landing on the decorative pull of the drawer in the bedside table. The slide of the wood was too loud as it revealed the items I'd hidden inside. The little jar. The library book. There was a pang in my chest as I thought of how excited Breck had been as he'd told me about the golden script inside. Something lower in me twinged as well, remembering how close I'd been to having my mouth on—

I coughed a few times and gathered both items out of the drawer, stuffing them deep inside my leather bag, underneath my clothes. I removed the ones I was wearing and climbed under the blankets, preparing for another restless night. Henry had promised to have one of his men dictate the clearest of instructions so I could find my way back home without my guide. Part of me was still clinging to the hope that Breck would return. That everything would be fine.

Something felt wrong, though. As I'd continued to think about it, I realized he'd never left me in such a way before. All the times he was gone for a long while, he'd known well ahead of time. He'd always made sure that I knew roughly when he would come back, be it a few days or longer. This time, there was nothing. Not even a note to explain things.

I turned onto my stomach, facing away from the low fire glowing in the hearth. It was too bright for me to sleep. I closed my eyes and pulled the blankets up over my head. If nothing else, I had already decided that I would certainly *not* be sleeping in any hay lofts on my journey home.

"*Peter*," came the whisper, along with a light pressure in the middle of my back. I stirred only slightly, stretching my legs out from where I'd had them bent up at the knees. "*Peter*," the voice came again, this time the pressure shaking me gently. I turned to look over my shoulder as I pulled the blankets down, the rush of fresh air making me cough. One eye opened as I squinted to see who was beside me.

"Breck?" I asked, my voice thick with sleep. The room was still golden from the light of the fire. I blinked a few times. No, it wasn't.

"*Peter. I need your help.*" I realized all at once what the soft radiance was coming from. *Who* it was coming from. Panic shot through my body like an arrow from one of the ancient towers surrounding the keep.

"*Elina. What's happened?*" I twisted around so I could sit up. She was perched on the mattress, barely making a dent despite her height. Her long, golden hair fell forward over her shoulder as she moved her hand back to her lap. "*Is he alright?*"

"*There's a situation. I think you're the only one who can help at this point. Will you come with me?*" She stood then, her graceful movement reminding me so much of Breck that my stomach lurched. I nodded and scrambled under the blankets for a moment, trying to collect my thoughts in my fog of sleep and emotions.

"I, em... I just have to... get dressed," I told her. She was still looking at me. I stared back at her.

"*Get on with it, then,*" she encouraged, making a hurry-up motion. I groaned and slid out from under the blankets, my hands coming down to cover myself the best I could as I went for my clothes at the far end of the room. My face burned as I pulled on my trousers first.

"*You humans and your modesty,*" she teased lightly when I turned around, fastening the buttons at the top of my shirt before I shoved the tails in my waistband. *"I've seen it all before, you know."*

"Aye, well..." I shook my head, too tired to finish that thought. I looked at my waistcoat, made a face, and reached for my jacket instead. *No time for the proper stuff now, Nan, I* thought to myself. I yanked on my boots. Elina reached both hands out for me as I crossed back to her. I took them and she tightened her grip in a squeeze that she didn't release.

"You'll feel strange. Your head will probably hurt. I can give you something for the pain. Just don't let go of my hands."

I didn't have time to ask any questions. One moment I was looking at her face, nodding, and the next, everything went sideways and the ground fell out from underneath my feet.

* * *

Elina's grip went loose. I completed my dizzy spell with a hard fall to my knees. My head jerked forward on impact. I stifled a moan and pressed my hands to the pain she'd warned about in my temples.

"Peter!"

Everything in me lit up at the sound of his voice. Even the pain seemed to subside as I turned in the direction I thought he'd called me from. There was no way for me to prepare myself for what I found when I opened my eyes.

We were deep in a forest, with trees so tall you couldn't see the crown of them even if you tried. Moss and thick vines of ivy covered most of their trunks, dripping from the branches like decorations. Sunlight filtered through, allowing ferns and other small plants to flourish. But that wasn't all. There were zips and whirls and sparkles of gold *everywhere* I looked. The bells and chimes from my vision at The Wishing Tree were back, filling the air as the littlest fairies moved about like birds and butterflies. No, those were real butterflies, flitting lazily from one soft, green perch to another.

I could feel the damp spots on the knees of my trousers from the moss as I got to my feet. Everything was so lush and beautiful. Soft. Magical. A slow-motion force came from behind as arms were wrapped around my shoulders. I turned when the grip they had on me loosened. Somehow, everything felt normal, but also not normal at all. A small, whimper of a laugh came out of my throat when I realized it was Breck holding me.

"*Am I fecked?*" I whisper-yelled at him. He just smiled and shook his head. The light had his cheeks and nose absolutely radiant with blue and silver sparkles. My grip tightened on him, fingers grasping at his clothes, as another wave of the dizziness passed over me. He held me closer.

"No. It's the magic. I can't believe you're here." He paused then, his smile fading. "Why are you here?"

I thought hard about this. My head really did hurt. "Elina came to get me. She said she needed my help." I brought my hand up to rub at my temple again. Breck sighed and put his forehead gently against mine. I wanted him to kiss me.

"I'm so sorry I couldn't return to you." He leaned up to place a slow, sweet kiss on the opposite side from where I was rubbing little circles, his lips lingering on my scar. "Eabha called us here. When that happens, we cannot leave until she says. Let's get something for your head."

He kept both hands on me, one around my waist and the other on my arm, as he guided me... somewhere. I tore my gaze from the lowest branches, where the fairies and other little creatures continued their easy, peaceful paths above us. Bird songs mixed with the delicate chimes now.

"What is this place?" I asked, my voice sounding far away to my own ears.

"This is where I come to train," he started, pointing out a moss-covered log so I wouldn't trip. "It's where the Seelie court meets." He paused again. "This is my home."

CHAPTER EIGHTEEN

Even after swallowing down the bitter green drink that Elina handed me, I still didn't feel quite like myself. There was a gentleness to everything that made me keep blinking my eyes to clear them, even though I was pretty sure my vision wasn't the problem. It made me think of the expensive paintings I'd seen on the walls at the castle. Too many soft edges made it hard to determine where one thing ended and the next began, only differentiated by color or movement, especially on things that were far away.

I held Breck's hand tightly to make sure he couldn't be one of those far away things.

He'd brought me inside what looked like ruins of another castle, so reclaimed by nature that you could only see some of the faded, gray stonework peeking out beneath the greenery. A side wall had collapsed completely. One step over the threshold revealed the magic hidden within.

Vines and moss still covered most of the walls and ground. What had appeared as empty space overhead from the outside was now intricately woven branches and vines; a natural roof that allowed the sunshine to peek through the cracks, leaving it bright but still peaceful. It reminded me of Breck's room at the mill, with rich browns complimenting the greens as tree trunks and thick roots seemed to have grown up from the earth to form places to sit. That's where Breck had placed me. I was trying my best to not disturb a large mushroom growing near my elbow.

Mixed with the greenery were swaths of shimmery, earthy fabrics draped across furniture, hanging across doorways, and – much to my delight – wrapped around everyone I encountered.

"It's out of respect for Eabha that we dress... *appropriately* while we're here," Breck mumbled after I'd spent too much time staring at him. I marveled at the way the cerulean vest hugged tight to his shoulders and chest, held together mostly by a crisscross length of golden twine at the front. It matched the shiny gold thread used to weave intricate swirls into the fabric. There was no shirt underneath to hide his freckles. The collar was ruffled with a sheer fabric that gathered back over each shoulder, forming a transparent cape of deep blues and golds. The cut of the garment ended at the top of his dark navy trousers in the front, but in the back it went much longer, down to his knees.

"Don't let him fool you," Carrick cut in, his tone that of a reproving older brother. "We still get to pick our clothes here." I'd never seen so much color spring to Breck's cheeks as I did then. It was adorable. I nudged his knee with mine.

"*I like it*," I whispered to him. At least, I think I whispered. It was hard to tell. He gave me a look then, showing his relief. I didn't care what he wore, but to see more skin and more freckles, I wasn't complaining. If anything, I was the one who should've been embarrassed. I hadn't needed my jacket. The weather was mild and comfortable. I didn't have to ask to know that it was like that all the time.

One thing I couldn't figure out, though, was what they were all doing. Murray was the only one up, pacing the floor along a wall with lots of windows. He reminded me of the way the horses looked when they'd been cooped up for too long, restless and ready to run the second they could. Everyone else was just sitting and waiting. They looked bored. Impatient, almost. Fallon wasn't there.

"Who wants to tell the lad?" Carrick asked with a sigh, shifting in his chair.

"I can," Elina offered with a gentle smile. She was still luminescent. Her clothes were mostly the same as what I had always seen her in, yellows and creams and flowing somehow, even as she sat still. Breck had already told me they'd been called together by Eabha, but not the reason why. How was I going to help with anything in their world?

"Is it something bad?" I asked, keeping my voice quiet. My head was feeling better.

"Eabha believes something very important needs to be shared before Breckabhainn stands before her. Fallon has some... reservations about this."

I tried to stop it. I really did. The thought came anyway, loud and clear to all of them who could hear the things going on inside my head.

Fallon wants us to break off our courtship.

Which would've been fine, except for the fact that I'd never actually made it clear to any of them that I was formally courting him in the first place. Not even to Breck. That term was intrinsically human. It also revealed my very *human* intentions.

With a little grin, Breck angled himself more toward me

on the seat we were sharing and pressed his face against my neck as the rest of them stared at us. Even Murray had stopped his pacing. I looked down, avoiding the mix of amusement and surprise on their faces. I wondered if my nerves could handle any more confessions within the span of one week.

"It's not *entirely* about that," Elina reassured me in a comforting tone. And then she giggled.

As if she'd been summoned to balance the joy coming from the fairy sitting across from us, Fallon brushed an arm harshly against one of the drapes hanging across a doorway. Our eyes met and she leveled her cool stare at me. It became even colder when she noticed Breck curled against my side.

"How did he get here?" she asked, speaking about me rather than to me.

"I brought him," Elina said, her bright attitude unwavering. I liked Elina a lot, but I found myself wishing that Finna was there to stick up for Breck and me. Not that Breck did a poor job standing up to her. "You need to speak with the lad, Fallon."

"He doesn't need to be here. Eabha is already unsettled. This will only make things worse."

"Can't you just tell us what the problem is?" Breck lifted his head from my shoulder to speak to her, but she ignored him, as well. He was about to say something else when the curtain shifted behind Fallon. Everyone got to their feet at once. I rushed to follow them.

"Elina was right to bring him. Hello, Peter. I'm glad to see you again." Eabha dipped her head at me. I returned the gesture, still unsure if that was the right way to greet her. My hands twitched against the seams on my trousers. She practically floated into the room, her dress trailing behind her in trains of gossamer and gold. Even the ends of her sleeves were long enough to reach the floor. She was every bit of a fairy queen as the ones in Lucy's books, down to the circlet in her hair.

Breck moved away as she got closer, making room. I cautiously stepped forward, angling my elbow away from my side as she wrapped her arm through mine, resting her hand on my bent forearm.

"Allow me to show you around so we can speak in peace," she said, her voice deep and smooth. I swallowed hard and nodded. I was too nervous to look at the rest of them as she guided me out of the room. If anyone could hear my thoughts, it would be her, so I tried to quiet them as much as I could. I focused instead on how my boots didn't make any noise as we walked down a long stretch of hallway. The floor appeared to be made from stone. Under my feet, it felt like grass.

We walked for a long while before she spoke again. We went through many rooms, some more grand than others, but all an intriguing blend of nature and refinement. I was nervous to trust the stairs, uncertain if they were real, but they held up all the same.

"You make our young Breckabhainn very happy. I can see it when he speaks of you."

"Aye—" I stopped, my voice going weak as I looked around. "He makes me happy, too." The final room was overflowing with more of the tiny golden fairies perched on branches, hiding in vines, and playing in a small fountain. A full rainbow of flowers bloomed around us; some I was certain I'd never seen before. It was a true garden in this upstairs room of the castle.

Eabha had found a place to sit amongst the greenery: a

chair with a high back, very similar to the ones I'd seen at the harvest festival in the woods. A proper throne. She gestured for me to join her by her feet. I settled onto the cushion of moss there, wrapping my arms around my knees as I pulled them up to my chest. Then I wasn't sure if that was appropriate, so I unbent and crossed them instead. That didn't feel right either, so I awkwardly got onto my knees and sat back on my heels, resting my hands atop my thighs. I was a feckin' disaster.

"You're aware that Breckabhainn will have his ceremony in a few weeks. To officially assume his position here with us in the Seelie court. To continue doing our important work."

I nodded, trying to ignore the strain I felt in my chest. The tinkling of bells came nearer to me. I turned my head to find a fairy hovering close enough to land on my shoulder. Like Elina, the fabric of their clothes was flowy and light, even as they remained still. Their wings, however, were moving so fast that they were only a blur behind their shoulders. The fairy swooshed away, back to the safety of a branch as if I'd startled it. Two other glittering figures went to circle the first excitedly. I could've sworn their fairy noises sounded like laughter.

"He was very upset that I took him away from your holiday together."

My attention snapped back to Eabha. Was it rude to agree? I kept my eyes focused on the hem of her skirts as I nodded just slightly, fighting the urge to move my hands against my thighs.

"He's been worried about it. His ceremony. I was hopeful that our time away would give him a chance to forget about it all for a while." My gaze flicked up to hers, which was a mistake, because she was looking right back at me. "Em, I mean, not *forget*, but… just relax, for a bit?" My response left me as a question, my voice going high at the end. It wasn't the whole truth, but it was certainly a part of what I'd wanted. She seemed to see right through my answer as she gave me a gentle laugh in response.

"Very thoughtful for a young man."

Without warning, a wave of what I thought was nausea came over me, but the only thing it produced was an intense urge to spill my secrets to her. I clenched my hands into fists to fight the unpleasant feeling. I had no choice but to let the words out.

"I care about him. More than I've ever cared about anyone before. And I'm scared that I'm going to lose him. That he's going to join you here and I won't get to see him anymore. Or if I do get to see him, it won't ever be the same again." I took a deep breath and coughed it out, trying to ease the pressure in my tight lungs. My confession didn't stop there. "I know we can never be joined because of the dark magic inside me. I also know that my life is better with him in it, and I don't want that to change. But he belongs here, with you."

I finally forced myself to stop rambling in time to realize that I had tears rolling down my cheeks. I wiped them away and balled my hands together on my lap again, growing furious with myself for crying in front of her. I chanced another look at Eabha when she didn't say anything. She was still watching me, her expression neutral but kind. The queasiness faded as quickly as it had come on.

Eabha raised her hand, as if to catch falling raindrops on her palm. A fairy swirled down to it without hesitation, paused, and then took off again out the open doorway. As her hand went back to where it had been resting, I noticed the rings on her fingers. Her hair was too thick to see if her ears were decorated. The silence stretched between us. I focused on the sound of the water in the fountain. The faint bells and chimes. The way my legs were starting to hurt from the position I was sitting in.

"You've been told that Breckabhainn was found in the woods. That Finna was asked to take care of him. To raise him as she would raise one of her own, while also allowing us to teach him and help him become the fairy he was destined to be."

My stomach felt uneasy again as I nodded.

"Breck is an orphan, by your human definition. His mother is dead. However, in our world, things work a little differently. Magic can be quite tricky, as you already know." The pain in my lungs served as a constant reminder of that. My hand instinctively came up to rub across my chest.

I finally found the courage to look Eabha in the face. "You said his mother," I started delicately. "What about his father?" I knew where human babies came from. I knew the steps involved. Were they not the same for fae? My eyebrows bunched together as I was about to ask. That's when Fallon came in, guided by the golden fairy Eabha must've sent to fetch her. She was more careful with her attitude when she was around their queen, which I appreciated in that moment. The look on her face was more panic than anger.

"What've you told him?" She glanced down at where I was sitting. Something about me must've given her the answer she wanted, because her shoulders relaxed a bit as she stopped in front of us. Her clothes were quite similar to what Breck was wearing, but instead of the blue, everything was gold-laced black. There was even gold ribbon running through the thick, dark braid of hair hanging over her shoulder. The ruffles of her collar ended at the back of her neck.

"I've only just begun," Eabha told her with ease. "The rest is not my story to tell."

I'd heard those words before when it came to Fallon.

I watched her jaw clench as she crossed and then uncrossed her arms, shifting her weight from one bare foot to the other. Finally, she sighed loudly and looked down at me again. I couldn't stop myself from flinching when she thrust her hand out in my direction. She was offering it to help me up. I was surprised at her strength as she pulled me to my feet.

"I'll be here if you need me," came Eabha's voice behind me. When I turned to thank her for her time, my heart stuttered. The throne where she'd been sitting was now covered with a tangle of nature. The spread of her dress, the fullness of her hair, it was all there, just made of vines and flowers instead. Tiny fairies were already coming down from their hiding places to settle within her leaves.

"Come with me," Fallon said flatly.

CHAPTER NINETEEN

We exited the ruins through a back door into a heavily wooded area. There was less sunlight here, but that also could've meant night was approaching. How long had I been there, anyway? Dread crept in as I thought about Henry and Sarah discovering that I was gone, too. I hoped they wouldn't do anything too drastic. I just needed them to take care of my horses until I returned.

I fought my way through the undergrowth in my struggle to keep up with Fallon, who was barely making a noise as she weaved her way between the trees. Just as I reached peak anxiety over the thought of them going through my bags and finding the book and the little jar, I tripped over a root and caught myself on a tree, coughing. I was out of breath.

"Fallon, wait," I called out. I pushed off the tree and kept going since she didn't seem to hear me.

The light faded quicker, until only a few minutes later I was having trouble seeing where I was going. A branch tangled up in my hair and scratched my cheek when I walked into it. I freed myself and started moving again, hopeful that I was still headed in the right direction.

I held my eyes open wider and wider until I had to stop because everything was completely dark. With my arms stretched out in front of me, I felt around for something sturdy to hold onto. My heart was racing to keep up with my labored breathing, and I wondered if Fallon had just left me for dead. I took a breath to call out her name when a hand grabbed my arm and pulled.

Only after my boots found a sturdier surface did we stop walking. She let me go and I stood still, blinking in the dark, unable to do anything except try to breathe through the burning in my lungs. I needed to sit down. I coughed several times and then shivered, a chill settling on my skin.

I turned around at the *whoosh* of a fire catching. It took only a few seconds to realize where Fallon had taken me. It almost made me laugh, if I hadn't been so unsure of what she was going to tell me – or do to me – in the cave she'd brought me to. Shadows danced on every wall as the flames grew stronger. A few pieces of roughly made furniture told me that this was a place Fallon probably spent a lot of time while they were at the Seelie court. I wondered what type of space Breck had claimed for himself as I moved toward one of the chairs closer to the fire.

I watched Fallon cautiously as I sat down, keeping my back straight and legs together. I didn't feel especially comfortable. The look on her face as she stared down into the trancing of the flames that separated us unsettled me even more. Her jaw was tight, lips pressed into a thin line. The only movement was the heavy rise and fall of her chest as she breathed. Then I noticed her hands. She had them in her lap, mostly hidden behind the bend of her knees thanks to her choice of a seat being too short. One of her thumbs was rubbing violently back and forth over the knuckle of the other thumb. Was she... nervous?

Finally, her eyes shot up to mine.

"Breck's mother—" she started, her voice quiet. Her gaze fell back to the fire. "Breck's mother made me promise that I would look after him. She made me promise that I would do everything I could to protect him." Fallon closed her eyes then, her features softening.

"You knew her?" I asked carefully.

A bitter laugh was forced from her chest. She opened her eyes again just to glare at me, but for some reason she couldn't make it stick, and it faded. "I knew her."

"What was she like?" I couldn't help the curiosity as it sprung to life. Had she been another member of the Seelie court? Was she also able to feel the river? Had she been killed by an Unseelie? I watched the tension in Fallon's body resign ever so slightly. She sighed and shook her head to herself, making a decision of some kind, it seemed.

"Let me show you." She held out her hand for me to take, palm down, waiting. I pushed off my chair and stepped closer, taking my place at a safe distance from her on the log she was using for a bench. She didn't look at me as I slid my hand into hers. She held on tightly. I closed my eyes and waited for her damp magic to surround me.

The crackling of the fire and the light of it beyond my eyelids faded to nothing. They were replaced by flashes of color too fast to decipher at first. My head started to spin, until it finally settled on one scene. One gorgeous scene by the river on a rare, cloudless day. There, on the grassy bank, sat a woman. Her skirts were gathered up around her thighs, probably to keep them from getting wet as she kicked her bare feet in the water, weight supported on her hands behind her. Long, golden tendrils stretched down her back. An echo of a giggle reached me as the woman turned to look over her shoulder. My heart seized in my chest as I saw her blue eyes. Her grin. Her freckles.

"*She was beautiful,*" I breathed, squeezing Fallon's hand without meaning to.

Another memory came next, of the woman in a much more elaborate dress, dancing as we had danced at Lughnasa that night around a large fire in the woods. I caught whisps of the music that was playing and more laughter. After watching her move, so happy and free, I realized that her freckles weren't sparkling as Breck's did when he was in their world. As she twirled, her half-pinned hair revealed that her ears were rounded like mine.

"She wasn't a fairy?" This took me by such surprise that I almost opened my eyes, but the colors shifted again into something else that made my body flash hot and then cold. My free hand came up to cover my mouth as I watched the new scene play out. As the woman smiled so hard that her eyes crinkled like Breck's sometimes did. As she knelt there in the dirt and leaves, her elegant blue skirts fanned around her. As she leaned in to rest their foreheads together on their hands bound with ribbon.

I pulled away from Fallon's grip as my eyes flew open to stare at the flames flicking in the ring of rocks at our feet. The erratic beating in my chest forced me into a fit of coughs so strong that I had to get up in search of cool air away from the fire. I realized, as I stood near the mouth of the cave with my hands on my knees, that my reaction was less than ideal. I straightened and turned to face her, finding that she hadn't moved other than to cross her arms tightly in front of her.

"She—" I swallowed, my voice rough from the coughing. "She was…"

"She was my mate," Fallon finished for me.

I took a few hesitant steps back in her direction. Breck's mother – his *human* mother – had been joined to Fallon before Eabha.

"He doesn't know," she started then, closing her eyes and opening the gates that were keeping the answers to my questions. I somehow managed to find another place to sit as I listened.

"Eabha had sent me to live in one of the villages experiencing hardship from the Great Hunger. I got to work immediately, playing my role and connecting with the humans, finding any way I could to get them to trust me so I could help with their miserable, unproductive crops. A strange, single woman arriving to a new village raised a lot of questions. Eventually they allowed me close enough to their fields to use my magic, but it wasn't enough.

"The humans were dying. They were starving, dropping out in the fields as they worked to plant and harvest food that wasn't even theirs to eat. What little they managed to grow for themselves was mostly diseased." She paused, taking a deep breath and letting it out slowly through her nose.

"This was how I met her. I was helping in the fields on a brutally cold day, sowing seeds we'd helped sprout above ground, when there was a scream. The eldest daughter of the family had collapsed right there in the dirt. I followed her father as he carried her to the shack they called a home, her limbs limp and dangling, her fingers and lips a horrific shade of blue. As they rushed around to gather warm water and blankets for her, I made use of the time we had alone to push as much magic as I could into her weak body. She was so thin."

Fallon made a small sound in the back of her throat. Something between a laugh and a moan. I looked up to find her eyes brimming with tears, catching the warm light from the fire. Her mouth was pinched into a grimace of a grin.

"When she opened her eyes, she smiled up at me and said, "Thanks, lovely," like I'd helped her up after she'd tripped, rather than bringing her back from the edge of her life. That was the moment I knew my heart would belong to her."

"What was her name?" I asked, barely above a whisper.

She finally blinked, sending the tears in matching tracks down her cheeks. She didn't reach to wipe them away. "Jo. Josephine."

Fallon went on to explain how from that day, she couldn't stand to be away from Jo. The draw of a human is irresistible to a fairy, especially after the fairy feels an attachment to them for one reason or another. I tried to tell her that humans felt love the same way, but she said it wasn't the same at all.

"Once a fairy forms a bond with a human, they start to change." She paused to study me in the low light, her eyes trailing down my body and then back up to my face. "What does his magic smell like to you?" Heat crept up my neck at the question. I had never really talked about that with anyone before. It felt strangely intimate. It was also the taste on his mouth when he kissed me.

"Fresh mint," I answered. She nodded slightly, as if she knew the answer already.

"And do you know what it smells like to me?"

"No."

"It smells like you," she said, the slightest hint of distaste in her words. My brows drew together. "It's one way that a fairy safeguards their human from others in our world. A mark of protection to tell other fairies that they cannot claim them." I blushed harder at the thought of Breck seeing me as his human to protect.

"But we're not... we've not been joined."

"Not every fairy views humans as equals. The tricks and deception are all a part of the Unseelie game to get whatever they want. As a result, these changes happen almost immediately." Fallon reached up brush her hair back over her ear where it had come loose from her braid. "When we sent Breck to you, some of the changes were to be expected. A fairy cannot work that closely with a human without feeling responsibility toward them. But when he came home stinking like the strangest mix of horses and honey, we knew."

"Is that what I smell like?" I resisted the urge to sniff at my clothes.

"Among other things," she confirmed.

When a silence settled between us, I rubbed my hands down my face and sat with my fingers covering my mouth and chin as I tried to process everything she'd just told me. I gathered my confidence to ask the question I knew she wouldn't want to answer.

"What happened to her?"

Fallon closed her eyes again, wincing as though my words had been physically painful. I wanted to tell her it was alright if she didn't answer, but she started talking before I could.

"We'd been joined for a little over two years when Jo said she wanted a baby. She'd always talked about having a family. Humans put so much emphasis on having children and carrying on their legacy, and I'd never understood that. I selfishly wanted her all to myself. If not forever, then for a while longer, at least. For several years after that it was our only quarrel. Our only sore spot. She would bring it up, we would get upset with each other about it, and then she would cry, and I'd tell her that soon we could find the magic to make it possible. Soon.

"But soon wasn't enough for her. After a particularly long session here with Eabha and the others, I returned home to her and... and I could *smell* it." Fallon said this last part through her teeth, a quiet rage brewing just beneath her stony exterior. "I hadn't seen her that happy since the night we were joined. She was radiant. And I was furious."

"She was pregnant," I mumbled, sorting the facts of the story out in my head.

"There was a safe way to do it. I'd known others like us who made it possible. But my foolish hesitance forced her to find her own way. We didn't actually talk about it for weeks. It hung between us like a heavy curtain, until one night in our bed I felt him kick against my hand, and I asked her what she had done to create this life that would be our child. My heart broke apart as she told me that she'd tied her ribbon on the Wishing Tree a whole year earlier. And a few months later, when he was born in the middle of the night, I held both of them as she took her last breath."

I was too stunned to speak. My mouth opened, but no words came.

"An Unseelie had granted her wish. They placed their dark magic inside of my sweet Jo, and she was blissfully unaware of what she'd done until the moment she was taken from me. Until the moment her life was taken so that he could live."

Fallon got to her feet in one swift motion, stepping away

from the fire and turning her back to me. I needed the moment to collect myself, too. I thought back to those meetings at Finna's cottage, when she was so cold about what had happened to Jamie, and I realized it was because she knew. She knew how I felt better than anyone else ever could.

"*I hated him,*" she whispered with venom, turning around. "I hated that baby with every part of me. All I could think was that he'd taken my Jo away. So I did the worst thing I could've done. I took him to the Unseelie and left him. I abandoned our son with those foul creatures. I thought they would care for him because he was made of their magic, but I was wrong. I watched from the shadows as he grew up mostly alone, fending for himself, becoming wilder by the day.

"I had to put a stop to it. I came up with this elaborate story about finding him in the woods and took him to Finna. She'd never known about him like the others, so I thought I could hide the truth. I let her raise him while I trained him to use his magic for good. So that he would always have a safe place with us in the Seelie court. So that I could right my wrongs and protect him the way I should have all along."

Breck's life had never been a mystery at all. It had been a horrible secret.

"Are you going to tell him?" My voice sounded far away again. Detached, like someone else had said the words instead of me. I noticed that my body felt a little bit like that, too.

"I haven't got a choice."

I raised my head to look at her, and she was staring back at me. "Why now?"

"Because he's willing to give up his magic forever to be with you. And I cannot let him do that."

CHAPTER TWENTY

My legs must have carried me back to the ruins. Everything in between was hazy and soft again, except for the little fairy Fallon sent with me to be my guide. I didn't realize how much trouble I'd had getting back until I walked into the sitting room and Elina gasped at the sight of me. As she rushed over, I looked down and saw the dirt on my clothes and the cuts on my hands. It wasn't funny, but I laughed.

"Go and fetch him more of the drink," Elina said somewhere nearby, or maybe far away, as I was led through a doorway. The curtain hanging there slid over my face until someone else moved it because I forgot to. Luckily, there were no stairs between the sitting room and wherever they took me, because my feet were heavy and awkward. I squeezed my eyes against the pain that had returned in my head. When I opened them again, I was staring up at the woven vines and branches above me that twinkled with enough fairies to look like the stars on a clear night.

I wanted to reach out and touch them, but someone was holding my arm down. I turned my head against the pillow to find Elina wiping at my hand with a rag. She was saying something about Fallon letting me walk alone in the dark when my pillow moved. I thought about how strange it was to feel heavy and light at the same time as my head was held forward and the rim of a glass was set against my lips.

"This will help." I blinked hard and found Breck's blurry face above mine. I accepted the drink as he tilted the glass for me, forgetting how nasty it had been until the thick, clumpy liquid touched my tongue. I fought back a gag as I swallowed, deciding that small sips would be much worse than taking it all at once. I exhaled hard after I got the last of it down, coughing a few times.

"It's so horrible," I moaned, grimacing.

"You'll feel better with it in your system," Breck reasoned, his hand finding its way to my hair. As I came back into my body, I realized that my pillow was actually his legs crossed beneath my head. I felt little tickles against the backs of my arms and legs. I blinked again, my vision sharpening, and looked down to discover that I was in the nip, spread out like a cat in the afternoon sun for all ten thousand twinkling fairies to see.

"*Shite*," I cursed under my breath as I pulled my legs up and rolled onto my side. "Where are my clothes?"

"They had blood and dirt on them. Elina took them to wash."

I grumbled and buried the side of my face in his lap, thoroughly tired of being exposed to fairies of any size without my consent. I brought my hand up to look at the fresh bandages wrapped around my palm. My walk back might've been too foggy to remember, but what I'd learned just before sat on me heavily, impossible to forget. I turned more to wrap both arms around Breck's waist and set my chin on my shoulder. His fingers continued to brush through the knots my curls had become.

"What is this made of?" I rocked my hips side to side as I tried to determine what exactly we were resting on.

"Clover and moss, mostly. With some leaves from the vines that fall when the fairies play too hard in them. I try to pick them out, but they're always making more mess to clean up."

"Your bed at home is made of the finest sheets I've ever felt, and here you sleep on *weeds*?"

He laughed. "It's not so bad once you get used to it. You know I don't sleep much anyway."

"Aye, now I know the reason," I teased as I sat up, pulling my legs to my chest. I let my gaze wander around the rest of the room. It was bigger than the whole upstairs of the mill, but still distinctly *his*, with greens and browns and soft fabrics all around. If you'd told me we shrunk down and found ourselves inside a tree decorated for a woodland fairy prince, I would've believed you.

"You're probably hungry," Breck said beside me, sounding almost guilty. "I can try to find you something. Wait here, I'll be right back."

I watched him leave, biting my tongue on my response about not going anywhere because I had no clothes. Some fabric that may or may not have been a blanket was jumbled up to my right. I pulled it across my lap and relaxed my legs as reality set in.

I was stuck in the fairy world. I had no idea how far I was from my home, or the estate by the sea, or how long I'd been missing. How long would they keep me here? Long enough to reveal Fallon's secrets so I could be there to support

Breck? What did she mean about him giving up his magic? I dropped my head into my hands.

"Does it still hurt?" I gave him a questioning look as he came back into the room. He rephrased his question. "Your head. Still hurts?"

"Oh, no. I'm just tired." Fatigue had settled on me in his absence. In one smooth motion, Breck bent his legs to cross them and sat down next to me with a bowl full of blackberries. He popped one into his mouth before holding them out to me. My heart warmed. Of course this was what he'd found for us to eat. I reached for one and put it on my tongue. It was twice the size of a blackberry from a bush in the human world and sweeter than syrup. I took another, then another.

We ate until the bowl was empty, neither of us pausing to talk. It was just the trick to settle the green drink still roiling around in my gut. Breck got up to set the bowl on a small table near the door and began removing his clothes. I ran my tongue over my teeth, brushing away a few blackberry seeds that had found hiding places. The last one was a little stubborn. As I sucked at it, the release of pressure made a squeak that sounded like the kissing noises Henry made for his horses.

Breck turned from where he was hanging his trousers in the wardrobe with a smirk.

"I thought you felt a certain way about that when others were around." He made his way back to the bed and knelt in front of me, his hands resting on my thighs through the blanket, voice shrinking to a whisper. *"They won't care, but they'll certainly hear us."*

"Oh—" I choked out, shaking my head a little. "I wasn't... I didn't mean anything by that. I was getting the seeds out of my teeth." I tried to replicate the noise I'd made with my tongue, but none of my attempts sounded the same, and I ended up more embarrassed than I was before. Breck's smirk grew into a smile as he brought his hands up to hold my face. My gaze slid over his sparkling nose and cheeks.

"*Alright. But I'd still like to kiss you. Can I?*"

"*Yes,*" I whispered back, too eager.

As his eyelids slid shut and our lips met, I tried to force away everything I'd learned. I tried to forget that Breck's mother had made a stupid human mistake and tied her ribbon to the Wishing Tree. I tried to disregard Fallon making the choice to abandon their son, only to change her mind later but continue to be so hard on him with his training.

And as my lungs started to burn while Breck deepened our kisses, drawing them out with long, sensual moments of his mouth against mine, I tried to ignore the fluttering of hope within my chest.

Dark magic lived inside us both.

CHAPTER TWENTY-ONE

Breck woke me up with another full glass of the drink that tasted like shredded grass and smashed bugs. I was fairly confident those were the only two ingredients as I chugged it like a first celebratory pint at the pub, squeezing my eyes shut tight. I almost couldn't keep it down that time. I wiped the back of my hand across my mouth and shuddered.

"Good morning," Breck said as he took the cup back. I glared at him bleakly.

"Right," I mumbled. I felt like I'd only slept for an hour or two at the most.

"Your clothes are here. Eabha has called a meeting, but I'll be back soon. There's more food on the table there for you." He leaned close and kissed the corner of my lips, glancing above us and keeping his voice low as he added, "I'd eat it soon before the little fairies come for it." Then he was on his feet, the translucent fabric of his cape flowing with his movement as he left me alone.

When I opened my eyes the second time, more light was spilling in through the branches above. I drew in a deep breath and coughed it out, rubbing my face with my bandaged hand. The taste left in my mouth from the drink was enough to force me up off the bed. I tried to decide if the spread of nature there on the floor was actually a bed or not as I dressed, glad to find that my clothes were clean and in fine condition, despite my best efforts to ruin them yet again.

Unfortunately, Breck had been right about the food. Only crumbs remained of whatever it was he'd left for me. I drank the water that looked mostly untouched, choosing to ignore the flourish of faint chimes as the tiny creatures laughed at me from the safety of their hiding spots.

"My sister will be glad to hear of your mischief," I told them.

I decided to leave my boots behind as I ventured out of the room. Bird songs echoed in the hallway. The cool, soft touch of nature beneath my bare feet helped me wake up more fully as I searched for the sitting room or any other place that felt familiar from the day before. When I thought I'd found it, I moved the curtain aside with my hand.

"Peter," Elina said in greeting, her voice mild. Carrick and Murray looked at me, too, and my stomach sank. No Fallon. No Breck. No Eabha.

"Where are they?" I asked, coming fully into the room and letting the fabric fall back into place behind me. Elina tilted her head with a weak grin. The kind you gave someone when you knew something the other person didn't. The kind that said, 'I've been keeping a huge secret from you and now I feel bad that you finally know the truth.'

"He hasn't come back yet, lad," Carrick answered.

"Why didn't anyone wake me?" I demanded, but I was already making for the door. I had no idea where I was going. This was the whole reason Elina had come to get me, wasn't it? To be there for him? And now they'd let me sleep right through it. A frustrated groan escaped me. I paused on a thick patch of moss, breathing hard. I looked up into the trees.

"Where is he? Where's Breckabhainn? Show me, please." I spun in place, searching for any of the fairies I'd seen so many of the day before. "Please!" I begged.

A few birds were startled from the trees at my shouting, flapping away to safety. I pressed my lips together. They probably weren't used to much commotion in a place so peaceful. What would anyone ever have to be upset about? Then again, with Fallon and Breck training together so often, they must've heard the raised voices of a heated discussion at some point.

My stomach twisted at the thought of them arguing while I slept. I took a few uncertain steps in one direction, the opposite of where Fallon had taken me the night before. It seemed that the woods went on forever. I kept my eyes on the ground as I searched for safe spots for my tender bare feet to fall.

Breck, where are you? I thought as I raised my head again to look around. Nothing was familiar, of course, but now I'd also lost sight of the ruins. A few coughs escaped me as I turned toward a large rock so I could sit for a moment and think. It was probably silly of me to have left the way I did, but I knew without a doubt that Breck would've come looking for me if the situation had been reversed. I was still reeling from learning the truth. How could he be feeling?

I pushed my hand through my hair and held the back of my neck, closing my eyes for a moment. An uncomfortable sensation moved in my gut. How long before the drink they kept giving me started to wear off again? What would happen to me if I went without it for too long?

I opened my eyes to start looking for the next path I would take, but instead they focused on something much closer that hadn't been there before. My sharp gasp made me cough hard and wince at the pain in my chest.

A young woman was standing in front of me, her face the same height as mine, even though I was still sitting on the stone. I averted my eyes when I realized she had nothing to cover herself with except for her mossy-green hair swept over one shoulder and a swath of sheer cloth wrapped around her hips. It left nothing to the imagination.

"*Baineann tú le Breckabhainn,*" she said, her voice as beautiful as she was. I didn't understand what she said, but the sound of Breck's name forced me to look at her again.

"You know where he is?"

She tilted her head curiously in response, taking her turn to look me down and back up. Her large green eyes blinked at me as she leaned closer, a slender hand coming up to brush her wavy hair behind the point of her ear. I instinctively leaned back a little.

"*Tá sé ag an abhainn,*" was her response. I watched her hand come up again as she reached for me. Her fingertips brushed at the material of my shirt on my shoulder. Then, she plucked at one of my curls before she used her finger against my jaw to tilt my head to the side. It occurred to me then that maybe she wasn't friendly. My heart sped up as she turned my head the opposite direction.

"I just want to find Breck," I told her, keeping my voice as calm as I could. She dropped her hand from my face and took a few steps back.

"*Tógfaidh mé ann thú.*" She seemed to wait for a response

that I couldn't give her. The woman pursed her lips and tried another approach, looking off to her left and then back at me expectantly. When I didn't move right away, she reached for my hand, pulling on me so I would get to my feet. I towered over her as she started us in the direction she'd indicated. Her skin was cold against mine.

She must've felt my hesitance fade a short while later. Her hand slipped away as she started taking longer strides, the cloth around her hips and legs somehow staying free of any snags on the underbrush. I was still searching for the pulpy spots to step on, hopping ungracefully in some places to accomplish the task.

Before long, the light started to shift. The beams of sunlight filtering through the treetops started to fade. I wanted to ask my guide how much farther we were going, but I kept quiet instead, knowing that whatever she told me wouldn't have made sense anyway. My answer came soon after when my ears picked up a familiar sound: the trickle of running water.

I stepped past the woman when she stopped, my feet coming to rest at the edge of a steep embankment. I could see where the grass and rocks ended and the fresh mud began, indicating that the water was much lower than it should've been. The narrow stream running along the riverbed reflected the color of the trees above. A break in the greens and browns caught my attention. It was a garment, blue and gold, abandoned across a partially sunken log. Nearby was another piece of clothing. Deep blue trousers haphazardly tossed into the mud.

When I turned to thank the woman for her help, she was already gone. I searched for a place that seemed easiest to climb down before I worked my way to the edge of the water. It was a slow process as I tried to protect my feet. More light disappeared above me as I approached Breck's clothes. I tossed them over my shoulder since I needed both hands to navigate the uneven terrain. This wasn't like the flat, easy bank of the river at home.

I nearly fell as my foot slipped on a slick rock.

Another shifted under me, and I felt the strain in my ankle as it twisted the wrong way.

The fatigue of my sore muscles and the uneasy feeling in my stomach all vanished when I finally saw him. His back was turned to me, shoulders hunched forward, perched on a stone sitting in the middle of the water. At normal river height, it likely would've been completely submerged, but the drop in the water exposed just how large it was.

I knew that my presence wasn't a surprise to him, so I didn't feel the need to announce myself as I underhand tossed his clothes up onto the grassy part of the bank and climbed awkwardly across the surrounding stepstones to get to him. I was out of breath and coughing by the time I hauled myself up to the top. I sat on a lower portion of the stone, looking up at him where he was staring at his hands in his lap, legs crossed.

Neither of us spoke for a long time. Truthfully, I had no words for what Fallon had told me. My human emotions were one thing, but how did Breck feel with the truth out in the open? He was so guarded with his personal life that I didn't want to upset him more by saying the wrong thing.

I'm here, I thought for him finally. I watched the subtle rise and fall of his shoulders as he breathed. I could only see the side of his face, but I didn't miss the way the muscles in his jaw clenched a few times.

Eventually we were surrounded by twilight. The lights of

the fairies in the trees were easier to see, though there weren't anywhere near as many of them above us then as there were at the ruins. They mostly stayed put, rather than dancing from place to place among the branches. Maybe they could sense how Breck was feeling, too. The water was still low. His pain was pushing the river away.

"Did you know that my name means *speckled river* in the fae language?" he asked finally, his voice rough with emotion and disuse. I heard him swallow some of it away. He straightened his shoulders a bit and looked out at the stretch of riverbed ahead of us. "Most fairies receive their name on their first birthday. After there's been enough time to discover their strengths and connections to nature." His head fell forward again. "I always wondered how they knew what to call me before they even knew me."

I couldn't stand it anymore. I clambered up to wrap my arms and legs around him. He hid his face against my neck, his hand gripping my shirt, and before long I felt his hot, silent tears fall against my skin. I rubbed his back in slow circles and let him cry, remembering all too well the physical pain of a broken heart. He'd been lied to his whole life by the ones who were supposed to care for him the most. His conception had even been kept a secret.

The river had gone still below us. The birds had all gone to sleep. The woods were eerily quiet for a moment as Breck's anguish reached its apex, a single, soundless sob shuddering through him. I held him as tight as I could, pressing my lips to his bare shoulder and willing my own eyes to stay dry.

Slowly, I felt his body relax against mine. The tension in his muscles and his fingers in my shirt loosened to the point that his hand fell to my thigh. I could feel his weight against me more, along with the rhythmic breaths against my wet collarbone. He was asleep.

Even though the pain in my stomach had returned, likely from not eating all day, I was flooded with relief that he was able to get some rest. I kept him close to me, and I closed my own eyes against the darkness of the night that had fallen so quickly once again.

CHAPTER TWENTY-TWO

Vivid swirls of color and the faraway sounds of the fairies filled my dreams while I slept. Even there, I could feel the effects of this magical place on my body. Everything was soft and flowy. My head was throbbing, and I was starving. Somehow, though, none of it registered as being unpleasant. I coughed because of my mouth being so dry, but I wasn't sure if it was in my dreams or in reality. I coughed a few more times. Then, a strange sensation forced my bleary eyes open.

Everything was completely blurry. I blinked hard and looked down, able to at least recognize the wetness I felt. Had I pissed myself? Worse yet was that I'd done it with my legs and arms still wrapped around Breck. Shame heated my whole body as I tried to move away from him, but the most I could do was mumble something unintelligible and let go, which sent me tumbling backward into the river.

A bit of clarity finally hit me. The water levels had come up to normal as we slept, rushing around our hips, reflecting Breck's emotions as he was able to relax. My confusion and dizziness made it impossible for me to right myself in the flowing water. Almost immediately, there were hands on me, and I was pulled back up to a sitting position on the rock.

"Are you alright?" Breck shook me a little. I couldn't answer him. *"Níl,"* he muttered under his breath, sounding like he was standing on the grassy bank of the river even though he was right next to me. I slumped against him, trying to find an angle that would relieve some of the pain behind my eyes. It didn't work. Breck made a desperate sound as he jostled me around a bit, likely trying to figure out how to get my dead weight to the edge of the water.

Finally, he seemed to make up his mind and grabbed my face in his hands, pressing his mouth against mine. I was too out of it to kiss him back. "Please forgive me if this hurts," was all he said. Then he took my hands in his, and I was swallowed by darkness.

* * *

The pain in my head was so severe that I cried out when I landed hard on my side in the grass. I curled in on myself and wrapped my arms around my head to try to fend it off, even though I knew somewhere deep down that the pain was internal.

I heard echoey voices above me, and then more hands were on me as I was picked up. I wanted to protest, but I found that an attempt to move my legs did nothing at all. I was at least able to groan when I was laid down somewhere softer. Nothing around me made sense until I swallowed the flood of thick liquid that was poured into my mouth. I gagged hard and it came back up with several wet, sputtering coughs. Only a short reprieve was offered before I had to drink again after the wasted portion was wiped away from my chin.

"His body cannot handle being here for much longer," someone said.

"Eabha has not yet made her decision." A short pause. "I brought the lad to make it easier, but I'm afraid it's only complicated things more."

Did that mean I hadn't been brought to comfort Breck after Fallon exposed her secrets to him?

"We're running out of time. He needs to return to the human world and regain his strength. This can be handled later." Carrick was serving as the voice of reason. I didn't want to leave until I knew Breck was going to be okay.

"Where's Breck?" The green drink was sitting at the top of my gullet like a dam ready to burst at any moment. I tried to sit up a little to encourage it down in the right direction.

"Recovering as well," Carrick told me. "First time he's carried someone else. It's exhausting physically and mentally no matter how many times you do it, but the first time... he might be out for a while yet." His gaze shifted, and I looked over to where Breck appeared to be sleeping, his body limp. I dodged more hands as I sat all the way up and crawled to him. I brushed his hair off his forehead and watched for his chest to move with some steady breaths.

"Peter, we have to send you back." Elina's gentle touch was on my shoulder. I wanted to shove it away. How could they send me back when he was hurting?

"I have to stay with him," I said, not bothering to look at her.

"Breck will be back to normal very soon. But right now, you're running out of time to return to your friends with your absence unnoticed."

That made me turn around. "What do you mean? I've been here for days."

"Time works differently here. If I take you back now, they won't even know you were gone. We must hurry, though." I looked back at Breck and brushed his hair aside again, my hand slipping to the side of his face. I ran my thumb across the shimmering freckles on his cheek. Leaving him then was the last thing I wanted to do. I leaned down to kiss his forehead. *I love you*, I thought for him, and then I got to my feet on unsteady legs. At least this time I hadn't messed up my clothes too badly.

Elina helped me over to my boots and I braced a hand against the wall as I put one on, then the other. My jacket was the last item to collect before I hesitantly put my hands into Elina's, and she held them tight. I gave Breck one last glance over my shoulder and then closed my eyes.

* * *

The bedroom was exactly as I'd left it. I shook my head a little to clear away the lingering pain. One step toward the window made me feel the weight of the human world on my entire body. It was like a strong, unyielding gust of wind blowing down on my head and shoulders. I gripped the windowsill to help support myself as I looked out onto the sea.

I'd left when it was dark. Now, I was greeted with the dim light of a cloudy morning. The water looked agitated, with heavy waves sending spray up over the rocks far below. Sea birds dipped and dived, picking away at their breakfast washed ashore. I hoped it wasn't an indication of a stormy day to come.

I splashed some water on my face at the basin and checked my reflection, trying to appear as though I'd only just woken up. I removed the worn bandage from around my hand and inspected my palm. I couldn't even see where a cut had been. I tossed the bandage onto the dressing table and checked my bag. Everything was still in its place, including the items I'd stashed away.

The saddle bag felt heavy over my shoulder as I took the steps slower than usual, trying to clear my mind of everything that had happened in the last few hours, which had been several days in the fairy world. It was so disorienting to think about that I tripped on the last step down, barely catching myself with a tight grip on the banister.

When I found Henry and Sarah at the breakfast table, they didn't give any indication that things seemed out of the ordinary. I draped my bag over the back of the chair Breck had used and sat down, stealing glances at my hosts as I served myself a generous helping of food. They were in the middle of their own conversation about something to do with the new house that was being built for them. Henry tossed a piece of tri-folded parchment down near his plate, which landed with a soft *tink* against his glass.

"Da picked this company on recommendation from one of his business partners. It's highly unlikely they'll let us be disappointed." I paused on chewing my mouthful of sausage when Henry turned his attention to me, waiting for the question to come about where I'd gone. He only gave me flash of his eyebrows and said, "Remember when we went to Dublin with school, and that place we stayed had one of those flushing toilets?" I nodded. "We're having our own water closet installed. Apparently, it's going to be a nightmare."

Henry's flippancy nearly made me laugh. "That place we stayed" was one of the finest hotels in the whole country. I remembered feeling entirely out of place, knowing what my family had sacrificed to send me on the weeks-long trip to get a real look at the history we'd been studying. Henry and Jamie had taken the wide, bustling streets and general finery in stride; I'd been relieved each night when I could escape to look up at the stars and think of our quiet home in the countryside.

"I don't understand why they'll have such an issue." Sarah dabbed at the corner of her mouth with her napkin after finishing a sip of tea. "Several of my friends have been very pleased with the whole process, even when they were only adding it to an existing structure."

I tuned the rest of their conversation out as my mind started to wander. Breck had been in bad shape when I left him, and I had no way of knowing if he was improving like Elina promised he would. The only thing I could do was get to Finna's as fast as I could and wait for him there. I'd told my brother I would be home in time for him to leave on schedule, so I planned to stop by Finna's once on my way, return home to trade the horses out for my young mare, check on my family, and then go back to the cottage.

My determination faltered when I thought of facing the chestnut mare's empty stall for the first time. I reached for my glass to help wash down my breakfast that had suddenly become difficult to swallow. The memory of the curdled mess I'd had to drink in the fairy world came back to me, and I set my juice back in its place with a weak hand.

The idea of leaving without Breck to travel home alone felt daunting, but part of me wondered if it was what I needed. I stood from the table and collected my bag from the neighboring chair. Henry and Sarah let their conversation fall silent as they got to their feet, as well, and guided me toward the gray morning and my waiting horses.

* * *

Finding my way home hadn't been as difficult as I feared. I'd left the estate with enough food to last for several days, though none of it had been as good as what I'd eaten on the first part of the journey. Clear directions and fair enough weather brought me steadily past places that were vaguely familiar. I left the coast behind in favor of the river, and I let it be my silent, steady guide in the absence of the one I really wished was with me.

In addition to the food, Henry had made sure to shove some coins into my pocket that he refused to take back. He said he wouldn't hear of me spending another night sleeping on the ground or in an old barn. I felt only slightly guilty as I checked myself into the inn on the first night. With the horses secured and my belongings safely stowed, I sat at the downstairs pub and nursed a dark beer that the keep promised was the best I'd ever taste. It was just alright.

My sore legs carried me up the steps toward my rented room. It was small but nice enough that I knew Henry would've been satisfied with my choice. I shut the door behind me with a soft click and rested my back against it for a moment as I worked the locks, before I stepped out of my boots and started removing my clothes. A heavy, floral perfume surrounded me as my head pressed into the pillow. I didn't want to imagine what other smells they were trying to mask with it as I turned onto my side and pulled the blankets up over my head.

I fell immediately into the trap of my thoughts. I understood Fallon's protectiveness over Breck now. She pushed him so hard to become like her so that there was never an opportunity for him to become something else. I wondered if the source of the magic a fairy was born with had anything to do with what they could be. Was he technically Unseelie? Or was the magic all the same, and the actions of the fairies themselves determined the rest?

I brought my hand up to rub at my chest. They'd said the magic in my lungs was dark. That was how it had always felt. From those first days in recovery, when each painful breath brought me closer to wishing for death even more than my illness had, some part of me had known that it wasn't right. But it was what kept me alive. It was a little like the green drink, I realized. Horrific at first, but it was the only thing that kept my body safe in their world. A necessary evil.

I tucked my hand up between the bend of my neck and shoulder and coughed out a slow sigh as I relaxed into the pillow. Maybe the magic inside me was dark only because it had been delivered by a dark fairy. My stomach twisted a little at my next thought.

A breath of Breck's magic was the only relief I ever got from the ache in my lungs. At first, I'd figured it had more to do with the cooling effect than anything else. Even a cup of mint tea left that sweet burn in my nose. Now, though, it made more sense. It was a meeting of kindred spirits when his magic touched mine. I closed my eyes and thought of our moment under the ash trees, when he'd lost himself and his power overwhelmed me. It had been a fleeting, frozen bliss.

Breck was made of dark magic. He was capable of the things children were raised to be scared of in the night. He could've learned to live forever by hurting and stealing and granting foolish human wishes with only himself in mind. But he was none of that. He was thoughtful. He was kind. Generous. Humble. Everything I wished I could be more of.

Fallon said Breck was willing to give up his magic for me. Forever. *Forever.* Is that what he wanted? My heart gave a little extra squeeze in my chest, and I buried my face deeper into the fragrant pillow to hide my grin from nobody.

CHAPTER TWENTY-THREE

I arrived home two days later as the sun was dipping below the horizon. The directions I had been given took me a different way than I'd thought, so I was surprised when I realized I was looking at the lights of my own village. The moment we rounded the final bend in the road, my eyes shot to the mill. All the windows were dark as I'd known they would be. The horses' hooves clopped across the bridge, their steps becoming more animated as they recognized the familiar sights and smells, too.

When the kitchen door squealed open, I expected to be greeted with my family sitting down to supper at the corner table. A low fire was still burning in the hearth, but the room was empty.

I carried my boots in one hand, saddle bags over the opposite shoulder, and passed through the kitchen to the short hallway that connected to the sitting room. It also sat quiet. I felt the lick of panic in my gut as I turned up the stairs and took them two at a time. I checked Lucy's room through the crack in her door, breathing hard. Empty. I dropped my things at the base of my own closed door and retraced my path, slinging myself off the last step down the opposite hallway toward William's study and the rest of the bedrooms.

Low voices finally reached my ears. I pushed the door to Nan's room open carefully, warm light spilling across my face as I took in the scene. Auburn, blonde, and silver curls bounced as the three of them turned their heads to look at me.

"Peter!" Lucy gasped, sliding from the bed to come and wrap her arms tight around my middle. I pressed my arm against her back to hug her closer before she pulled away and reached for my hand to drag me in. Her voice was soft when she spoke. "Come and look. The barn cat had her kittens in Nan's room!"

I approached carefully, peering into a basket I remembered from my childhood that was lined with blankets. It wasn't enough for Lucy, so I relented and got to my knees as the cat looked up at me with heavy eyes and loud purrs. Four balls of fur squirmed next to her. I gave her a sympathetic look.

"That's what you get for rubbing up against every lad you come across," I told her.

"Peter," Nan warned me harshly.

I glanced up in time to catch Anne's grin that she tried to hide.

"William already said I can keep one of them," Lucy said, practically vibrating with excitement. I wrapped my arm around her shoulders and hugged her against me again. She leaned close and scratched the barn cat under her chin.

"Hungry," Nan said as she got up from her chair with some effort, not quite asking a question. I looked at Anne again where she sat on the bed, exchanging a silent hello with her in the form of a head nod, before I got up to follow Nan back to the kitchen.

"Sarah's family owns a castle," I told her as I slid onto a stool, watching her work in the low light. "They've been restoring and renovating it. It was like something out of Lucy's books."

"Did you have a nice time, then?" she asked, not impressed with the show of money.

"Aye, we did." My slip of words apparently didn't go unnoticed as her green eyes lifted to mine. I tried to recover. "The four of us toured the grounds and spent time at the beach. Henry was so glad to have his team back with him."

I could feel her words coming before they left her mouth. "When you find a nice girl to settle down with, you'll see how important it is to maintain separate interests. It's not healthy to spend too much time together."

"You and Grandad didn't like to do everything together?" I teased her lightly. She slid a plate in front of me with two slices of warm soda bread slathered with homemade butter. A bowl of the stew she'd kept warm over the fire followed close behind. I dipped the bread in the steaming broth.

"Our hobbies rarely overlapped. I had no interest in catching fish or fooling with horses, and he would never dream of stepping foot in the kitchen or mending clothes."

"Maybe because your hobbies sound like more work than fun," I reasoned.

"And that's exactly why you need to find someone to build a home with soon. I won't be around to feed and clothe you forever." She turned her back to me again.

"Someone," I echoed quietly before I took another bite of bread. She was right, though. I hadn't the first clue about cooking for myself, or cleaning, or repairing all the clothes I seemed destined to ruin. Running a house was a huge under- taking. Was this something I could balance with Breck? We both had our own responsibilities to tend to, as well.

"Did you ever feel like he wasn't doing enough to support you?"

"He was one of the hardest working men I've ever known," she responded with a tenderness I rarely got to see in her. "As was his son. As are his grandsons." I felt the swell of pride inside me at her words. "There is no such thing as 'enough' when you give everything you can each day. The rest, you figure out together."

I walked a delicate line with my next question.

"What if both of you are the hardest worker? How do you know where to pick up the slack?"

"You'll know," she said simply. "If you're committed to making it work, you'll know."

I finished my meal quickly and told Nan I needed to check on the horses. I collected my boots from where I'd abandoned them and slipped out the front door.

* * *

I could see my breath for the first half of my journey to Finna's. The weather had grown colder. The trees had let go of their leaves. The solstice was a heartbeat away, and it showed, but not everything had changed. I paused on the bridge to listen to the water rushing down the falls. It was a comfort I hadn't realized I missed until I heard it. I'd forgotten what it was like to return after being so far from home.

My fingers and nose were numb by the time I reached the

red door of the cottage. Two knocks and a few seconds later, the door opened. Finna's face lit up with a smile. She stepped back to let me in; I watched her excitement fade as her eyes shifted to the empty space behind me. She searched for only a moment before she shut the door and turned to take my coat, but I was already hanging it up.

"Breck isn't here," I told her. I'd been working up the nerve to tell her everything on my walk, but my confidence was shaky at best now that we were face-to-face. "Could I have some tea?"

"Sit," was all she said, placing a gentle hand on my back to send me toward the sitting room as she went for the kitchen. I sat on the sofa and tucked my fingers underneath my thighs to try and warm them. Finna returned with two cups. I took mine with both hands and let the heat soak into them as I took my first sip.

"They're all with Eabha," I started after the tea had begun to settle in my stomach. "Breck was called away. I didn't know anything until Elina came for me. She said that she needed my help. I thought Breck was in trouble, so of course I went."

"She took you to the fairy world?" Finna's reaction was a mix of surprise and disbelief.

"He was fine when I arrived. But..." This was the part I was unsure about. Had Finna been covering up the lies, too? Fallon had said she never knew, but Finna was smart.

"Go on," Finna urged from her seat by the hearth. I took a steadying breath.

"Fallon is Breck's mother." The words tumbled from my mouth quicker than I'd intended. Finna's eyes went wide. She blinked at me a few times. I wanted to take my last gulp of tea, but it felt like poor timing. Finna opened her mouth to say something. Closed it again.

Finna had raised Breck as her own. He was her son more than anyone else's, if you considered all the things she'd done for him. Their relationship with each other was special. The last thing I wanted to do was interfere, but she deserved to know, just as Breck had. Nobody gave him that option, and I wasn't about to let it happen again.

"I'm sorry, Finna."

She responded with a tight shake of her head, lips pressed together. I could see the light of the fire catch in the tears pooling in her eyes. One of them escaped when she blinked and looked at me again.

"How did he take the news?"

"Not well," I admitted. Memories of finding him on the rock came flooding back. "Did you know?"

"I… I wondered," she said quietly. "But I never dared to ask. If they had wanted me to know, they would've told me. I just never understood how she found this little lad all alone, and he couldn't remember anything about his life. He didn't understand a word I said. He refused to keep clothes on or stay inside when he needed to. He was feral. And sometimes I think that still lives deep inside him."

"Fallon's mate was the one who carried him. She'd wished for a baby, and an Unseelie granted the wish." I swallowed as emotion thickened in my throat. "Fallon had to say goodbye to her mate so that Breck could live."

Both of Finna's hands rushed to cover her gasp with shaky fingers. My gaze slid to her cup, which remained where it had been when she let go, frozen in the air in front of her. She made another sad sound before she swept her fingers over her wet cheeks and reached for the cup, setting it down safely on the table by her chair.

"*Dark magic*," she whispered as she shook her head and looked at the glow in the hearth. "Jo was such a sweet thing. But strong."

"Aye. Fallon told me."

"I'm surprised. She never talks about her to anyone now." Finna looked at me. "I was led to believe that Jo was taken by a human illness. She was bedridden for months." She gave a weak laugh. "I suppose it was a pregnancy they were trying to hide, then. No wonder she wouldn't allow me to see her so I could try to help." I could practically see all the loose ends tying themselves up in Finna's head. Her grief turned to something lighter as she spoke.

"Blonde hair, blue eyes. That cute nose. He looks just like her. I should've seen it before." Finna was on her feet then, reaching for both our empty cups to take them to the kitchen. I got up and followed her. She took her frustration out on scrubbing in the sink, her hands buried in soapy water. I sat in my usual spot at the table to offer my quiet support.

"She used to be happy, you know. Jo's death changed her." She brushed her thick hair away from her face with her forearm. "But now, to know what really happened. Oh, my dear friend."

Finna continued to speak about Fallon as if she were in the room with us. By the time she was done, the kitchen was spotless and I had a newfound softness for someone I'd only had tense encounters with before. She'd told story after story about the love between Fallon and Jo, starting with the one Fallon had told me herself about the moment she knew Jo was the one.

"You should've seen them on the day they were joined. In all my years, I've never laid eyes on a happier couple."

"I can't picture Fallon smiling about anything," I confessed. I'd propped my elbow on the table, my chin and cheek cupped in my hand. Fatigue was catching up with me, but I didn't want to go home in case Breck came back.

"She puts on an impressive show, but she has a good heart underneath it all. She cares far more than she lets on. It's what makes her a good leader." Finna finally ran out of things to clean, so she joined me at the table after lighting a few extra candles on the windowsill.

"Tell me more about that night?" I asked, my tired voice coming across as wistful. I leaned back in my chair and crossed my arms loosely, fighting a yawn that turned into a cough. Finna hummed a thoughtful noise as she drew on her memories.

"Jo was radiant in her dress. She made all her own clothes."

"She made that blue dress?" Even the dresses Sarah and her sisters wore at the wedding hadn't been as captivating.

"Ah, you saw it," Finna said with a grin. "Fallon found the fabric for her as a part of their commitment gifts. Jo wanted to make her a dress, as well, but Fallon never wears such things, so it wasn't appropriate for the tradition."

"Tradition?" I tried to contain the spark of interest that word set off in me. I clearly failed as I noticed the shift in Finna's expression to something more knowing. She held up the back of her hand toward me and wiggled her fingers, her jewelry catching the warm light from the candles.

"Fairies do not exchange rings like humans do. By tradition, the commitment gift is to be something handmade or deeply meaningful. Something that shows how much they care for their future mate. Fallon gave Jo the fabric for her dream dress, and Jo gave Fallon a leather-bound book filled with handwritten poems, stories, and love letters for her to read when they were apart."

"That's sickeningly romantic," I said with a chuckle.

"As I said," Finna concurred, smiling at the fond memories. She glanced at the darkness outside and then turned her attention back to me. "Shall I fetch a blanket and pillow for the sofa?"

"I don't want to be in your way," I hedged.

"Nonsense. Breck still does it all the time. Besides, you're much too tired to walk all the way home at this time of night. Come." With a big puff of air directed at one candle, Finna put them all out at once. The resulting curls of smoke from the wicks threatened more coughs from my lungs, so I hurried to follow her out of the kitchen. I removed my boots and put them near my coat. It took just enough time for Finna to return with her promised items.

The thought that Breck had used them last was a comfort as I settled on my side. The blanket wasn't very long, but the sofa was too short for me to stretch my legs out anyway. I bent my knees up and shuffled my feet around until they were both securely underneath the blanket.

Finna's fingers ruffling my hair took me by surprise. "Sleep well, love."

I tucked the blanket up against my chin and settled my tired gaze on the hearth. Before she could get very far, I shifted against the pillow. "Finna?" She paused and turned back to me, listening. "Would you come to my house for supper? My family wants to meet you."

Her whole body seemed to soften at my offer. She pressed her lips together with a grin, nodding. "I would enjoy that very much."

CHAPTER TWENTY-FOUR

The next day was spent catching up on everything I'd missed. I had worried that it would be overwhelming, but luckily Thomas was ready with his high-society gossiping ways to lay it all out for me. Somehow, even the most mundane of topics seemed scandalous the way they dripped from his tongue.

"*And*," he continued, lowering his voice as one of the hands walked a horse I didn't recognize past us, "you'll never guess who is newly boarded with us as of yesterday."

"Go on," I encouraged, not really wanting to know but feeling obligated to listen since he'd done as I asked and managed my lessons in my absence.

"None other than Ant Byrne! Can you imagine it?"

Anthony Byrne was a name I'd known since childhood. Any lad who'd even glanced at a polo mallet knew who he was. He'd once been a hero to us all, until a season-ending injury sidelined him. For a while it was a question if he'd ever walk again, let alone ride. He hadn't played professionally since, but he still made his appearances and remained heavily involved in the sport.

"What's he doing here?" I asked, finally pausing in my task to give Thomas my full attention. It seemed to light him up.

"That's the best of all. Word is that he's made a deal with William. Instead of boarding fees, he's willing to directly fund an upgraded training arena here on the property, in exchange for our open spot on the team next year."

This sent a wash of surprise through me. "Ant will play with us?"

Thomas stepped closer and poked a finger into my chest. "He's *begging* to play with us." He flashed his eyebrows and gave me my personal space back, returning to his own horse. The only response I could manage was a cough as the information settled. In his prime, he'd been nearly unstoppable. Now he was interested in being on our team?

"Walshe." I turned at the familiar, harsh voice. John Wallace was halfway down the aisle and already inspecting my mare, as if to check and see how much damage I'd done to her on our journey. My early return was likely a surprise to them all, but nobody had asked me about it directly. I was happy to keep it that way.

"Wally," I greeted him back. "Thomas has been filling me in on all the good news."

"Aye, plenty to go around. Bring 'er along." He didn't slow down as he passed us. I untied my mare and turned her around to follow him outside. Wally's short legs had already carried him across the yard to the fence. His arms were crossed along the top rail. He didn't look up at me when I stopped next to him. The silence stretched between us for some time.

I tried to think of something to break the silence. "William must be—"

"I didn't want to sell the horse, lad, but I didn't have a choice. I had to get the money to settle the deal I made with 'er. I would'a paid it on my own if I'd had it to spare."

"I know that," I reassured him. It was strange to hear Wally so vulnerable. He let out a heavy sigh and reached into his pocket, fishing around for something. Realization hit as he produced a small coin pouch. He shoved it at me, giving me no option but to take it.

"That's everything left after the debt was paid." He spoke over me when I started to protest. "I didn't earn a bit of it. You put in all the work. Keep what you deserve." With that, he left me standing at the fence. I stared at the bag of coins. It wasn't what I wanted, but it could be a start toward saving up for a new horse. One like Henry and Thomas had. A horse like Ant was sure to ride for the season, too.

I pulled at the collar of my shirt and tucked the pouch inside, feeling it slide down and settle where the tails were tucked into my waistband, and brought my mare's reins over her head as I put my foot in the stirrup. Thomas had already found the mounting block and was waiting for me at the mouth of the trail. His mouth was running again before I could reach him.

"How's married life treating our dearest friend?" he queried, his horse falling into stride beside mine.

I snorted a laugh and shook my head, trying to pick the right words. "I've never known a man more suited for being a husband. He's grown a full beard and everything."

Thomas barked out a laugh. "Has he? Now that is something I cannot wait to see. When do they plan to return? They've been gone an exceptionally long time, even for a couple of their status. I would expect that Henry's father is getting impatient for him to start his work."

"They should be along soon." Their reason for delay brought heat to my cheeks. Anne, and now Sarah. Even the little barn cat was doing her part in bringing new life to the world. I hadn't noticed until that moment how I was surrounded by it.

For a rare moment, Thomas was silent. Then I was hit with, "Can I trust you with a confession?" Despite the grimace my face so badly wanted to make, I maintained my composure. Thomas and I had spoken more to each other in Henry's absence than we likely had in all the previous years of knowing one another. I started to wonder if it had been my own fault.

"Aye, what've you done?" I asked, trying a gentle prod like I would've done with Henry. It didn't help the serious look on Thomas' face, but his shoulders did relax some. We crested the first hill of the trail and curved back around toward the river before he finally worked up the nerve to speak.

"I am wholly inexperienced when it comes to matters of intimacy."

I waited for him to continue. When he didn't, I glanced over to find him staring back.

"Is... that all?" I asked with uncertainty. Thomas looked away then, his back straight as a board, jaw tight. I wasn't sure if my words were the reason for his reaction, so I continued. "I thought you've kissed Emma Clare before, haven't you?"

"Once," came his clipped response.

"Well, once isn't nothing," I reasoned with a shrug.

"Tomorrow is my twenty-first birthday, and I am utterly

pathetic when it comes to romance. I haven't the first clue about how to properly court a lady. I've been unable to ask Henry for advice since he's been gone for so long." Thomas let out a frustrated sigh. "And asking you seems useless, because you somehow maintain the status of being the most sought-after bachelor, all while finding no interest in women aside from your nighttime flings."

"My *what*?" I challenged, heart beating harder in my chest at this flood of information.

"We all see how you act most chivalrously in a social setting, but everyone who's anyone knows that Peter Walshe is a downright scoundrel after dark. Can you even remember them all? Do you know their names, or do you simply lift their skirts, have your fun, and slink back home in the early hours of the morning? I imagine your newfound fame has helped."

Anger welled inside me to the point of wanting to shout, but I swallowed it down. This, *this* was exactly why I would never fit in with the rest of the people I called neighbors. This was why I refused to attend any social events unless it was at Henry's request. His words hadn't even come across as accusatory. He was almost envious.

"None of that is true," I said, forcing my voice to come out as neutral as possible. I knew defending myself against what he'd said was a waste of my breath, but I couldn't let my own integrity be challenged so heavily. "Who is telling you these things?"

"Well," Thomas faltered, "I don't know any of them personally. But I know the people who heard it from someone else. And *they* say that all the young ladies are wanting their share of you. If they haven't had it already, that is."

Embarrassment flamed across my chest and up my neck. I breathed in too sharply, causing me to cough hard several times. I found myself teetering on the ledge I'd walked since I first realized that I was different. My secret hung in a delicate balance, and my grip on the rope of silence became more frayed with each tug, each joke, each moment like this, when I wanted so badly to use the truth to free myself from the salacious rumors being spread by people who pretended to know me.

"They're lying." It was all I could manage.

Thomas laughed and made a high-pitched noise that conveyed his suspicions.

"Consider yourself lucky to be so desired. Most often, they only gossip about which of us they find most revolting for one reason or another."

"I cannot imagine why," I mumbled. I felt a numbness creeping through me.

Thomas spent the rest of our ride talking about other people that ran in his circle of friends, stirring the drama even more if I'd cared enough to listen. By the time we returned to the stables, the back of my throat and nose were raw from holding in my emotions. How anyone could voluntarily be a part of a community that thrived so heavily on hearsay and scandals, I would never understand.

Typically, I never left my untacking and grooming duties to the hands. It was one of my favorite parts of the process, bonding with my horses, knowing their bodies so I could easily recognize an injury or ailment if one ever popped up. This time, I could barely manage to dismount before I was in the tack room, throwing my gear into my box with more force than necessary. Thomas' presence as he turned through the doorway made the room feel even smaller than it already was.

"You should come to my party tomorrow evening. Everyone will be there." I could hear the familiar scrapes of him changing out of his riding boots behind me.

"No thanks," I said, empty of all emotion.

"Well, at least give me some words of advice, then. Emma Clare has decided that we should make it a most special night, and I want to—"

I was across the room in seconds. I ripped Thomas around with a rough hand on his shoulder so that he landed with a yelp of shock and protest, back was against the wall, sitting awkwardly on the bench where I'd had my own first intimate moments with Jamie. I got in his face and lowered my voice to nearly a whisper.

"My advice is to keep your hands and every other bit of you away from Emma Clare until you've properly courted her. Show her some respect like the young lady she is. Set up times to meet with her and a chaperone. Get to know each other. Bring her flowers. If I hear otherwise, and certainly if Henry hears otherwise, you'll be lucky to have a wedding night to remember someday."

"But she—"

"She is a *girl*. She doesn't know what she wants, other than to fit in with the rest of her friends, who are all claiming to be more sexually active than they really are." Thomas swallowed and looked down, breaking our eye contact. I clenched my hands at my sides and let them relax again.

"I do like her," he admitted finally.

"Then show her you do. What's her favorite flower, Thomas? What does she like to eat for breakfast? What makes her smile when she's upset?" His silence was all the answer I needed. "Trust me. If you hope for any kind of future with the lass, do not lie with her just to say that you did."

I returned to my things long enough to put on my other shoe, which I'd abandoned in my haste, and left Thomas to stew with his thoughts. I couldn't handle one more second of him.

CHAPTER TWENTY-FIVE

I didn't care that it was only early afternoon. I went up to my bedroom, careful not to slam any doors behind me to draw attention, and buried my face into my pillow. What I'd been subjected to that morning had been the last emotional weight I could carry without having to let some of it go.

When my lungs started to burn, I moved my pillow to one side and rested my cheek against it instead, sniffing at the wetness that trickled over the bridge of my nose.

I needed to know that Breck was alright. I had to find a way to communicate with him somehow. I tried to think of everything I'd learned about fairies and magic. Of course, there was one way I knew I could get his attention without question, but trying to drown myself in the river was an extreme I wasn't willing to risk no matter how badly I needed him back.

My face was wiped dry against the pillow as I shifted from staring at my wall to looking the other direction out the window.

The hypocrisy of my words to Thomas weren't lost on

me. Given the chance at sixteen, I would've had my hands and mouth on Jamie anywhere he'd let me put them, if we hadn't still been caught up in the secrecy of our feelings for one another. At twenty-one, that ship had long ago sailed.

My reaction had been fueled by Henry and Sarah. By what they would've done if they found out I knew about this unceremonious union and done nothing to stop it. Emma Clare was a shameless flirt, as were the rest of her sisters, but that didn't mean her reputation and future were something to risk for the thirty seconds it would take Thomas to prove himself a man on his birthday.

I groaned and pulled my pillow up over my head. Closed my eyes. Slowed my breathing. The next thing I knew, my mattress was dipping by my hip. I startled, shoving the pillow aside.

"What's the matter? Did you have a bad dream?" Lucy was climbing up onto the bed, inviting herself into my space. I rolled over and made room for her.

"I'm fine," I told her, my voice betraying me.

"You were crying though." I made a face to object, but she frowned at me. "Your nose is all red, and your eyes are puffy."

"Alright," I admitted under my breath. No use in arguing that. She settled back against the headboard and opened her book to a middle page, quietly picking up where she left off. I bunched my pillow underneath my head again. As her eyes tracked the words on the page, I wondered when she'd grown up so much.

"What's this one about, then?" I asked, reaching to tilt the cover enough so I could see it. "I don't recognize it. Library book?" She shook her head, giving me a temporary answer without breaking her focus until she finished the page, turning to the next.

"It's a collection. Anne said it's very special because she's never seen it in English before. I think I'd like to learn another language to read more stories from older books. Do you think I could?"

"I'm sure you could do anything you put your mind to, Luc."

She smiled and continued with the story, reading aloud now so I could hear it, too. I let the details of it fill my mind. I forgot about everything else except for the fact that my littlest sister was taking the time to try and lift my spirits. It was almost enough to get me choked up all over again.

When Lucy got tired, I took over, and we finished just as the dreary light outside had faded too much to read by. She closed the book on her lap and turned to look up at me.

"Why did she say no to all the other suitors, but when the flower prince put his crown on her head, she said she would marry him right away?"

I had to think for a moment before I responded. "I suppose she was looking for the perfect someone to make her happy."

"He was also very handsome," she added, as if she'd known that was the answer to her own question.

"That probably didn't hurt either," I agreed with a grin.

"Fairy princes are always so handsome."

My mouth went a little dry at the thought. "To match the beauty of the fairy princesses, of course." Something Finna had told me came to mind then. "You know, when fairies are going to get married, they don't exchange rings like we do. They must give each other a very special gift to show their love. I'll bet the flower prince gave her his crown as his gift, and it was what she'd always wanted."

"But then he also gave her wings? That's two gifts. She didn't give him anything at all."

"Well, they probably just didn't include it in the story." I paused. "What do you think she could've given him to show that she loved him?"

Lucy's lips scrunched up to one side as she gave my question some serious thought. If anyone knew the answer, it would be our resident fairy expert. Her face brightened as she settled on something.

"I would make my prince a delicious meal, because fairies love to eat, especially things that humans make with ingredients from the woods." I thought she was done as she made her way off the bed and held her book tight to her chest, but she added, "And, I would give him something to wear so that he would always think of me any time he put it on. Maybe a beautiful piece of sparkly jewelry."

"Isn't that a little too much like the rings?" I asked as I got to my feet, too.

She huffed and gave me a look that said I was being ridiculous.

"Well, *I'm* not a fairy, after all! Why can't he wear a ring for me, and I'll wear his crown?"

How did my eight-year-old sister have a better grasp on this concept than I did? She skipped toward the door when Nan's voice carried up the stairs to let us know that supper was ready. With her hand on the knob of my door, she pulled it open and gave me one last glance.

"Please tell the miller thank you for my new book when you see him."

Surprise froze me in place. The book was a gift from Breck? I spun around and reached my bedside table in a handful of strides. The white envelope sitting there sent a thrill through me. I hadn't noticed it earlier in all my misery. I tore it open and didn't bother to sit down as I unfolded the parchment, my eyes scanning the words twice before I slowed down enough to read them.

Please allow me to
make this up to you.
We have much to discuss.
B

CHAPTER TWENTY-SIX

I ate so fast that I barely had time to taste the food before I swallowed it. I blamed a headache for the odd schedule I'd kept that day when Anne asked, and then I excused myself, making for the barn until I was sure nobody could see me through the kitchen windows.

I was panting through the pain in my lungs as I crossed the bridge. It was forgotten in an instant when I saw the light in the upstairs windows of the mill. I kept my balance down the hill and sprinted the rest of the way.

"Breck!" I called, coughing after at the strained effort. I was seven footfalls from the weathered door when it opened, allowing me to leap clear over the steps and land unsteadily inside the storeroom, grasping in the dark for any part of him I could reach first.

A sob of excitement wrenched from my chest when I felt his hands grab me, turning me around. I blinked at the outline of him as his arms wrapped tightly around my neck. Our kiss was desperate, too short thanks to my gasps for air, which quickly turned into more coughs. We sank to the floor together in a heap of tangled legs as I tried to catch my breath.

The chilly curl of his magic started at my ankles and wrists, moving with more purpose than I was used to. By the time it wrapped around my heaving chest and whispered across my neck, I didn't have to wonder why. The relief was instant as the cold air reached my lungs. I tried to take deeper breaths, but it was still too much. Instead, I let Breck do the work. His magic seemed to flow in even on my exhales, seeking out the pain. A deep shiver went through my whole body.

"Come on," Breck said quietly, attempting to unravel himself from where I'd collapsed against him, my forehead on his shoulder. I let him help me up. He kept both hands on me as we climbed the stairs, my shoes making an obnoxious amount of noise compared to his bare feet. I was settled on the rug with a blanket around my shoulders and fresh mint tea in my hands before Breck said anything else.

"Why didn't you ever tell me that my magic helped your pain?" He seemed upset with himself over the question. I let my arms rest against my thighs and swallowed before I answered.

"I guess I thought you knew," I said, bunching my shoulders a little. "Is it… because of…"

"You remember what Finna told you. Light and dark magic cannot mix." I nodded. How could I forget? "If our magic had been so incompatible, it likely would've made the pain even worse." He shook his head, staring at the rug beneath us, his fingers toying with the thick fibers of it. "I don't know how I didn't realize it earlier."

"You cannot blame yourself in any of this," I told him, becoming protective. "New information can't change the past. As much as we might like for it to." I used my free hand that wasn't holding the tea to shuffle my weight away from the fire in the stove and closer to him. Our shoulders touched as I leaned against the side of the bed. I took another sip from my cup and pulled in a slow, steady breath. "But it can change the future, I suppose."

This earned me Breck's full attention as he looked up from the rug, his eyes meeting mine and lingering, searching. Something deep in me begged for a smirk to quirk up the corner of his lips. For that mischievous twinkle to light up in his eyes. Anything to tell me that he was having the same thoughts I was. Instead, he remained serious for a moment longer before he stood and went to busy himself with something in his kitchen.

I brought my thumb and finger up to massage the bridge of my nose, letting out a slow sigh. Breck was alright. He had been released from Eabha and the others, a bit more melancholy than I was used to, but safe. For that, I was endlessly grateful.

Breck returned to our temporary camp on the floor, landing gracefully at my side. A bundle of parchment was open in one hand that he held up between us. "Finna made more apple cake for you. She went a little strong on the walnuts and cinnamon, but I think you'll like it."

I reached for my piece and brought it to my mouth, taking a healthy bite. Breck's note said we had a lot to discuss, but I was content to just sit with him after being apart for so long. It felt like being whole again. Even after I'd licked my fingers clean, neither of us spoke. I finally decided to start with something easy.

"Lucy wanted me to tell you she loves her new book. She read some of it to me this afternoon."

"I'm glad she likes it. I thought she might." This brought a small twitch to his lips.

"It must be easy to get presents for someone when you can look into their head and see exactly what they want," I said, nudging his arm with mine. "I'll be glad to have your help when birthdays come around. I'd like to be good at giving gifts for a change." My thoughts shifted to other birthday news, which wiped the smile from my mouth. I told him about what happened with Thomas earlier in the day.

"Tall, dark, and mysterious is working in your favor," Breck finally teased back. I scoffed at him and let the blanket fall from my shoulders now that I'd been sufficiently warmed.

"First of all, I would hardly consider rumors like that to be in my favor. And second, I think you forgot the part about being *handsome*." I adopted a haughty tone for the last part, which finally made him grin.

"My apologies. From what I understand, that part is usually to be expected in a man who finds himself rumored to be popular with the ladies."

"Aye, well." I paused to lean far enough over that I could place my empty cup safely on the hardwood floor. "I suppose since it's only natural in your world for everyone to be flawlessly attractive, the other attributes probably hold more weight." I shifted my hips so I could turn to face him, pulling one leg up to cross it underneath the other. Breck was busy folding the empty parchment in half again and again with precision, smoothing it against his thigh as he'd done on our trip.

"I'm sorry for the mess I created of your holiday." His soft voice was full of regret. "I know how important it was to you."

"You've nothing to apologize for. I still had a good time. We had fun, didn't we?" I thought about the highlights of the trip, trying to project them for Breck to see all the good memories we'd made. He didn't make any reaction to indicate if he was getting them or not.

"I never wanted to show you my world that way. The Seelie court is so special to me, and I didn't get the chance to bring you on my own terms. To show you how incredible it can be."

"We can go back," I encouraged, moving closer to him yet. My bent knee rested against the outside of his crossed thigh. "Once it doesn't nearly kill you to take me places, of course." The look he gave me conveyed how serious he was about this. I brought my hand up to his jaw, rubbing my thumb against his cheek. "Elina thought it was important. But we can make it special again. Next time."

Breck leaned into my touch, but his eyes remained cast down until he closed them.

"That's what you want?" He sounded so uncertain.

"Of course, it is. Whatever you want is what I want."

"How do you know? For certain?"

I gave it some thought before I answered.

"I know because of the way my whole body aches for you when you're gone. I know because the moments of my life with you in them are infinitely better than the ones without. I know because, in the end, I would rather be with you, wet and reeking of pig shite, than anywhere else if it meant I could have you in my arms."

This earned a rare, genuine laugh from Breck that was heavy with emotion as he brought his hands up, one to the side of my neck as the other slid into my hair at the back of my head, pulling me toward him. My eyes closed as our lips met, noses mashing cozily. I was only partially aware of our bodies moving and Breck's magic enveloping us until I was on my back, the high pile of the rug cushioning my bare shoulders. My eyes opened at the unexpected sensation.

Breck was straddling my hips, as naked as I was, grinning at the objects he was holding. In one hand was the book from the library at the castle. In the other, the little jar. I'd had them both tucked safely in the pockets of my coat, which was now hanging neatly over the back of a chair with the rest of our clothes. He looked between them again for good measure before he arched an eyebrow down at me.

"I think you're better at giving gifts than you realize," he murmured, his smirk growing. I let out a breathy laugh, adjusting to all that his magic was capable of in such a short time. I slid my palms from his bent knees down toward his ankles.

His attention returned to the book, cradling the spine of it carefully in his palm as the pages opened all on their own. His freckles sparkled in the fire and fairy lights as his eyes scanned the golden words that must've appeared on the paper, tucked in the margins. He made a show of clearing his throat. "Shall I begin?"

My grip tightened on his calves as the words began dripping from his tongue. Could words be delicious? I closed my eyes briefly to soak in the sweetness of them. When my pulse was humming, I forced myself to look up at him again. Somehow, I found the clarity to speak.

"Correct me if I'm wrong, but that all seems awfully eloquent for records of births and deaths."

Breck giggled and closed the book gently, setting it aside as he leaned forward onto his hands, which he placed on either side of my head. The brush of his body against the newly sensitive parts mine had me inhaling sharply through my teeth.

"That's because I wasn't reading from the book," he explained. As he leaned down to kiss my neck, his voice shrank to a whisper. *"I was describing all the things I'd like to do to you right now."*

I groaned and tilted my head, capturing his mouth with mine. One of his hands found my chest, slowly working its way down, and I caught his wrist in my fingers. He wasn't about to go one step further without us picking up where we left off at the estate before he was called away.

"I'm sorry, but I have a debt to pay before any other services can be rendered."

Breck's lips returned to my neck, placing feather-light kisses against my pulse. "Repayment is not necessary."

"That seems like poor business to me. You'd never allow that downstairs, would you?" I grinned at my own attempt to keep things playful, but the slide of the tip of his tongue along my collarbone brought me crashing back down. My brows furrowed and I brought my arms up, one hand sliding across his back while the other tangled into his hair.

"I keep a tab for a reason," he murmured, nudging my jaw with his nose so he could even things up on the other side of my neck. I happily obliged. "Sometimes it's more worth it to me to make the customer happy than it is to collect their payment."

I swallowed and nodded a little to show my understanding, breathing hard. "I see."

"This is especially true when I'm trying to make them a lifelong customer." The double meaning behind his words set off little sparks in some part of my brain, but I had no time to acknowledge them. Breck moved his body down my legs and took me in his mouth so swiftly that all I could do was accept defeat and bend one arm underneath my head so I could see him better.

I watched with heavy lids until the hand he wasn't holding me with moved from my hip to between his own legs, which sent a heavy wave of want through me. I pushed up onto my elbows, and Breck seemed to understand. He let both of us go and crawled up to kiss me.

"*I want you inside me, mo ghrá,*" he whispered against my lips.

If I'd been at all coherent, I would've finally asked him what those two words meant. Instead, his request took over my body and mind completely. I reached for the little jar faster than a horse could kick a man and unscrewed the lid as Breck climbed onto the bed, making a show of it. I nearly dropped everything I was holding as I watched him.

"Aren't you coming?" he asked. I realized I was still sitting on the rug.

I was on my feet then, uncapping the jar as I came around the side of the bed. I set the lid on the windowsill over Breck's head and bent my knee as I climbed atop his fine bedclothes, which were already mussed. We both took a turn collecting some of the contents of the jar onto our fingers and got busy with slick hands and slow kisses. I was out of breath by the time we pulled apart. It gave me an idea.

"Your magic," I panted, sitting back between his bent knees. "I want you to use your magic."

His eyes searched mine for a moment, lips parted, chest rising and falling much smoother than my own, but still showing his exertion. His hesitation was marked by the way he drew his bottom lip in between his teeth, dragging along

✴

the kiss-swollen skin until it popped loose again. A shaky breath escaped me at the sight.

"Alright," he said finally.

I leaned forward to press my lips to his as he settled onto his back. His tousled hair fell away from his forehead, revealing more freckles to kiss as his legs worked their way around my hips. I sat up and reached between us, working him for a few strokes with my silken hand before I did the same to myself. With my eyes closed to the anticipation of the pleasure I was one tick away from, I felt Breck's magic on me.

The sensation was familiar now, but I still felt the goose-bumps spring up along my bare limbs, making me quiver. I knew the sight waiting for me as soon as I opened my eyes, as well, so I kept them shut a little longer, saving it for the right moment.

My hips found a rhythm as his magic seemed to discover new places on my body it had never been before. The skin between my shoulder blades, the dip of my lower back. I stifled a sound of surprise as it slipped between us and found my most intimate places to caress. Breck gave a gentle laugh at my reaction, indicating that he'd done that one on purpose.

After he'd had his fun, I felt the moment he sent the brumal conjuration swirling up to find my lungs. I took a deep breath and opened my eyes, thoroughly overwhelming myself with everything that Breck was. His freckled cheeks glittered like the sunlight reflecting off the river on a cloudless day. He was watching me with such adoration that I felt something clench in my chest and then burst, spreading all the way out to my fingers and toes.

Nothing could've quelled my urge to lean down and kiss

him in that moment. His parted lips met mine with an unfamiliar hunger. I had to reclaim his bottom one; I had to feel it between my teeth as I tugged at it gently, which made him moan in such a way that pleasure twisted low in my stomach from the sound alone. Vaguely, I recognized that my labored breaths were no longer painful as our bodies moved together.

The grip his magic had on me was more powerful than I'd ever felt before. It was as though he wasn't just using it on me, but he was *sharing* it with me. I felt it in my chest, my head, my heart. Is this what it was like to hold the strength of a fairy?

"We have to go," I said urgently as I broke our kiss. I reached for Breck's hand and all but dragged him off the mattress. I couldn't explain the uneasiness that had come over me by being on the bed, inside the mill, but I had to fix it. He followed me silently down the steps and out the door.

The sting of the night air bit at my bare skin only slightly. Breck's magic had already chilled me inside and out. There wasn't even a misty trace of my breath on each exhale. An innate sense of need pulled me toward the thick stretch of trees that the mill was tucked into. I blinked into the darkness, not bothering to worry about anything painful I might step on along the way.

Breck's fingers lacing between mine was the first thing to somewhat break my focus. His free hand wrapped around my forearm, pulling himself close enough to me as we walked that my arm was pressed against his body. He didn't seem concerned about my odd behavior.

I kept going until I felt a shift inside me. That uneasiness seemed to settle as my feet came to rest in an entirely nondescript location. The trees stood sentry around us, as they had for hundreds of years. The only sound was our breathing. I turned to face Breck, trying to figure out a way to explain myself to him, when a little glimmer of light caught my eye. Then another, and another. I looked up to find a handful of fairies in the branches above our heads.

I'd led us to a place with more magic. The golden light of the fairies created just enough of a glow for me to see the details of Breck's face. He looked calm. Peaceful. Sultry.

The fire of passion flickered in me as I remembered what I'd interrupted. Without thinking, I leaned into him, pushing him a few steps until his back was against the nearest tree. I kissed him deeply and sank to my knees, taking him in my hand first, my tongue teasing his bollocks, before I slid it flat up his length and took as much of him as I could in my mouth. Feck the little fairies. They could watch if they wanted. I needed the world to know that Breck was mine.

I worked on us both at the same time, taking full advantage of the fact that my lungs weren't screaming in agony yet. I gave one particularly long drag on Breck before I felt him shudder under the hand I had wrapped around the back of his thigh.

"Peter, stop," he panted, his voice hoarse. "I'm going to—"

I was on my feet in seconds, albeit a little unsteady. Breck turned around to face the tree, peering at me over his shoulder as his hands gripped the rough bark. The curve of his neck, the thick dusting of freckles across his shoulders, it was all nearly too much as I slid my leg between his to part them more.

The deep nagging I felt ebbed as I brought us together again with our feet firmly in the dirt. My toes curled into it for good measure. I felt my heel catch neatly in the crook of a root from the tree supporting Breck's weight. Something deep inside said that this was exactly where we needed to be. I wasn't about to argue.

My hands found Breck's hips as I rocked into him. He abandoned his hold on the trunk and let his shoulder take more of the burden as he jerked himself in his left hand, each exhale a stunted noise of pleasure, until finally he whimpered out, "*Is é mo chroí leats—a—hah—*"

A whip of cold only comparable to the shock of falling into the river washed over me, sending us both soaring to our fate. I pressed my face into the back of Breck's neck as I came, the first time in nearly three years I was able to experience it without the pain and coughing. It was even better than I remembered.

Breck turned slowly in my grip. He was more out of breath than I was, his eyes barely open as his head fell back to the rough bark. Though I'd never felt more sated, I still couldn't keep myself away from him. My lips found his jaw, the stretch of his throat, the light sheen of sweat across his chest.

"What did you say?" I asked him once we'd settled more.

"*I didn't,*" he breathed. I had to admit I felt a little smug over how spent he was.

"I mean before, when you… you know," I tried to explain.

"Oh." I couldn't tell at first if his response was a reaction to him remembering, or to the way I was sucking gently on the skin just under his ear. "It was, uh… *mmh*. Ask me again tomorrow." His hands came to my face, and he pulled me up for a proper kiss, slow and lazy and full of unspoken promises.

CHAPTER TWENTY-SEVEN

Mathew arrived for his lesson promptly the next morning, and to my surprise, he made quick work of tacking up his horse with little guidance on my part. I watched him work, giving him an encouraging nod when he caught me looking.

"My father said I should be a good lad and try to impress you today, or else I would be stuck with the other trainer again," he grumbled as he worked to get the girth buckled on his saddle. "He's not very nice."

I barely managed to hold in my snort of a laugh.

"Sorry I had to leave so suddenly last week." I stepped closer to help when he seemed to struggle. The mare was making it difficult for him to get the buckle prong in the correct hole. "Wait until she lets her breath out before you tighten the strap." He nodded his understanding and did as he was told.

"I've been talking to her, like you said. I think she's starting to like me."

"Aye, and the little treat you slipped her helped, as well," I chided. Mathew shrugged innocently and hid his grin. "Just don't do it too often or she'll want to eat nothing but sweets."

Mathew was guiding his mare to the mounting block when a flurry of activity at the far stables drew our attention. I recognized Ant Byrne leading a small posse, including an over-eager Thomas at his heels. Maybe he'd finally found someone new to bother.

"Who is that?" Mathew asked with mild interest. I returned my focus to our lesson as he awkwardly swung his leg over the saddle. He spent too much time bent over, helping his boots into the stirrups, and huffed as he sat up.

"He's another polo player boarding with us. I think he might join our team next season."

"Is he as good as you are?"

I chuckled at that, wishing so badly that Henry had been there to hear it.

"He used to be one of the best. Ready?"

I let the duo into the training ring. Mathew seemed to hesitate at first, but then he encouraged his horse into a walk along the fence. I stopped in the middle after shutting the gate, following with my eyes as they came around. "Trot next," I instructed after several minutes, and Mathew eased her into the next gait without trouble. She was stunning, able to listen to her novice rider much more readily now that he had some clue about what he was doing. "She looks grand. Canter now," I called, the intense focus on his face relaxing some at my praise.

The mare's three-beat was music to my soul as they circled at a steady pace. I knew I couldn't take most of the credit just yet, but I was proud to be a part of this blossoming of a bright future between a young rider and his horse.

A low whistle made me turn. Ant was at the fence, ogling the mare as she made her laps. He turned his attention to me with a bright smile. "How's it, Peter? Good to see you again."

"Anthony," I greeted him back with a dip of my chin.

"I came searching for that chestnut of yours when I heard she was for sale. Turns out I was too slow or too cheap, whichever you'd consider worse." He laughed at his own words and adjusted his stance. "I decided I'd have to settle for training alongside you instead. But it appears I'm late to that, as well." We both watched Mathew as he rode between us on another pass.

"I'm certain you're not looking for lessons," I said, hinting at disbelief.

"A man's never too good to make improvements."

The confidence he wore was bordering on arrogance, already rubbing me the wrong way. His mention of the chestnut mare had soured my mood even more. I tried not to let it show.

"This is a private session, but I'll find you later so we can catch up," I told him dismissively. I called for Mathew to bring his horse back down to a walk. He looked relieved. Ant was still watching from the fence as we left.

I found Nan sitting in the garden on my walk back from the stables after I'd finished my work for the morning. She was bundled in so many layers to fend off the cool weather that I barely recognized her. At first glance, she looked more like a pile of wash that was waiting to be hung up to dry.

"What're you doing out here?" I asked, coming to stand beside her and the chair she'd dragged out from the kitchen to sit in. Her tired fingers were working steadily, the *click-clicking* of her wooden knitting needles bringing back fond memories of my childhood. She didn't look up from her project when she finally answered me.

"I decided that you were right."

My brows went up in surprise. "About?"

"I've done a poor job lately of keeping up with the things that I enjoy. Ever since the illness, really." She drew in a deep breath and sighed it out, her head tilting slightly. "I came across my old needles, and I thought maybe I would venture to the fabric shop in the village."

"That's great, Nan." A smile spread across my lips as I crouched beside her, inspecting the bundles of yarn in the basket resting by her feet.

"There are so many more options now than there used to be. I was trying to decide between a pale yellow and an even lighter pink, and the strangest thing happened. A draft from the door opening blew so hard across the display table that this color rolled right onto the floor."

It was a calm sage green. I gave the ball closest to me a squeeze, as one does. It was exceptionally soft. When Nan tugged on it to loosen more length to work with, the fibers caught the midday light.

"Does it have some gold in it?" I leaned closer to confirm. The thinnest whisps of shimmery, golden fibers were woven in. My newfound association with the color piqued my interest even further. How curious that this would've been the yarn to find a way to make itself known.

"Beautiful, isn't it? I bought all of it that they had. It'll be perfect for a baby blanket."

I straightened, leaning in to place a kiss to her temple after I located it underneath her bonnet and two shawls.

"Don't stay out too long. Your fingers must be cold," I guessed.

She made a dismissive noise. "Anne's in the kitchen."

Anne was indeed in the kitchen, chopping up vegetables for supper. I pulled a stool out to sit on and bent one arm close to my chest atop the counter, supporting my chin in the other hand.

"Nan's taken the day off. Can you make me something to eat?" I asked, using my sweetest voice.

Her closed-mouth laugh came across as unimpressed, but she grinned anyway. "You really haven't the first idea about making yourself food, have you?"

"It is one of my many flaws, I'm afraid." I reached for a piece of sliced carrot that she'd slid to the side and popped it into my mouth. When I went for another, she swatted my hand away.

"Alright, alright, give me just a moment, you pest. You're starting to make me question why I missed you while you were gone." My mouth fell open in mock hurt, and she rolled her eyes. "Come now, of course I missed you. It's certainly not the same when you're not here."

"Do you mean that?"

Anne paused to look up at me. "How could we not miss you? You're a big part of what holds this family together."

"I guess I've always felt more like everyone's responsibility. Always needing you and Nan to look after me. Feed me. Even Lucy takes her turn tending to me these days."

"That's what people do when they care about you." She went back to cutting, her fingertips tucked neatly away from the sharp edge of the knife as it came down swiftly on another carrot. "Are you alright, by the way? Lucy said you'd been crying yesterday."

"Of course, she did," I sighed under my breath. "I'm fine. I was just annoyed with Thomas. He was being a complete eejit over something he'd regret."

"I've heard talk that he's expressed interest in courting Emma Clare."

"Aye, and he was thinking of *expressing* it tonight at his party."

"Proposing?" she asked wistfully, ever the romantic.

"Propositioning," I corrected, which made her cheeks go slightly more pink than usual. "Though, from the way he tells it, Emma Clare was the one to suggest it."

"My, those sisters sure do have a way of working their charms on the men in this village. I must admit, I'm glad you seem to have escaped their advances." Anne set aside her knife and wiped her hands on her smock before she started her next project. I resisted stealing another piece from the vegetables piled up nearby.

"You've nothing to worry about there."

Anne made a thoughtful face before she lit up again. "And so soon we get to meet your Finna. I'll be delighted to finally see the type of woman who can hold your attention. Though, I do hope you're doing this in the proper way, with speaking to her parents and all."

Apprehension swirled helplessly within me. There were so many ways to tell Anne she was wrong about Finna, spanning from bold lies to the hard truth, but none of them would make me feel better. Not in that moment, at least. I settled on a tight, short grin of acknowledgement and hoped that she would drop the subject. Thankfully, she did.

The supper they planned had been set for the following weekend, which fell only a few days before Breck was to have his ceremony. I'd told him I understood if he would be too busy to come, but he had said he wouldn't miss it for anything. I was already a wreck about it. Knowing he would be there was the only thing keeping me from begging to cancel it altogether. I needed to talk with Finna about the finer details, namely the fact that my whole family thought I was going to ask for her hand any day. I could already imagine her response.

The slide of the plate as Anne pushed it toward me broke my spiraling thoughts. I looked down at the jam covered crustless bread cut into four pieces and thin slices of apple with the peel removed. It was a meal fit for a wee child. I gave her a bland look, and she smirked.

"Sorry, just practicing." She rubbed her belly affectionately and turned back to preparing for supper. I picked up a piece of apple and threw it at her, which made her squeal in surprise, and took my plate up to my room to eat alone.

CHAPTER TWENTY-EIGHT

The evening before the big supper party, I found myself pacing around Finna's sitting room as though I'd been tasked with wearing a hole through her rug. Too many thoughts had piled up in my head, and worst of all was that Breck had been gone for several days, yet to return. I'd already had three cups of tea.

"Love, why don't you sit down and tell me what's bothering you?" Finna's calm, raspy voice of reason came from where she was sitting in her favorite chair by the hearth. She looked cozier than I was used to, wrapped in a thick shawl over her simple white dressing gown. Her hair had somehow been wrangled into two thick braids, which were resting over her shoulders. I'd arrived later in the evening than I'd planned to and woken her up from bed. "You're only working yourself into a worse state with all these circles."

I resigned with a sigh and sat on the sofa, elbows on my knees to support my head in my hands. My fingers tangled into my hair and then loosened as I ran them through.

"Are you sure you want to do this tomorrow?" I asked, staring at my feet.

"Meet your family? Of course. I've already made three desserts to bring along."

I lifted my head. "I mean are you sure you want to be a part of the horrific tangle of lies that is my personal life? I understand if you don't, honestly, I do."

Finna slid off her chair and came to join me on the sofa. She took my hand between her small ones, resting them on her knee. Her top hand patted mine several times before she spoke again.

"As your friend, I will be happy to support you however I can." A weighty pause. "As Breck's adoptive mammy, it's incredibly hard to watch both of you struggling with keeping everything a secret."

My stomach turned at her confession. "I'm sorry."

"I understand the way things are in your world. The way a relationship between the two of you would be seen by others. But there are ways to make it work, if that's what you both wish. I've seen it happen many times."

"How did Fallon and Jo make it work so easily?"

"Sacrifice. On both of their parts. Confiding in Jo's family and friends they knew they could trust, and being willing to lose those they couldn't."

"What if that was my family? Nan or William? Anne and Lucy. How could I possibly give them up? How could I hurt them so, when we've already suffered such loss."

"Peter, look at me." Finna's voice was more stern than it had been before. She met and held my gaze, her double grip on my hand tightening for a moment. "People who truly care for you will still love you no matter what. Your Henry is a perfect example, is he not?"

I thought about Henry's mild reaction when I'd told him about Jamie when we were fourteen. How unashamedly supportive he'd been of me when I told him about Breck. The way he'd practically begged me to not keep my feelings a secret in their company at the estate.

"What about my career? I'm not good at doing anything else. What if Wally refuses to manage me, or nobody allows me to play on their team ever again?"

"Not *everyone* needs to know, love."

"The polo field is where secrets go to die, Finna. That's where everyone gets their gossip during the season. It would be impossible." I sighed again, helplessly. "Can't you mix something up? Some kind of salve or potion to make everyone forget about me so I can just live my life in peace?"

"I'm afraid not," she said, sounding truly sorry about it. "But, wouldn't it be better for your heart to be happy, rather than living with the secrets so you could continue to be a part of the society you've never wanted to fit into anyway?"

I wasn't sure how to respond to that. It was the only life I'd ever known. The grandeur, the parties, the spectacle of it all. I'd never enjoyed any of it. I loved what I did because I loved my horses. I loved Henry. I'd loved Jamie, and my father, and even auld Wally. They were the ones who kept me going when the rest felt like too much.

I slid my hand from between Finna's and got to my feet, taking a few steps toward the fire in the hearth. If there was one thing I'd come to know about myself, it was that change terrified me. Loss was the monster hiding under my bed at night. I'd become so scared of my world being shaken that, somehow, I'd decided being miserable was better than facing uncertainty. Routine was safe. I'd placated my fears with familiarity, because it had been the only way I'd known how to come back from my illness with any sense of the life I'd had before.

The truth was, I'd known for so long that I deserved more than that. Breck deserved more than that. His efforts were the only thing that had pulled me from the monotony of my life. He'd shown me how much fun it could be to forget about responsibility for a while, without the abuse of a few drinks too many. He'd helped me see how exhilarating it was to escape into the woods, or climb a mountain, or go on a ridiculous adventure with nothing but a few bags full of food and a loosely thought-out plan. And somehow, in the end, everything always turned out.

A bit of a laugh, bit of a sob escaped me. When I turned around, Finna was watching me with her own tearful expression. She must've been able to see the shift in my emotions, which I still couldn't fully understand.

I closed the distance between us and got down on both knees in front of her, sock feet crossed under my arse like a child at story time. It was my turn to take one of her hands in both of mine. With another pathetic noise, I pressed my forehead to our bundle of hands and kept it there while I tried to gather my thoughts. *Don't cry, don't cry, don't cry,* I told myself as I looked up at her again.

"I need your help."

"What do you need?" Her sympathetic smile grew, as if she already knew the answer.

"I have to speak with you and Fallon. Before the ceremony."

* * *

Everyone had taken part in getting the house ready for guests. The double doors to the formal dining room, which sat empty for years, were thrown open days beforehand. The crisp, white table linens had been washed, chairs had been wiped clean from dust, and places had been set. I was staring at it all when Anne spoke, startling me.

"Excited?" she asked, ignoring the fact that she'd made me jump as she passed by with a few freshly washed and dried stemmed glasses in her hands. She set them around the plates and cutlery in a tasteful way. I coughed a little and nodded shortly.

"Em, of course." It wasn't my best acting. Anne grinned up at me anyway.

"You look great," she complimented as she reached up to smooth a hand over the folded lapel of my nicest waistcoat. I'd argued my way out of wearing a dinner jacket with it, but I'd lost against the matching neckcloth. If I had known this was an affair I'd have to dress up for, I might've fought harder against it. Then again, the way the rest of my family had been fussing over the event during the days leading up to it had brought a certain joy to the house. I'd even caught Nan smiling a handful of times.

"You, as well," I offered with a small grin. Anne had done up her hair, exchanging the bundle of yellow curls she normally wore at the nape of her neck for a higher, statelier bun with some smaller pieces framing her face. She'd painted her lips and cheeks, adding to her natural flush. I was starting to realize that this party was as much for my family as it was for our guests.

Lucy flitted in wearing her prettiest dress. A crown of two braids across the top of her head were decorated with ribbons of the same pinkish color. The gauzy material of her skirts added to the lightness of her movements, and for a moment, I was convinced my sister had been granted her wish of becoming one of the fairies she so deeply loved. But then the Walshe in her came shining through as she tripped and fell, catching herself with her outstretched hands.

"Lucy, that is *not* how a young lady behaves at a party," came Nan's admonishment as she entered the room. My mouth fell open as I took in the sparkling necklace at her throat, complimented by matching earrings. She hadn't worn them since William and Anne were married in the back garden.

"Nan," I gasped. She shot me a warning look that I ignored. "You're a vision of beauty."

"Enough of that," she waved off. "Get yourselves to the sitting room so we can properly greet our guests when they arrive. It should be any minute now."

We did as she instructed. William was away on business, so it would be just the six of us. Part of me was relieved by his absence, considering the only person I knew who hated social gatherings more than I did was him. He likely would've sat silently through the meal and excused himself at the first opportunity. As my insides churned with anticipation, I silently wished I could do the same.

A faint knocking caught our attention all at once. I sprung from the arm of the chair I'd been perched on and made for the entryway. A deep, calming breath only made me cough as I opened the door. Finna's bright smile helped sooth my nerves, but what my attention landed on next made them vanish completely, if only for a moment.

"Please, come in," I managed, fighting my cheek-achingly large grin as I stepped aside to let Finna and Breck in out of the cold. Both of their arms were full of various items. I saw my family crowd around in my peripheral. "Finna, this is my Nan, my youngest sister Lucy, and my brother's wife, Anne." They all made a polite nod and dip of a greeting as I introduced them. "William is unable to join us this evening, I'm afraid."

"So wonderful to finally meet you all," Finna gushed. "I hope it's alright that I've brought some desserts for everyone to enjoy. Peter has such a sweet tooth, I figured it must run in the family!"

We all gave a laugh that was appropriate for company before the four most important women in my life swarmed neatly together toward the kitchen, leaving Breck and I standing alone in the faint glow of the fire coming from the sitting room. There were a hundred things I wanted to say to him, but I settled on something safe enough for the rest of the party to hear, just in case.

"Is this what I think it is?" I asked, reaching for the unmarked green bottle in his right hand.

"Finna thought it was the perfect time to break out the good wine." His soft voice washed over me like the relief of climbing into bed at the end of a long day.

"Too bad we'll have to share this time," I told him with a smirk, drawing up memories of the last time we'd shared a bottle between just the two of us. He chuckled and nodded, looking at the bouquet of flowers in his other hand.

"These are from her garden, so technically I think they'd be fine without water for several days. But is there a place I can put them?"

"Aye, come on."

I led Breck through the kitchen, watching as his eyes wandered around, taking in the intricacies of the place I'd grown up. It was strangely intimate to have him in my house for the first time. Anne took the flowers graciously and went in search of a vase, instructing us to go and sit down in the places at the table we'd been designated. Breck's seat was on one side of me. Finna's was on the other.

The flowers found a home near the head of the table, a spot where they could be appreciated but not block anyone's view. Next came enough food to rival the spreads we'd enjoyed at the estate with Henry and Sarah. I was shocked that they'd had enough time to prepare it all in one day.

"Peter told us about your... special diet," Nan said, directing her attention to Breck, clearly unaware of how condescending she sounded. "I hope you're able to find enough dishes that are suitable."

"I'm certain it won't be a problem, thank you," he replied easily.

"She thought I was joking when I told her," I explained with my own lofty retort.

"I've just never met a man who isn't desperate for meat and potatoes at the end of the day." With everyone seated, we began the delicate dance of serving ourselves. "Although Peter often fights eating properly, as well. I believe he would live on bread and dessert alone, if given the chance."

Finna giggled at this as she passed me the basket with the sliced bread in it. "That is probably the truth," she agreed. She looked as lovely as the rest of them in her evening dress. Unlike Breck, she hadn't been forced to abandon most of her jewelry, either. Her bracelets tinkled together at her wrists as she accepted the bowl Lucy was passing to her across the table.

To put it simply, my sister was captivated by our guests. She split her attention evenly between them, watching their every move, being more still and silent than I'd ever seen her, aside from the times she had her nose in a book. Just as I was starting to worry that she knew more than we realized, Anne picked the conversation back up.

"So tell us, Finna. Is Peter being a proper gentleman for you? He's never been one to divulge the details of his personal life, even with us." The sparkle in her eye as she spoke forced me to take a steadying breath. I'd known this was coming, but I still wasn't ready for it.

"Oh, he's been a lovely friend to me, yes. I so enjoy the time we spend together."

Anne and Nan exchanged a look that made me want to crawl under the table. Finna and I had talked at length about the questions they likely would ask and how we were going to respond to them. We would keep our answers vague and, whenever possible, try to redirect the conversation.

"Have you any sisters to escort you, dear?" This was Nan's contribution.

Finna laughed again, sweet and unassuming. "Actually, I'm quite old enough to escort myself. But Breck is the closest thing I've got to family. He's often the one to look after me, when the situation requires it."

The shift across the table was palpable. Another tactic we'd briefly discussed was indicating that Finna was much too old for me. She'd clearly decided to run full speed with that one. To my relief, Nan decided to hold her tongue on the disagreeable statement I could tell she was bursting to voice. Anne recovered much faster, though I could see her trying to deduce Finna's age in her head.

"Well. If your wish is for a family, then you mustn't delay your intentions much longer."

"Ah, pardon my manners," Finna exclaimed, waving her hands in a forget-everything-else-I've-just-said type of way.

"I failed to offer my congratulations on your own happy news!"

Any talk of the baby was guaranteed to distract them, and it worked flawlessly. I sighed slowly and tried to relax against the back of my chair, releasing the tension I'd been holding in my shoulders and jaw. When I felt a chill on my ankle, my relief doubled. I risked a glance at Breck.

Thank you, I thought for him. He allowed a faint grin to cross his features but remained focused on the conversation and the spoonful of cooked vegetables he was bringing to his mouth. His magic traveled slowly upward, and my relief transformed into something else as I realized the direction it was headed. Before I could react, I was treated to an icy embrace between my legs.

By some miracle, I was able to hide any indication of what was happening under the table, aside from the blush I knew was staining my cheeks. I shot another look in his direction, his smirk hidden behind the glass he'd raised to his lips as he sipped casually at his wine.

Dirty bastard, I scolded. This was ultimately what made him look at me, and when he did, I could barely contain myself. He'd styled his hair in the same way he'd done for Henry's engagement party, showing off the freckles on his forehead and the human curve of the tips of his undecorated ears. My eyes fell to his choice of clothes for the evening. Formal enough for a dinner, but not quite nice enough for a high society event. It was almost as if we'd coordinated. Luckily for him, though, he hadn't been forced to wear a silly, poofy necktie.

"This is interesting," he said, reaching up to touch said necktie, rubbing the silk of it between his thumb and finger.

"Nan likes when I wear it," I grumbled, keeping my voice low. "Don't you dare say it suits me," I added in warning.

"I won't say it," he promised. As I tried to decide if he meant that he wouldn't say it because I told him not to, or because he couldn't lie to me, I felt his fingertip brush ever so gently against the skin at the top of my starched collar before his hand returned to his lap. That simple touch was enough to send my whole body into hyperfocus.

I snapped my attention back to the rest of the party. Reaching for my wine glass, I looked up to find Anne watching me. Her eyebrows arched slightly, gaze shifting very obviously to Breck and then back to me, before she reached for her own drink. *Feck.*

"Breck's birthday is next week," I blurted, saying the first thing I could think of to rejoin the conversation. Finna paused what she'd been saying to allow for the interruption.

"We shall have another party," Lucy cheered. We all laughed politely again.

"I'm sure he has his own plans already, Lucy." Anne set her glass down and resumed her role of playing co-host. "Now, help me clear the table so we can have our dessert."

They made quick work of it, leaving little time for us to linger uncomfortably in the silence that happened when nobody wanted to say anything at the risk of leaving the absent members of the party out of the conversation. Finna had joined them to help bring out the sweets, carefully unwrapping them as they came back with clean plates and forks.

"Peter is very fond of my spiced apple cake, so I've brought some of that along, as well as some berry tarts." The last bundle of parchment was left untouched. "I'll allow Breck to reveal that one."

He offered a modest look to the rest of us when we turned our attention on him. With the twine and parchment undone, he picked it up carefully and held it out across the table.

"I made this for Anne, but it's for everyone to enjoy, of course."

With a look of surprise, she took his offering and peered inside. Her gasp was enough to make us all worry, but then she smiled and reached into the depths of the mystery bundle with her fingers.

"Chocolate caramels," she cooed. Manners fully abandoned, she put the entire piece in her mouth and closed her eyes, a look of pure bliss overcoming her.

"I want one!" Lucy lost her patience before the rest of us. Anne took another before she passed them down the table, savoring this one a little more. Silence spread again as we all chewed. I didn't know if it was because of my feelings toward who made them, but I thought they were even better than the ones William had brought her as a gift.

"They're wonderful, Breck. Thank you." She gave a most genuine smile.

"I'm glad you like them."

CHAPTER TWENTY-NINE

Supper was such a success that they begged Finna to stay longer for a chat in the sitting room, which meant that Breck and I were expected to leave them alone. We were much too old to go up to my bedroom, so the logical solution was for us to retire to the study. I went in first, candle in hand so I could light the others that were scattered helpfully around the room. By the time Breck shut the door behind us with a sturdy click, I'd completed my task, setting the space aglow.

I remained in one spot as Breck began to wander, looking high and low as he inspected the room I was so familiar with. He ignored William's desk and the mess of business papers on it entirely. His focus was on the books. With a slight tilt of his head, he began reading the spines, touching some of them with gentle fingertips as he went.

"We probably haven't got any books with special writing in them," I began, keeping my voice low to avoid being over-heard, even though I knew this was the safest place for us to talk in the whole house.

"No, afraid not," he agreed. "But there is a lot of history. It's not entirely untouched by magic."

"The river?" I guessed. I set down the candle I was holding and came around the desk to join him. He'd crouched to inspect the books on a lower shelf, pulling one out to flip through the pages.

"I suspect that the Walshes have always had open minds about my world." He replaced the book and stood up, moving on to another shelf. "It's hard to explain. There's just something I can feel when I'm somewhere in the human world that welcomes me."

"Lucy has probably brought enough positive energy toward fairies and magic into this place to last for several more generations. You must've noticed the way she was staring at you all night."

Breck turned to me then, smirk firmly in place. "You almost sound jealous."

I let out a little squeak of protest. "I am not *jealous* of my little sister's obvious affections for you. That is, unless you heard her thinking something I should know about?"

He let out a thoughtful hum and paused his searching when he came upon our family photograph. He picked up the frame and studied it like it was the most important thing he'd ever seen. My throat got a little tight, so I attempted to clear it before I spoke again.

"That's the only one we have of the whole family," I told him.

"You all look very much alike," he noted, holding it closer to his face.

"Dad always said there was no denying us." I laughed softly and stepped closer to look at the photo with him, our shoulders touching. "Though I'm not sure how I ended up being as tall as I am. Mammy and Dad were both perfectly average in that."

"Perhaps it's because you were the last son. Every last drop had to be used up before the sisters arrived."

I snorted. "The biggest disappointment in that regard, no doubt."

"How do you mean?" he asked, carefully setting the frame down where he'd found it.

"A son is expected to be so many things. Someone who follows in his father's footsteps and grows up to be a good provider for his wife and children. Like William."

"There are plenty of men who never marry or have children." Breck's attention was fully on me now. I hadn't meant for this conversation to turn so serious.

"And you can find them all lingering around the pub every night, dirty and miserable from work, knowing that they'll go to bed alone and wake up the next day to do it all over again."

Breck searched my face, his eyes shifting back and forth between mine several times.

"That's an exceptionally narrow view of things," he said quietly.

My face heated with embarrassment. "I know it is. But... for someone like me, it could easily be a reality. You have to know that's the truth."

"The truth is that lonely men at the pub are the way they are because they've lost their loved ones. They've been injured, or fallen ill, or cannot do the work that will provide a comfortable life. They are victims of circumstance, as anyone could be." Breck hooked a finger under my chin, making me look at him after I'd hung my head. "You cannot be a disappointment to the people who truly care about you."

"And if I'm unable to live up to someone's expectations?"

"Then I would guess that's not someone who brings happiness to your life."

Why did he make it sound so simple? Finna had told me basically the same thing.

"You're right," I managed. "I'm sorry I'm so complicated."

"You are everything," Breck returned just as quietly. He used his finger under my chin to pull me forward, closing the gap between us for a kiss. It was soft and sweet, comforting in exactly the way I needed it to be.

"*I missed you,*" I whispered as I kissed him again. I longed to sneak him upstairs and show him just how much I'd missed him, but the only path would take us past the sitting room. It was likely that they'd already sent Lucy to bed, as well, and the thought of being with Breck while my baby sister slept just across the hall was enough to sour my stomach. But then, something not entirely different went on in the privacy of Anne and William's bedroom below—

Breck laughed and nuzzled his face against mine. "You never stop thinking, do you?"

"Sorry," I pouted, even though he couldn't see it. I brought my arms up to wrap around him, settling for a long hug. He returned the favor, holding me close, his breath tickling the skin below my ear on each exhale. We remained like this long enough for my thoughts to have come alive again.

"Tell me something?" I asked, pressing my lips to his neck before I pulled away so I could look at him. He nodded, waiting for me to continue. "Why have you given my whole family presents?"

"Whatever do you mean?" He sounded uncertain, but the sheepish grin on his face told the story.

"Lucy's new, apparently very rare and special book. The

perfect yarn for Nan in the fabric shop. And now you've somehow mastered the art of making chocolate caramels for Anne?"

"Well, I did not actually give her the yarn. It just happened to fall in her path."

"By way of a magical wind?" I asked flatly.

"Exactly. I thought she would've found it too forward if I gave it to her directly. She's quite a proud woman. I would hate to offend her somehow."

I allowed a quiet laugh and lowered my voice. "So the fact that I've had my way with you more times than I can remember isn't the part you're worried will upset her delicate sensibilities?"

Breck giggled and bunched his eyebrows together. "I wasn't planning on us telling her that part, but if you feel that we need to, I'll be supportive."

* * *

We remained in the study for the socially appropriate length of time before Breck helped me put out the candles. When we rounded the corner to the sitting room, Anne let out a sad sigh.

"Must the evening be over already? It's been so lovely."

"Not to worry. I'd be happy to come 'round again, any time." Finna helped Anne to her feet, and they embraced more like sisters than new acquaintances. I'd always known they would get along.

"Oh, please! It's been hopelessly dull being stuck in the house waiting for the baby to arrive. My other friends all have children of their own, so the time they can spend visiting is very limited."

Finna and Breck gave their thanks again for the meal and good company, followed by another round of cheek kisses and clasped hands, before I finally shut the door behind them. I braced myself for what I knew would be next.

"Peter, you *must* marry her." Anne was besotted. "She's so perfect for you. She can cook, and care for a house, and she's not even put off by your obsession with sweets."

"Why would that be off-putting?" I argued weakly, frowning.

"Nan, tell him he has to propose. We'll go in the morning to pick out a ring."

"Anne," I tried, but she kept going.

"We can have the wedding here in the garden, same as we did for William and me. It doesn't have to be anything big. We all know how you dislike grand events. Of course, you'll have Henry as your best man, and since she doesn't have any sisters, perhaps I could stand with her as matron of—"

"Anne!" My raised voice finally quieted her. She seemed to realize then how she'd been acting, and it nearly brought her to tears. We were still getting used to the swinging emotions of her delicate condition.

"My apologies. I got carried away." She rested a hand on her chest, as though her heart must've been racing to keep up with her excitement. My own was beating heavily at the thought of trying to continue with this sham we'd created. It was getting wildly out of hand faster than I'd imagined.

Nan had already left us for the kitchen, probably to finish tidying up for the evening. The two of us stood in silence for a moment. I could've said something. In the end, I shook my head dismissively.

"It's alright," I told her. "I'm going to bed."

I took the steps two at a time and was out of breath when

I reached my room. I shed my nice clothes, starting most aggressively with the neckcloth that had been choking me all evening. I bundled it up in my hands and threw it against the wall. It slid down into a delicate heap that I was angry at, somehow. After I'd come out of my waistcoat and trousers, I was halfway done with removing my shirt when I looked at the little pile of silk again.

When I picked it up, the fabric slipped easily through my fingers. I stared at it as I made my way to the bed. I kept staring after I'd climbed in under the bedclothes and curled up onto my side. I rubbed the fabric between my fingers and thumb. The nicest thing I could say about it was that Breck had touched it and said it was interesting.

I realized that my anger stemmed from what it represented. Even though it was just a strip of cloth, it was part of the society I did not fit into. It was yet another example of why I would never belong in the world of wealth and fine things. Henry often complained that he hated dressing up, but he still did it every chance he got. He thrived in social gatherings. He lived for the next opportunity to show off. It was what made him happy.

I rolled onto my back and stared at the ceiling. What made me happy?

Breck. My horses. Being in nature. Sweets. My friends. My family.

My grip tightened on the silk where I'd been mindlessly running it through my fingers.

I had all the things that made me happy. I didn't need to be wealthy. I didn't need to dress up or impress people. I didn't need to surround myself with things that, in the end, were kept mostly to make a statement to others about who I was. The people who mattered already knew. And they loved me. Not for who I thought I should be, but for who I had already become.

* * *

After standing in the dark hallway for entirely too long, I forced myself to knock quietly on Anne's door before I could lose my nerve completely. There was a slight shuffling noise from the other side, and then the strike of a match.

"Come in," she called out sleepily.

I pushed the door open and stepped inside, closing it back with a sense of finality that had my fingers quivering. Anne was sitting up in the bed, her blankets pulled high to cover her nightgown.

"Is everything alright?" she asked, the tone of her voice indicating that she knew it wasn't. I made my way to the edge of the bed and sat down as gently as I could by her knees. My hands immediately started tracking nervously up and down my thighs. She reached out to grab one of them and I balled my fists. I was starting to wish I'd been pickier at dinner, because I felt like I could be sick at any moment.

"Tell me what's wrong." Anne used her free hand to tuck her blanket underneath both arms so it wouldn't fall before she reached to turn me more toward her. I gave in and turned. Her look of concern grew, likely because she could see how wet my eyes were then.

"I cannot marry Finna," I said feebly.

"If this is because I pushed you too hard earlier, I am unbelievably sorry."

I shook my head. "It's not that."

"What is it, then?" Her confusion only made this harder. How had I possibly kept my secret so well from her that she was completely oblivious to why I could not do as they hoped I would? My frustration only created a new wave of tears, which escaped down my cheeks without my permission. I felt it was only right to make a pitiful noise in the back of my throat to go with them.

"I cannot marry her, because I am in love with Breck." I closed my eyes and turned my head away, unable to face whatever her reaction would be. My voice, on the other hand, had apparently found all the confidence it needed. "He is the one I've been seeing in secret. He is the one I have found happiness with. And I intend to keep it that way, for as along as he will have me."

The silence that followed was enough to make me wonder if I'd died right then and there. My mind started to spin with all sorts of excuses and ways to back out of my confession. Maybe the wine had been off at supper, and I didn't know what I was saying. I was having a walking dream and talking nonsense in my sleep. I'd been put under a magic spell to tell lies.

"Why didn't you say anything before?"

I turned back to her in shock. She did not look murderous, or repulsed, or even angry. If anything, she looked a little hurt.

"*What?*"

"You let me make a fool of myself this evening over the wrong person. I saw the way you looked at each other at the table. It certainly was not the look of friendship. Nor was it the first time I've seen such an exchange between the both of you."

My whole body went scarlet. I opened my mouth to say something, but no words came. Anne huffed a bit of an impatient sigh and gave me a decided look.

"I read Jamie's letter. I did not realize I was going to find something so personal when I opened it. When he gave it to me, he was acting so very odd, and my curiosity got the better of me."

I was full on shaking now. "You knew?"

"Oh, love." She reached for me again, but I couldn't feel her hand on my arm. "Nobody cries the way you did that day unless their heart has been broken."

There were tears in her eyes now, too, and all at once we both fell apart. I collapsed into her embrace, burying my face into her shoulder. She held me so tightly that it almost hurt before she started rubbing my back in the most comforting way. I let myself cry the same way I had when she'd told me Jamie had died. I let myself mourn the years I'd lost from keeping my secrets so fiercely protected.

My voice was rough and stuffy sounding when I sat up to dry my eyes with my sleeve.

"If you knew all along, why didn't you ever ask me about it?"

Anne wiped her own eyes and sniffled. "It's not appropriate for a woman to ask a man those kinds of questions, of course."

"Yet you've still been working with Nan to marry me off to whichever lass will have me for the last three years? That hardly seems appropriate, either."

"There are men who enjoy... both. I suppose it was wrong of me to assume that you are one of them?"

I covered my face with my hands. She was right. Her asking questions like that felt very inappropriate and wholly embarrassing. "I do not enjoy both," I ground out from behind my palms.

"Oh, Peter, will you ever forgive me? If I had known then

surely I never would've... it's just that... it seems that sometimes, when that is the preference, men do still like to marry
and have a family. But then they... well, they enjoy the
other... on their own time."

"Wherever did you learn that?" I asked, incredulous.

"I read," she answered plainly. The neat stack of books on
her bedside table took on a bold new presence in the room.
What kinds of stories truly existed on those pages she loved
so dearly? And why had I never bothered to learn more
about them?

I dropped my hands to my lap. "Does Nan know?"

"She doesn't. I'm not sure she would even understand.
You heard her response to someone being a vegetarian." We
both laughed weakly at that.

"You don't hate me?" I asked finally, teetering on the edge
of my emotions.

"I could never hate you. You're the little brother I never
had and often wished for."

"I'm sure you liked Nicholas better than me," I moped.

"Nicholas was never as nice to me as you always have
been. You're more than just a brother by marriage to me.
You're a very dear friend. And I'm glad you felt you were
ready to tell me all of this."

"Can we please stop forcing me into marriage, then?"

"I'll never mention it again." She paused, tilting her head
with a bit of a smile. "But now that I know who you *really*
fancy..."

I groaned. "Breck has enough to worry about as it is right
now. The last thing he needs is for you to start being all
strange about it."

"Who said I'm going to be strange about it? And why, is
something going on?"

I stuck my tongue between my teeth. Was now the right time to tell her the rest of the story? I drew in a deep breath and let it out slowly, coughing only once.

"Em, well, remember when we had that whole conversation about fairies?"

CHAPTER THIRTY

Three days before Breck's ceremony was set to take place, I was sitting in Finna's favorite chair with a full cup of tea in my hands that had long since gone cold. I'd ridden directly there from my lesson with Mathew, which meant I was still in my waistcoat and riding breeches. Just as I remembered Fallon's comment about me smelling of horse sweat all the time, the door opened, and I jumped so hard that I nearly dropped my tea.

I set the cup down before I could make good on that mistake and got to my feet. I focused my fidgety energy into straightening my clothes and running a hand through my hair. It was getting too long for me to do anything useful with it. I was due for another cut.

Fallon dipped her head at Finna, who had been keeping busy in the kitchen until then, and then she turned her focus to me. I watched as she came around to sit on the sofa, tucking into the corner that was the farthest away from where I was standing. I was starting to rethink the entire thing when she cleared her throat.

"Peter."

"Fallon," I returned hurriedly. "Thank you for agreeing to meet with me."

"I was not given a choice in the matter." She gave Finna a pointed look as she brought a fresh cup of tea, which Fallon accepted and then immediately set down. Stars above, I was not ready for this. I took a few steps to place myself directly in front of them, while leaving enough room that if one or both decided to throw something, I would have a slim chance of ducking to safety.

Finna grinned up at me from where she'd settled next to Fallon on the sofa. "The lad has something he needs us to hear. Aren't you grateful that he included us both? It must be something terribly important."

Fallon was still watching me with her usual stoic expression. I took it as a good sign that her arms were uncrossed for once, at least. "It's a very busy time for me to be sitting for a chat, so I hope it is terribly important."

I'd been going over what I wanted to say in my head every night for a week. Longer than that, to be perfectly honest, but now that the time had arrived, I'd gone so blank that I might as well have pulled it out of my arse anyway. I tugged at the hem of my waistcoat one more time for good measure, and then I began.

"Breck is the most important thing in my life. That hasn't always been the case. Even until recently, I was focused more on things like my polo career, my social status, and what other people thought of me. Ever since we met, he's been committed to helping me learn how to let go of those things. And I know that it's a part of his responsibility and his training, but also, it's more than that.

"He's shown me that it's alright to take risks and do

things for other people, even if I'm afraid to do them at first. He's given me the confidence to see myself in a life that I live just for me, not for others who think they know what's best for me. He's allowed me the chance to learn who I really am. What makes me happy. What will continue to make me happy. And at the top of that list is him.

"He's the most generous, thoughtful, and supportive man I've ever known. That's saying a lot, because my father embodied those things, as well. Unfortunately, I cannot look up to him anymore. But now I have Breck. And I intend to keep him in my life for a very long time."

I flailed a little to indicate that I needed them to excuse me for a moment. I rushed over to my leather satchel that I'd left by the door. As I opened the flap, I returned to my place in the middle of the room, pulling out the three wooden spools I'd purchased at the fabric shop. Each held a length of shimmery ribbon in a different shade of purple. I dropped my bag as I tried to manage all three at once, and then nearly tripped as I stepped over it to present the ribbons to Finna. She gasped as though they were the nicest thing she'd ever been given, which I knew couldn't have been true, but I appreciated it all the same.

With that part done, I crouched next to my bag to fish around for the rest of what I'd brought. I scooped up the small linen sachets in both hands. After giving myself a second to close my eyes and breathe, I stood up and turned around, offering them to Fallon. She looked at them, then at me, and then at my hands again as she reached up to take them from me.

"You always say how much you don't like when things smell bad," I explained. "I asked Finna what types of smells you do like, and she said you like lavender, so. You can put them inside shoes, for example, or underneath your pillow."

Fallon raised one of them delicately to her nose. The shop owner had said the buds would stay fragrant for quite a while, and I hoped that would be even more true with her extraordinary sense of smell. Finna reached over and picked up one of the pouches for herself, taking a deep whiff after she squeezed it a few times.

"That's divine. Excellent specimen."

I hadn't taken my eyes off Fallon. She brought the pouch back down to her lap, shuffling it around in her fingers as she seemed to be inspecting it for flaws. Then she looked up, blinked once, and spoke.

"Is this your way of asking if I'll accept you and Breckabhainn being joined before Eabha?"

"Em..." I started, but I was unable to finish. I nodded instead.

"This was unnecessary. My answer would have been the same regardless, as Eabha has already made her decision." She stood off the sofa abruptly, but to my relief, she took the sachets with her. The door opened, allowing a gust of almost-winter air inside, and I was certain she was about to slam it shut on my hopes and dreams. But then she turned, her dark braid falling over her shoulder and hanging down the center of her back. "He is the only one you need to impress with your commitment gift. Make it something he will never forget. He deserves nothing less." And then she was gone. I remained staring at the door until I became vaguely aware of Finna's arms around my middle.

"Did she...?" I asked. I could feel my heartbeat in my throat.

"She most definitely did!" Finna's voice squeaked on the

last word as she pressed her cheek against my chest. My lungs did not appreciate all the squeezing. I coughed several times and patted Finna's shoulder politely until she let go. We shared a smile, hers bright and mine unsteady, before I felt an overwhelming wave of dizziness. Finna must've recognized the shift in me and safely guided me down.

I spent half an hour with my feet dangling over the arm of the sofa, a cold rag over my eyes, and an herby salve carefully dabbed onto my chest and neck.

"Finna," I said finally. "What can I possibly give him that will be good enough to show him how I feel?" I pulled the rag off my face so I could see her. "I'm terrible at giving gifts as it is."

"Nonsense! I love my ribbons. They're sparkly, and beautiful, and you picked my favorite color."

I groaned and draped the damp rag back over my face. "I thought *this* was going to be the hard part." I waved my arm around to indicate the conversation we'd had there in the room.

"Oh, hardly. We both already knew this was coming."

The rag landed on the floor. "You did?"

"Of course. You heard Fallon. She already had her answer."

I dragged my legs over the armrest and sat up, supporting myself with both hands on the cushions to either side of me. I felt exhausted. A proper sleeping and eating pattern had been out of the question for the days leading up to this meeting. It seemed like it wasn't going to improve much now either, even though I'd gotten the response I was hoping for.

"What did Carrick's mate give him? I need some ideas."

"I believe it was a very expensive bottle of whiskey and a new grooming kit. He's quite easy to please, as it turns out.

And so is Breck. I think you're worrying more than you need to."

"I just want him to understand how important he is to me."

"He will. But let's think, shall we? You want it to be something meaningful. Something that will convey your feelings in a big way." Her bracelets clinked together as her hand came up, fingertips tapping against her lips. "Oh! I have something that might help." She disappeared into her bedroom and returned with an object in her hand. She dropped it into my waiting, upturned palm. It was a stone so clear I could see through most of it; cool to the touch and shiny enough to catch the light.

"What is this?" I asked, holding it up.

"Quartz. It's a crystal. Keep it close to you and sleep with it above your pillow tonight."

"What does it do?"

Finna smiled. "We'll find out, won't we?"

* * *

I laid in bed that night wishing for sleep. A gentle rain was falling, which meant I couldn't see anything as I stared out the window. My hand slipped under my pillow, and I pulled out the crystal Finna had given me. I'd tried to sleep with it above my head like she'd instructed, but it kept sliding down into my hair, so I'd settled for what I hoped was the next best thing. I turned it around in my fingertips, focusing on the difference between the parts that were rough and smooth.

"*What do you want, Breck?*" I whispered into the darkness of my room. I wrapped my fingers around the stone and put my fist against my forehead on the pillow. My eyes slid closed, finally heavy enough to let me get some rest.

I dreamed in swirls of color. I heard the bells and chimes of little fairies. The sun was warm on my bare shoulders. Blades of grass swayed lazily in the breeze, tickling my legs and feet.

"Peter," he said, thick and dreamy. And there he was beneath me, freckles dazzling like gems, eyes soft, alluring smirk curving the corner of his lips. He shifted his head to the side, hand coming up to steady the woven spikes of wheat and red flowers nestled into his hair. It was the crown he'd worn the night of the harvest cele-bration. The night I'd fallen in love with him.

"You are the prince from the fairy tales," I told him. As though he didn't already know.

"I am yours, mo ghrá. From now on until forever."

"So happily ever after really does exist?"

His smile crinkled the corners of his eyes. "If that is what you wish."

"More than anything," I said.

"Then that is what you shall have."

My eyes opened on a gasp, which sent me into a coughing fit. I sat up and stared down at where my feet were under the mussed blankets as I tried to calm my lungs. I squeezed the crystal I still had a grip on. "Thank you, Finna."

CHAPTER THIRTY-ONE

I was more than an hour into listening to Thomas boast about what fun his party had been, *again*, when a collection of hoofbeats came from the dirt road outside the stables. My glance in Thomas' direction to exchange a look went unmet. I set down the stiff brush I'd been using on my mare and wiped my hands on my breeches before I went to investigate.

A mix of joy and relief spread from the center of my chest.

"Boyo!" Henry crowed from the back of his horse as he woahed his team in front of me. I grinned and reached to take ahold of his horse's reins as he slid expertly from his saddle.

"Well, isn't this a nice surprise," I said, running a hand down the mare's face. Henry made some obscene noises as he twisted his back and stretched out his legs.

"Aren't I always?" he asked, flashing that crooked grin of his with a wink.

I made a show of peeking around at the horses. "Did you lose Sarah along the way?"

"As it turns out, a lady in a delicate condition much prefers to ride in a carriage, rather'n on the back of a horse." There was a flash of the young lad I once knew behind his eyes before he gave me a proud look.

I chuckled and shook my head. "You've really done it now, haven't you?"

He laughed and clapped me on the back, taking his horse from me and leading the team toward the open double doors. I turned my own horse out so I could help him with the task of untacking and grooming his after they'd all had their fill of some fresh water. Thomas had started in on him immediately with all the news and gossip he could think of.

"And in case you haven't already heard, Ant Byrne is boarding with us now, and he'll be joining our team next season. I hope you're both ready to be even more successful and admired."

"Why is Ant Byrne going to have anything to do with us bein' either of those?" Henry asked, as unimpressed with Thomas as always.

"Because he's a legend, of course." Thomas seemed shocked that he would ask such a thing.

"He's also a feckin' tool."

Thomas gaped at him and quickly wrapped up what he was doing, leaving us in blissful silence for a while after he left. Word spread of Henry's return fast enough. Wally came 'round to say hello, as did many of the stable hands. After his horses were tended to and securely put out to the pasture, we stood at the fence and watched them.

"So," he began in a leading way, keeping his attention on the horses.

"Things are grand," I told him, not being entirely facetious.

"I'm glad to hear it. Haven't stopped thinkin' about it all since you left us."

I turned to look at him then, brows furrowing slightly. "Why's that?"

"What, I'm not allowed to worry about me best friend?" He said this with a mock defensiveness that made me laugh.

I let the moment settle before I spoke again, my face warming instantly as I did.

"I'm going to ask him to marry me. Or well, the equivalent of getting married in the fairy world."

"*Ahh*, I knew you'd come around. Fantastic news. I'll prepare a speech."

"It doesn't exactly work that way, but I do appreciate it."

"I'll throw the stag party then, at least." He made a face and then continued with a more measured tone. "Seein' as how you're both lads and all, will it be a joint affair, or...?"

"I... don't know," I admitted.

"No bother. I'll host, and you can decide. Has he any friends to invite?"

This was getting complicated. The thought of having Carrick and Murray over to Henry's house for a night of drinking seemed like a terrible idea. Not that they would even accept the invitation in the first place. Would Breck want to ask them anyway? Did he have other friends I'd never met that he would like to invite instead?

"Would you be terribly upset if it was just the two of us? For auld times' sake?"

Henry smiled at that. "Whatever you want, Pete. I would like to speak with the lad at some point before it's all official. Remind him that just because he's taking claim, that doesn't mean he gets to steal you away from us to some faraway, magical place."

His voice had gone quiet on the last bit. I stared down at his profile again.

"He's not stealing me away from anything. Besides, shall I remind you that you're the one who just disappeared with your new bride to a feckin' *castle* for long enough to grow a proper beard?" I reached up and flicked at his chin and the thick layer of fiery orange hair he was sporting there. He swiped at my hand in vain, too slow to make contact, so the next best thing was to shove me and then grab my cap off my head, flinging it over the fence into the pasture.

"And aren't you glad to have me back?" He gave me a smug smirk. I sighed and ruffled my fingers in my newly exposed hair, rolling my eyes dramatically because I knew he'd find it funny.

"Immeasurably," I told him as I stepped up and swung my legs over the fence, landing on both feet on the other side.

"Thought so," he added, climbing up onto the bottom slat to watch me. I picked up my cap and thwapped it back and forth against my thigh a few times before I put it back on. Henry digressed smoothly back to where we'd started. "Have you already bought him a ring, then?"

"I won't be giving him a ring," I explained as I made my way back over the fence.

"That's an arse move of you," he said, coming to Breck's defense.

"Rings are not the tradition. They call them commitment gifts. And I've had a shit time trying to figure out what to give him. It's supposed to be something incredibly meaningful, and you know this is not an area of strength for me." Henry hopped down from the fence and matched strides with me as I walked us slowly in the direction of the river.

"Aye, you really are terrible at it."

I gave a short laugh. "Thanks."

"You haven't thought of anything at all?" he pressed.

"Well," I began cautiously, feeling shy over my idea as it had come to me in the form of that very intimate dream. "I have one thought. But it's very hard to explain it to you without divulging a bit more than I'd like to."

"It's something for the bedroom," he guessed, voice slightly suggestive. I groaned.

"*No*. It's not. It's just... something from a night we shared together that I think would mean a lot to him, if I can pull off what I'm picturing in my mind. And then I'll have to properly explain myself with it. I don't know, Henry, I'm bound to mess it up somehow."

"If he hasn't been put off by how often you muddle things up by now, I doubt he's going to change his mind," he offered helpfully. I knocked my fist against his arm.

"You're the worst," I complained, making him laugh.

"Sorry, but Thomas will forever hold that record." He didn't know how right he was. I stared down at my feet as we walked, weighing the risks of telling him what had happened between us. Then I remembered my promise to myself about not keeping any more secrets from him.

"Speaking of," I started tentatively. "Thomas and I had an interaction that proved very concerning the other day. He was oversharing about his birthday plans, and sort of bragged to me that he was planning to take things too far with Emma Clare." Henry's head whipped up to look at me. "I'm mostly sure that I was able to put a stop to it. But I needed to tell you. I'm sorry."

"That feckin' donkey. I'll kill him," Henry threatened.

"I just don't want her reputation as a young lady ruined by the likes of Thomas Dougal. They're two of the most obnoxious people I've ever known, but she doesn't deserve to have her life ruined."

"You're a good man," he said, working very hard to keep his temper contained. "I owe you one."

I waved my hand to indicate he didn't owe me anything at all. We walked and talked for nearly an hour, catching up after being apart for so long. We'd made it all the way down the river to the point nearing where it forked off toward the mill on the other side of the trees. Henry must've caught me staring in that direction, for I could hear the amusement in his voice when he spoke.

"You really can't get enough of him, can you?"

I gave him a sheepish grin as my hand came up to clasp the back of my neck. That bucket inside me that had once held all my feelings toward Breck had been refilled anew, and I nearly let them all spill in a gush of praise and desire at the urge of Henry's question. Instead, I decided simple was best.

"He makes me so happy."

Henry laughed warmly and nodded, glancing in the direction I'd been staring.

"Well, let's hear your idea for his gift, then. I'll see what I can do to help."

"Promise you won't make fun of me," I hedged. He gave me an impatient look. I took a deep breath, coughed, and told him what I was planning. I could feel myself including too many details, but secretly it felt nice to share them with someone. When I finished, he crossed his arms and then uncrossed them, shifted on his feet, and then finally landed with his fists propped on his hips, elbows wide. Then he turned away from me and paced a few steps, hands still firmly in place.

"Henry...?"

He cleared his throat loudly, repeating the action a few times. I remained quiet after that. More rough noises framed what I could've sworn was a sniffle as he turned around and came back to me. Slowly, I pressed my lips together to hide a small grin.

"Uh, I, uh... I think that's grand," he said shortly, not meeting my eyes as he spoke, which was very unlike him. When he started to blink hard, I took my opportunity to step in and hook my arm around his neck, pulling him close to me. For a few seconds, he remained still, and then he gave in and hugged me back, his fist tapping hard between my shoulder blades several times.

"You'll always be my best friend. You know that, right?"

"Aye, I know that," he answered indignantly, pulling away.

"Fatherhood has made you soft already," I teased gently. I expected some smart reply, but what I got instead made his reaction all the more understandable.

"So much has changed. This time last year, we were just two lads who liked to feck about and ride horses. And now look at us." His face pinched briefly with emotion. "I thought once that I'd lost you. This feels a bit like that again. But then you have to go and tell me such a sweet story, and I see how feckin' in love you are, and... how can I be so selfish?"

"I felt the same way about you and Sarah," I admitted. He looked at me then.

"You did?"

"Of course, I did. I know how happy she makes you, and I'm so proud of the life you've created for your new family. But I never want to go so long without seeing you again."

"I don't expect we'll be traveling much anymore," Henry quipped, coming back around to his normal self.

"You know what I mean," I told him, and he nodded.

He took another moment to collect himself before he grinned.

"Ma still grows her prized amaryllis in the covered garden every winter. I'll bet they're just startin' to bloom."

CHAPTER THIRTY-TWO

The solstice arrived on an appropriately blustery day. I'd nearly taken flight with one strong gust on my way to Finna's. The wind had caught my cloak at just the right angle, sending me stumbling and clutching the scarf Nan had insisted that I wear to keep my neck warm on the walk over. I'd told them all that I would be out for the evening, and that I'd most likely return the next day, to make sure they weren't waiting up for me.

The box I was carrying was the first thing Finna's eyes landed on when I shut the door behind me. A fire was roaring in her cozy sitting room. She ushered me in, taking the box so I could unwrap all my layers now that I was safely inside.

"So good to see you, love. Everything is set out for us. Care for tea?"

"I think I'd like to get the hard part over with first, if that's alright," I said, trying to keep my nerves from showing in the smile I offered her. She returned it brightly.

We crowded into the kitchen, my gaze sweeping across

the ingredients she'd so carefully organized and laid out on her counter for us. For me. I washed my hands, partly because I'd still had to do my chores that morning, and partly because I was stalling. Next came the task of rolling my sleeves up to my elbows to get them out of the way. Finna stepped in to help, which unfortunately made the process much faster.

The flour, sugar, butter, and all the rest came together easier than I'd imagined as I'd tossed around under my sheets the night before. Finna offered words of encouragement from her seat at the table, allowing me to do the work myself as I referenced the handwritten recipe card no less than a hundred times.

"The next part is very delicate. You mustn't work the dough too much. Gentle hands."

I did as she instructed as I turned the dough out onto the counter, which I'd carefully covered with a fine layer of flour. Watching my own hands work on something so new to me felt disorienting but oddly satisfying.

"I might like to try this again sometime, I think," I told her. She giggled.

"I knew you'd like it. Baking is a bit more fun than making lube for your friend," she reasoned cheekily. I glanced at her, willing myself not to turn scarlet. "Always remember to put the love in, though! The most important ingredient of all."

I read the little card again, making a flat, even circle with the dough. As even as I could manage, at least. I used a special tool that Finna had to cut out more circles, and then she talked me through the proper way to arrange them onto her baking tray that looked to be older than Nan.

I heaved out a sigh and a few coughs as I closed the door on her oven.

"Now what?" I asked, inspecting the dough that had taken up residence under my fingernails.

"Now, we wait. Tea?"

I accepted her offer this time as I settled into my chair at the table. The weather was still miserable outside her large window. It was a good thing Breck's ceremony wasn't taking place in the human world. Not that I was ready to venture back into the fairy world so soon after the experience I'd had. Aside from wanting to support Breck on the most important day of his life, the only thing making me feel better about it was Finna's promise to give me a different concoction to drink before I left that she claimed would work much more effectively, last longer, and not taste like something out of a horse's rear end.

"Can I see it now?"

I pulled my attention from the window to where Finna was waiting with poised hands over the box I'd brought along. I hesitated for a moment before I nodded. She opened the box carefully, peering inside as though she didn't know what she'd find.

"Oh, Peter. It's lovely."

"I hope it'll hold up on the journey," I said, rubbing my thighs slowly under the table.

"It should be fine. And once we've arrived, the magic there will keep it pristine."

I picked up my honeyed tea and took a long sip, closing my eyes as I swallowed. I'd worn another outfit I hoped would convey that I was trying to look nice, but not *too* nice. Breck seemed to like that best. Finna was wearing her deep purple gown again, along with what must've been every piece of jewelry she owned. Her lips had been stained a deep red color.

"Can I ask you something?" I set my cup down carefully.

"Anything," she said from her seat next to me.

"I keep telling myself that I'm being ridiculous. That it doesn't really matter. But Breck… well, he hasn't ever told me that he loves me. I've started feeling like a fool when I say it, knowing I won't hear him say it back."

"I imagine he never will," she started, grinning at the way my eyebrows bunched together. "He's never said it to me, either. Fairies do not say "I love you" the way people do. They feel it's another watered down phrase that humans have butchered the meaning of over the centuries."

"Oh," I said weakly. I'd always thought of them as quite powerful words.

"Perhaps you've heard him say something else in those more intimate moments?"

"Mo ghrá." It was the only thing I'd heard him say in his language enough times to memorize. "What does it mean?"

A sweet laugh bubbled up out of her chest. "That's a question for the man you're about to commit yourself to, not an auld witch like me." She reached across and patted her hand on my forearm a few times before she got up to check inside the oven. "Only a few more minutes, I'd say. Come and look."

Those minutes passed, and Finna showed me how to protect my hands with a towel so I could pull out the tray that, to my genuine surprise, held some perfectly shaped blackberry scones. Finna said they were more purple than hers because I hadn't been as gentle with the fruit as I could've been, but that they would taste good all the same. We set them out to cool just as the front door opened.

"Hello!" Elina called out in greeting, coming around the

corner and looking as though the cold weather hadn't bothered her at all. I supposed it made sense for someone made of sunshine. Carrick followed behind, also wearing little more than he usually did. I was starting to feel overdressed, but then I remembered what Finna had said about Lughnasa. Dress code was unimportant.

"Hello, my dears," Finna said warmly, embracing both of them when they stooped to kiss her cheek. "I can hardly believe the day has arrived. Our Breck is all grown up."

"He'll be glad when the day is over," Carrick said after offering me a nod in greeting. I didn't look away from him as Elina hugged me around the shoulders.

"Is he alright?" I asked.

"As alright as he can be. Fallon hasn't let up on him yet. I think she's still afraid he's going to get in front of Eabha and embarrass all of us. We'll be lucky if he keeps his clothes on long enough to finish the ceremony," he jabbed, chuckling to himself.

"Have some faith in him, Carrick," Elina rebuked with a frown. "Have you forgotten your own ceremony already? You were nearly too nervous to speak."

"Help me pack up my basket and we can be on our way," Finna said, changing the subject. "Peter, come along and get your drink." I decided not to watch her making whatever it was I had to swallow down until she lifted the lid on a small jar nearby, pinched out some of the powder, blew on it, and sprinkled it into the glass. With the twirl of her finger, the entire thing mixed itself. "There we are," she said as she held it up for me to take.

I brought the glass to my lips and squeezed my eyes shut as I tipped my head back. The texture was still unpleasant, but upon the final gulp, I realized that it tasted like nothing at all.

Finna had packed up the scones and my box into her large basket, its handle resting safely in the crook of her arm. Next to Carrick, she looked like a wee lass holding her father's hands. Elina was waiting for me with that patient smile she always wore.

"This time will be better, I promise. Just don't let go," she reminded me. I nodded my understanding as we clasped our hands together. I felt the air move around me as I closed my eyes again, and then the smoke of all Finna's candles being put out reached my nose, before everything went sideways.

* * *

The Seelie court's castle was bustling with activity when we arrived. I could barely hear the chimes of the littlest fairies and the songs of the birds over the chattering of words I mostly couldn't understand. I brought my hand up to rub at my forehead and the dull ache there. It was much less severe than the last time I'd arrived in the fairy world.

Fairies and other magical creatures were all around us. They rushed to greet Finna like she was royalty, touching her face and hair and clothes. She accepted them graciously. When Elina stepped away, exposing me to the masses, there was a slight pause in the commotion. My heart started to pound heavier as I felt their eyes on me. Then, a few seemed to remember me from the night in the woods, and they approached me with the same grabby hands and unfamiliar words. I tried to greet them back the best I could as I straggled behind the others toward the ruins.

I took a few calming breaths after I'd passed over the threshold, reacquainting myself with the floaty, strange feeling of my body. It was much quieter inside, but still busy. I recognized the preparations of a massive party thanks to all the times I'd been early to an event hosted by Henry's parents. There was more food than necessary, beautiful instruments being tuned and tested, and the excitement in the air was almost thick enough to touch. It came upon me to reach my hand out and test that last bit for myself, but the rational side of me decided against it.

A gentle touch at my elbow made me turn around.

"He's in his room," Finna said, holding out the plate full of scones in her other hand. I took them and leaned down to kiss her cheek, which she'd turned up for me.

"Thank you," I told her quietly as I set off, weaving through the action in search of Breck.

I found my way with little difficulty. The door was open just a crack, enough for me to see him standing with his back to me. There were two winged fairies helping to straighten out his clothes, zipping up, down, and around to adjust this and that. One of them was fussing with his hair as I pushed the door open, knocking it with the back of my hand a few times.

I nearly dropped the plate when he turned around.

"*Peter*," he breathed, his smile crinkling his eyes and making my heart leap.

"Look at you," I said, recovering as quickly as I could for him. I let my eyes trail over what he was wearing before I met his gaze again. He had on a vest made of velvet that was such a dark blue it was almost black. The neck of it was high, nearly up to his chin, and the shoulders were stiff enough to hold their shape. Gauzy, white sleeves came down both arms and collected neatly at his wrists. Stitched silver details were swirled across the velvet, matching the buttons on the vest and the jewelry he was wearing.

"It's a bit much," he started, looking down at himself. "And no pockets. I don't see how you manage it with your riding breeches."

I took a few steps to close the distance between us. Breck reached out to hook his finger in the band of my own black trousers, gently tugging me toward him.

"I'm sure it's harder for someone who has a habit of keeping his hands tucked away in them most of the time."

"What've you brought me?" he asked softly, lifting the linen napkin covering the scones. When he realized what they were, his eyes lit up. I didn't have to encourage him to take one. I held my breath as I waited for his reaction, but he simply let go of my trousers, moving to sit on his bed and motioning for me to do the same.

I settled next to him. "Do you like it?"

"They are my favorite," he said easily before taking another bite. I must've had an odd expression on my face, because he slowly stopped chewing and blinked down at the scone before he gave me a worried look. "Why? Is there something different about them? Has Finna fixed them with magic to ease my nerves?"

"I made them," I confessed with less confidence than I'd hoped for.

"You... made them?" He swallowed down what was in his mouth and inspected the treat further before he looked down at the plate where I'd set it on my leg.

"Happy birthday," I said then, not entirely sure why I was feeling so melancholy. "I know it's nothing like the rest of the feast they've prepared for you, but. If you're anything like William or Henry were on their big day, you've not really eaten anything, and I couldn't have you feeling peckish before—"

I didn't get the chance to finish what I was saying. Breck was kissing me, his fingers tangled in my hair at the back of my head. I managed to move the plate from my lap to the floor before we knocked it over. I wasn't sure where to touch him that I wouldn't mess up his clothes or his hair, so I kept my hands to myself, leaning into him and tilting my head more to the side.

"You didn't have to make me anything," he murmured against my cheek as he rested the side of his face against mine.

"I wanted to. It wasn't terrible, actually. Finna is a good teacher."

"Have you tried one?" He sat back and put the rest of the one he'd been eating in his mouth before he reached for another, holding it out for me to take a bite. I leaned in and did just that, wasting no time in comparing it to the ones Finna had perfected. It wasn't the best, but it was decent enough to keep eating it.

"Not terrible," I decided, wiping at the crumbs I felt stuck in the corner of my lips. Breck laughed lightly and touched his mouth to that spot.

"Give yourself more credit, *mo ghrá*."

My eyebrows went up, and I was just about to say something about those words when the two fairies from before came back into the room, followed closely by Fallon. She assessed our situation with a bland look and then addressed Breck directly.

"It's time."

CHAPTER THIRTY-THREE

When I emerged from the ruins, dusk had taken over where the sunlight had been. Floating fairy lights had been arranged artfully amongst the trees, which were full of the little golden fairies that seemed too excited to stay in one place for very long. The guests in attendance were milling about, some with drinks in their hands. I was desperate for one of my own, but I wasn't about to risk counteracting Finna's concoction so early in the evening.

With her petite fingers resting against the inside of my forearm, Finna and I proceeded toward the front of the crowd. Some of the instruments I'd passed by earlier were being played off to my right, balanced by more on the other side of the clearing we'd entered. There were no grand fires burning this time, which seemed counterintuitive for an outside event on the first true day of winter, but as it had been on my previous visit, the weather was mild and comfortable.

"Relax, love," came Finna's voice as she patted my arm. I looked down and realized that my grip on the box I'd been carrying was turning my knuckles white. I loosened my fingers and coughed out a heavy breath.

"There are so many... here," I said, stopping myself before I said people, or fairies, or creatures.

"Events as important as this one don't come around very often. The last one was for Carrick, if you can believe it." We came to a stop within throwing distance of a half-moon arrangement of thrones. I stared at the empty seat Breck had occupied the last time I'd stood before the Seelie court and my throat tightened.

When a hush came over the crowd, we all instinctively turned to see what was happening. Fallon was leading the procession, her eyes trained forward despite the way the fairies around her were vying for her attention with waves and head bows. Behind her was Elina, glowing and acknowledging the partygoers with occasional waves and smiles in return. Next came Murray, who appeared to be damp enough that he might've come directly from the sea only a few moments prior. Carrick was behind him, towering over everyone as he wore his self-confident smile that matched his stride.

The murmurs around us went silent as the last of them came into view.

Breck's cheeks caught the light even more than usual. This was what had taken me by surprise when I'd seen him. Someone had dusted the tops of his cheekbones with a shimmery powder, scant more swiped across his eyelids and the very tip of his nose. If I hadn't been mistaken, there'd also been a touch of stain on his lips. His hair was perfectly mussed, as always, and the cut of his outfit was so precise that it made my skin flush thinking about the body underneath I was so familiar with.

Remembering that potentially anyone around us could hear or see what I was thinking, I swallowed hard and tried to focus. Breck swept his sheer cape out of the way before he sat down, his posture trained in a way that I knew was unnatural for him. He was likely itching to pull his legs up and cross them. With his hands on his knees, he finally allowed himself to look around. He found me instantly.

I missed you, I thought for him. The faintest smile graced his mouth, and then I felt the curl of his magic around one of my wrists. It was all I needed to remind myself that everything was going to be fine.

When Fallon stood up, the whispers that had started again went quiet. All eyes were on her.

"Today is a most special day for one of our own. Breckabhainn has come of age. He has proven himself through his commitment to his training, great improvements in his magic, and the loyalty he has shown to both the fairy and the human world. As his mentor, I can say with confidence that we could not wish to pick someone more fit to take a place on the Seelie court."

Eabha appeared then, from where I couldn't say, and Fallon dipped her head to pass over the responsibility of addressing the crowd. She took her seat, back straight, eyes forward. I wished that I could offer her some comfort. How difficult it must've been to maintain her secret about Breck in that moment.

A collective head dip from the crowd was returned by Eabha, gracious and unhurried. Before she spoke, she turned and invited Breck to join her. He took his place at her side.

"We have all known Breckabhainn since he was a young fairy. We have seen him transform from a little sprout who enjoyed nothing more than playing in the dirt, to an adolescent who desired greatly to hone his magic, and now to a member of our society who we can all look up to."

Finna sniffled next to me and wiped at her eyes.

"In my lifetime, I am quite certain I've never met another fairy who works as hard as Breckabhainn. He seeks out every opportunity to be helpful to others, magical beings and humans alike. Often, his help goes unnoticed, and he never expects recognition. A true model for the rest of us."

I could tell by the tightness in his jaw that Breck was uncomfortable with all the praise.

"While many of us would like to take credit for who Breckabhainn has become, we cannot say any more without recognizing Finna." Eabha found her in the crowd and offered her a gentle smile, which Finna returned. She'd accepted her fate and was letting her tears roll freely down her face. Eabha turned her attention back to the masses and raised her hands, palms upturned.

"As tradition would have it, now would be the time for me to recite the ceremonial speech and present Breckabhainn with his crown. But I believe there's someone who has requested to say a few words before we begin. Peter?"

My own name echoed in my ears.

The small collection of fairies in front of me stepped or fluttered aside to clear a path. I bit the inside of my bottom lip as I stepped forward, taking over the spot Eabha had been standing in as she offered it to me. Breck turned fully toward me with a look of wonder.

"*What's all this?*" he whispered, his eyes searching mine.

"I love you," I began. I didn't worry about talking loudly to address the crowd. Everyone who I wanted to be a part of it was close enough to hear. "You have changed my life. You know as well as anyone what a wreck I was. I was practically a recluse, going through the motions because that's all I knew how to do anymore. Then, one day, I volunteered to get the flour, and I met you, and my whole world turned upside down in the best imaginable way."

I bent to set my box down between our feet because I couldn't stand to not be touching him any longer. I took his hands in mine and squeezed them. He squeezed back tenderly.

"Recently, I've realized that the life I was struggling so hard to fit into was making me miserable because it's not where I belong. It's not where I've ever belonged. I belong with you. Being with you makes me happy not only for the human things I'm escaping, but for the *you* things I'm gaining. Your kindness, your thoughtfulness, the way you never put yourself first, even when I wish you would."

Breck huffed out a laugh at that, and I dropped his hands to cup his face instead.

"What I'm trying to say is that I know you're worried about balancing your life with me and your responsibilities. Fallon told me that you wanted to give up your magic forever to be with me." I slid my thumbs against his cheeks, carefully avoiding his added sparkles. "I never want you to feel that way again. Of course, I miss you when you're gone, but Anne misses William when he's gone too, and he's only off making business deals and trades. He's not off making the world a better place like you are."

With the last shred of confidence I had left, I knelt onto the moss below our feet and opened the box, carefully lifting out the crown made of woven twigs and vines. A gasp swept through the crowd around us, mixed with a few hushed murmurs. The five impressive, snow white amaryllis blooms Henry had fetched for me looked even more alive than they'd been when I'd secured them in place with twine. When I pulled my gaze up to Breck again, he was staring at what I'd made with an expression I couldn't read.

"I want you to take your place on the Seelie court, Breck. I want you to keep helping others the way you've helped me. But when your responsibilities are met, and your work is done for the day, I want you to always come home to me."

Ever so slowly, with a grace only he could manage, Breck sank to his knees. My pulse raced as I watched him bow his head, silently accepting my offer. I placed the wreath of flowers on his hair. He brought one hand up to hold it in place as he sat back on his heels.

"I will, *mo ghrá*. I will always come home to you. To the one who has my heart."

I decided to feck their traditions one step further as I pushed the box out of my way, shuffling up to him on my knees and pressing my mouth and body to his. His free hand found its way to my hip first, then my lower back as he pulled me closer. Only after we broke apart did the cheering of the crowd break through the fog of elation clouding my mind.

We helped each other to our feet. Finna had burst through to be the first one to reach us, trapping us in a group hug. Formality kept the others securely in their seats, but Elina was beaming, and even Fallon had the slightest grin at the corner of her dark lips.

Eventually, Eabha managed to quiet everyone so she could finish the ceremony. I listened to her foreign words, but mostly I watched Breck listen to them with a poise that hadn't been there before. He bent forward slightly when Eabha presented him with his true crown; a tangle of silver vines and leaves forming a circlet that fit perfectly over his hair and came to rest against his forehead. He replaced his flower wreath before he righted himself, wearing both as though he felt they were meant to be a matching set.

The celebration that ensued was thoroughly overwhelming. I stuck to Breck's side, his hand never letting go of mine, as we faced the endless string of felicitations. My clothes were tugged, my face and hair touched, and my free hand shaken so many times that by the end of it all, I wanted nothing more than a bath and the solace of a bed – mine, Breck's, or anyone else's, I wasn't picky.

"Will you be sleeping here tonight?" Elina asked, which made me laugh a little, since the sun was already starting to lighten the sky above the thick branches overhead as the party finally ended.

"I need to take Peter home," Breck answered, the smirk he slipped me telling a longer story.

"Very well, let's find Finna."

The ache in my head and mild, queasy feeling in my gut told me it was perfect timing for us to go. The drink was starting to wear off. I let Breck drag me along to wherever Finna was, and I felt my hands transfer to someone else's for the journey back to the human world.

* * *

We'd only been back at the cottage for several minutes, but I'd already been served a steaming cup of tea, and Breck had disappeared to Finna's bedroom to change into clothes he'd left there earlier. I was sad to see the other outfit go, but his typical brown trousers and white shirt with the open collar provided a sense of comfort to both of us.

As he sat beside me, I noticed that he'd removed the circlet but kept his flower crown on.

"Alright?" he asked, pulling his legs up to fold underneath him on the sofa. I nodded.

"Tired, is all. Head hurts a bit. The tea will help."

Breck tucked in closer and placed a long, gentle kiss to my temple. We sat and listened to the crackling of the fire across the room. Our comfortable silence was everything I needed. That, and Breck's hand resting on the inside of my thigh, his thumb rubbing in a small circle.

He spoke after a while. "Would you mind very much if we went outside? I think I need some air."

The darkness of the night had brought some calm with it, replacing the strong winds from earlier that morning. It was still a bit cold, however, so I'd wrapped up in my cloak and scarf. The last thing I needed was to be out for one night and catch a cold. Nan would never let me forget it.

Breck took my hand and walked us around the side of the cottage to the small gate that led into Finna's sprawling back garden. As I marveled at how the pea stones didn't hurt his bare feet, Breck's magic brushed over my ankles and meandered up my body, giving me goosebumps. I shivered and stepped closer to him, despite the fact that he was the cause of my chill.

"You did great today," I told him.

He made a thoughtful sound. "I think you were the one who made the biggest impression."

"Fallon said you deserved nothing less than the most memorable thing I could possibly give you. I hope I managed well enough," I said, grinning to myself.

"I'm just sad I didn't get to eat the rest of your scones." He truly did sound disappointed.

"They weren't *that* good," I chaffed, bumping my shoulder against his. He chuckled and bumped me back, before he brought our joined hands up and kissed the back of mine.

"They were. And they were for my birthday. I've never had a birthday gift before."

"You haven't?"

"No. Fallon pretended to pick the solstice at random, I suppose, so we never knew for certain. And fairies don't really celebrate birthdays anyway, aside from the first one when we're given our name. I guess when you have so many, it doesn't really matter. But now that we know it is today, it felt sort of special to get a gift."

I stepped in front of him then, my shoes shuffling around in the gravel, and my hands found his hips before they ventured lower, settling on his backside.

"You should know that birthday gifts can come in many forms," I told him. He tilted his head to the side as I leaned in, providing more room for me to kiss his neck.

"Aye, but I really wanted the scones," he said. I could hear the smile in his voice. I scoffed playfully and let him go, but he reached for me and pulled us back together, his forehead resting against mine. "I will gladly accept any more gifts you wish to give me. But there's something I want to show you first."

We continued through the garden until we came to the vine covered archway that led out into the orchard. Breck let me go first and then took my hand again so we could walk beside each other.

"Has Finna discovered a new type of apple that she's been secretly growing for me?"

"Apples do not grow in December."

"Not even magical ones?" I badgered on, blinking up at

the dormant trees that stood in perfect rows around us. What could he possibly have to show me amongst them when nothing was blooming, and in the middle of the night to top it off? Eventually, we passed by all the fruit trees. Breck stopped walking. I looked at him in the faint moonlight.

"*Close your eyes,*" he whispered. I did. His magic swirled around me faster than I was used to as he guided me along. I focused on placing my feet safely in front of me, one after the other, until Breck let go of my hand. His arms came up around me from behind as he laid his fingers over my eyes, guaranteeing that I couldn't see anything as he moved both of us forward.

When he asked if I was ready, I nodded, and his hands slid from my face to my shoulders. I opened my eyes and had to blink hard several times so they could adjust. Hundreds of them, fairy lights and real fairies, were concentrated into the trees above us so densely that it nearly could've passed for daylight. Their little chimes and bells seemed to be mostly in sync, as though they were working together to create a soft melody for us.

My gaze fell from the branches and time slowed.

There, in all her indignant glory, stood the chestnut mare.

My hand flew to cover my mouth, but it wasn't enough, so the other one slapped on top for good measure. In my attempt to say something, anything, I managed a strangled whimper. Breck's hands slid down from my shoulders as his arms wrapped across my chest, his nose nuzzling behind my ear before he kissed the sensitive skin just below it.

"For you, my love," he said. In that instant, I knew without question that those were the words he'd been telling me all along. *Mo ghrá. My love.*

I turned in his arms and wrapped mine tightly around his neck with enough force that we almost toppled backwards. I kissed him, quick and sweet, over and over until he giggled and made a little yelp of surprise as his crown fell off and landed by our feet. Only then did I realize that I'd nearly bent him in half, my hand supporting his weight at the small of his back. I pulled him up and turned us just enough that I could see the mare again.

"Go to her," he encouraged with a final kiss on my cheek.

As I approached her, she flicked her ears forward and relaxed them again. A simple rope halter was the only thing she had on. Her mane had grown long enough to fall down the side of her neck and over her forehead. I let her sniff my hand before I placed it on her muzzle, which she quickly bumped away with the toss of her head. Breck was still the only one she liked touching her face, then. It really was her. I took a few steps, running my hand along her back. She was in grand off-season condition.

"When... how long have you had her?" I asked, finally finding my words.

"Since she was sold. Carrick is a surprisingly convincing horsemonger, the way he tells it."

"He bought her from Wally?" I felt cold shock splashing around with the tea in my stomach.

"Well, yes. But I paid for her." He reached down for his crown of flowers and put it back on, straightening it with care. "She's the most precious thing I've ever bought with human money. And now she belongs to you."

I was about to protest, saying that I couldn't possibly afford to pay him back, when my surprise faded away and the reality of the situation fell over me. This was more than a gift.

This was *the* gift.

A soft gasp escaped me as everything clicked into place.

"Finna will be glad to have this secret revealed," he continued, coming over to pet the—*my* chestnut mare's face. "She was very kind to let me keep her here until tonight. You can imagine the fun we had trying to steer her clear of the garden."

"I don't know what to say," I admitted.

"I did have a speech prepared. In case I went first." His grin made his cheeks sparkle in the fairy lights. "But it seems that we both had the same idea."

"You've been planning this since we left on our trip?" I thought back to when I'd first told him about Wally selling the mare, right after we had set out from the cottage. Breck glanced down at his feet, grin turning sheepish. His lack of an answer made my heart do that funny little something in my chest. "I stand by what I said. I cannot possibly deserve you."

"Shall we take your new horse home?" He reached to untie her rope from the thick branch it was looped around and held it out for me.

"What will I tell everyone when they see her back in her stall tomorrow morning?"

"You could tell them that the man who bought her decided she was more of a menace than what she's worth? She did try to bite Carrick on the first day he brought her here."

I laughed and looked back at my mare as she trailed calmly behind us. The news was hardly surprising. "Has anyone ridden her?"

"That's why she tried to bite him."

CHAPTER THIRTY-FOUR

Breck and I had been committed to each other for just under a month when everything started to change.

I was returning from a ride when I heard shouting from inside the stables. I dismounted in a rush and urged my gelding along behind me, which he obliged, though it was slower than what was helpful at the time. When I came around the corner, one of my riding boots slipped a bit in the mud just outside the wide double doors. I found Henry right up in the personal space of our newest irritation. Ant had a smug look on his face that I wanted to punch off him. I ran toward them before Henry could act on similar thoughts.

"Come on," I said in his ear as I wrapped my arm around his shoulders, steering him outside and away from the confrontation.

"Aye, that's it, pup," Ant called behind us. "Run along with your biggest admirer. Always here to save the day."

The words stung. Henry was more than capable of looking after himself, especially in a fight. He didn't need rescuing. What he did need, however, was someone to bring him back down. His red hair and matching personality almost always guaranteed that Henry would have his say if he wasn't stopped. This tension between them had started almost immediately after he and Sarah had returned home, and it was only growing more intense. If I didn't step in, the unraveling would surely become a physical one. I honestly wasn't sure who would come out of it worse off.

We didn't stop walking until we reached the bank of the river. My gelding wasted no time in lowering his head to search the roughage for something to eat when I let him go. Henry ducked out from underneath my arm and started away from me, then turned back, repeating this several times as he paced out his anger. I stood silently, watching him wear a path in the stunted winter grass. He was still flushed and breathing hard, his hands animated at his sides, clenching and unclenching, fingers flexing wide and relaxing.

It was at times like this that I understood why Breck liked having the ability to listen to the thoughts inside someone's head.

Henry finally paused long enough to look up at me. My eyebrows went up sympathetically, showing him I was ready to listen, but he just cursed and turned away again. I was starting to wonder if maybe there was more to his frustration. A short distance behind me were the rocks where I'd shared my first kiss with Jamie. I slid my feet back those few steps and sat down. The stone sent a chill through my thin breeches to my skin. I shivered slightly.

When he was ready to speak, he stopped in his tracks and turned toward the river, his hands coming up to plant on his hips. It was hard to say if the confidence was real, or if he was putting it on to get through whatever he was about to tell me.

"I don't want this life, boyo," he said. My stomach sank.

"What do you mean?" I asked carefully, trying to mask my fear and surprise.

"I haven't worked this hard to spend the rest of me life answering to other people. Da said that when I came back, he'd turn over a lot of his projects to me. The ones I'd been helpin' with already. He said I'd be his partner in the business. And to think I feckin' believed him!" Henry's hands came up to push back through his hair before they fell to his hips again. He turned to me. "The only work he has me on is fetchin' things for him like I did when I was a lad. Transcribe this, copy that. I'm not his feckin' secretary."

He huffed out a sigh and came to sit next to me on the rocks. I turned a bit so that my back wasn't to him as he plopped down.

"And this shite with Ant," he said, flinging his hand out in the direction of the stables as his voice deepened. "I can tell you right this minute that there'll be no room on the team for the both of us come next season."

"You want to quit the club?" My reply was weak. His shoulders drooped.

"I don't *want* to. But I almost feel I haven't got a choice. Not if I'm expected to make any money with the little business Da did relinquish to me, look after Sarah, manage the new house. The time left over for fun right now isn't enough to continue the way things were before. I barely have the opportunity to come all the way down here as it is these days, let alone get back into our full training schedule in a few months."

He was right. The care of his horses had largely been turned over to the stable hands. I was lucky if I saw him every couple of days. We hadn't been on a ride together since the one we'd taken at the estate. But if he left the team, then what? Would he sell his horses, too? The cost to keep them would certainly be more than what was acceptable for an occasional jaunt along the river trail. And then what excuse would he have to come 'round? This wasn't about me, not really, but I was feeling very selfish at the moment.

"I thought we said nothing else was going to change."

Henry's hand landed on my shoulder with a squeeze. "Sarah and I have been talking about it. Nearly every night. Between my stress-induced insomnia and the heartburn she's experiencing, we've been missing a lot of sleep. But we're trying to work some things out. Can you promise me something?"

I nodded, not meeting his eyes.

"Promise that you'll decide what makes *you* happy. Don't think about anyone else for a change." Before I could ask what he meant, he pushed himself up to his feet with a loud sigh. "Thanks for makin' sure I didn't bash his head in."

"What was it about this time?" I was up then, too, moving toward my horse to collect him. Henry groaned and shook his head, pausing before he answered.

"You'd think cleanin' up after himself would give him an incurable disease," he started. "There's no way recovering from a broken leg made him forget how to dump out his soap buckets or wipe his shears so they don't rust. Everywhere he goes, it's a trail of chaos left behind. So I decided to tell him as much."

"Clearly he appreciated that," I said dryly.

"I don't give two shites *what* he appreciates, unless it's the fact that the world doesn't revolve around Ant Byrne."

A small grin formed on my lips. "Someone should let Thomas know."

"Don't even get me started."

Thomas had taken a turn for the worst. To say he was infatuated was far too gentle. He'd attached himself to Ant like a foal to its mother, trotting along just waiting for any opportunity to impress the man. Ant was taking full advantage of this, but in all honesty, I couldn't bring myself to feel bad for him. Thomas had used up every speck of benevolence I had left. All I knew was that I was glad to stay out of their way.

* * *

Another supper party had been planned for two days later, this time with a rare appearance from my oldest brother. William sat stiffly in his chair next to Anne, moustache working as he chewed a bite of Finna's gingerbread pudding creation. It was warm and gooey and perfect. A fine balance for the brumal gusts of wind that were beating themselves against the stone walls of our house.

"If this weather doesn't let up, you're both more than welcome to stay the night," Nan offered nonchalantly. "I'll have two of the bedrooms turned down for you." Too many thoughts hit me at once. First was the concern over Nan forcing her tired knees upstairs to prepare two extra beds. A quick second was that at least one of those beds would be put to no use, because there was zero chance I'd have Breck sleeping in a bed in my own house that wasn't mine. But Nan didn't need to know that bit.

"That's very kind of you," Finna smiled. She was on Anne's other side. Their friendship was growing with each call Finna made to the house, offering Anne the company and support she so badly needed during her stretch as a shut-in.

My gaze shifted to Anne in her middle seat across from me. She'd been quiet for most of the afternoon. Her fatigue was chronic at this point. Some discomfort that Finna said was perfectly normal had been keeping her from doing much of anything, but she'd insisted on helping prepare for the gathering. Nan had relented and let her chop vegetables. We nearly had to break her legs to force her down onto one of the stools at the counter rather than standing up on her swollen feet to complete the task.

Breck's knee bumped mine under the table. When I turned to look at him, his focus was not on me. His jaw was set. Expression hard to read. I remembered this look. This was the look I got when he was trying to figure out what was wrong with me the day I'd first met the others at the cottage. The day I'd been clumsy and accidentally sliced my fingers open on a bale tie.

"*Alright?*" I whispered to him, talking under the conversation happening around us. The slightest tilt of his chin had my focus shifting back to Anne. I realized that her fair cheeks looked even more flushed than normal. Her shoulders were hunched over just enough to indicate her unease, now that I was looking for it. Her hand was at the side of her belly.

Finna felt the shift and followed my attention to the woman beside her. She raised a supportive touch to Anne's shoulder.

"How frequently is the pain coming now, love?" Her tone was calm but serious.

Anne swallowed before she could answer. "Maybe every few minutes," she managed.

We cleared from the table in record time, the women assisting Anne slowly toward the bedroom at the far other end of the house, while the rest of us crowded into the sitting room. I was surprised that William decided to stay there with us instead of retreating to the privacy of his study. Our company did little to calm his nerves, unfortunately, if that was what he'd been hoping for. After half an hour, I offered to fetch him a strong drink, and he readily accepted.

I hadn't been prepared to share a space with only William and Breck, so we sat mostly in silence. Or rather, Breck sat on the floor by the chair I was in while William wandered around the room, nervously clutching the short glass in his hands against his chest. The restraint I showed in not reaching out to run my fingers through Breck's hair was enough to earn me some kind of award, I was sure of it. His steady presence was the only thing keeping me from following William around the room step for step.

"Finna has helped with these situations many times before," Breck said after a while. "I'm sure this time will be as successful as the others."

William nodded tightly, draining the last sip of his drink. I thought for a moment that if he was squeezing it any tighter, the glass might shatter. He seemed to realize the same thing and set it down on a side table as he fell onto the chair across from us. Hunching forward, he held his head with his elbows on his knees. I didn't know how to comfort him. The uncertainty of it all made it hard to offer the supportive words I'd provided on his wedding day. I couldn't honestly say that everything would turn out just fine.

A wail of pain a while later startled us all out of the semi-sleep we'd fallen into. Breck picked his cheek up off my leg before anyone else could notice. Not that William was in any state to be noticing things. He'd leapt off the chair and had resumed his pacing as though he'd never stopped.

I twisted to glance out the window behind me. The wind was carrying on. Everything was still dark. I yawned and settled my head in the corner of the high back of my chair, made easier by the fact that I'd slumped down into it as the hours had passed. It seemed inappropriate to excuse ourselves up to my bedroom with everything else going on, as much as I would've liked to – for sleeping purposes, of course.

My arms uncrossed then, and my hand found its way along the outside of my thigh until the knuckles of two curved fingers reached the back of Breck's neck. I stroked the freckled skin there, just beneath his hairline.

Thank you for staying, I thought for him as William made another pass between us and the hearth, casting us in the briefest shadow as he blocked the light from the fire. I let my hand fall to the cushion beside my thigh before William turned and started back the other direction. The curl of Breck's magic around my wrist warmed me, despite the chill of it.

Another cry from the end of the hallway and the ensuing footsteps got our attention. I was on my feet the moment I saw Finna in the doorway, her wild hair trying to escape her attempt to tame it at the nape of her neck. At least she was still smiling. She searched all three of our faces before landing on mine.

"She's asking for you."

A wave of uncertainty passed through me, made worse when William shot me a glare.

"Me?" I asked dumbly, and Finna nodded. She held out her hand toward me and waved it in a way that said come on, hurry up, so I did. I rubbed my hands along the seams of my trousers the entire way to the bedroom, trying to calm my nerves. Why would Anne want me?

Finna pushed the door open a crack, but then paused and turned to look up at me in the low light.

"I know how you are about blood and the like. Do not look anywhere but her face and you'll be just fine. I've given her something for the pain, but there's only so much I can do. She just wants comfort right now. Support. She needs her dearest friend."

I didn't have time to process all those words before the door was opened to a scene I'd never witnessed anything like before. The room was hot, the air thick and damp. Lucy was by the hearth with the fire blazing, heating water. There were blankets and rags, both wet and dry, draped across every surface. When the deep red color of one punched me in the gut, I averted my eyes until I'd shuffled quickly around to the far side of the bed. I sat with my back turned to the activity behind me and looked only at Anne's face as Finna had instructed.

Her tight blonde curls were wet and clinging to her forehead and cheeks. She looked exhausted, her chest heaving beneath the blankets. The dip of the mattress as I'd sat down drew her attention. She gave me a weak grin but didn't say anything. I returned the gesture, but it quickly faded as Anne's face pinched in agony. I reached for her hand without thinking and she responded with a tight squeeze.

My heart was racing with uncertainty as Nan and Finna offered various instructions and words of support. I didn't dare look away from Anne as my senses were overwhelmed. I just held her hand in both of mine and watched as her expressions changed, cycling through weariness and an odd mix of what I could only describe as pain and determination.

Anne fought back another scream. The bones in my hand neared their breaking point as she squeezed again. I hoped I didn't look horrified as her head pressed back into the pillows, the sound she'd been trying to contain ripping from her chest.

And then it was over.

And then there was silence.

And then, a little whimper of a cry. Then another. Anne's hand slid from between mine. Nan adjusted the blankets, carefully folding them down. I only had the sense to look away as she parted Anne's dressing gown, exposing her before I could realize what was happening.

I kept my head turned until Anne said my name. When I looked back, the blankets had been pulled up again, and snuggled beneath them on her chest was the most magical little creature I'd ever seen. And that was saying a lot, all things considered. I watched and watched for what felt like forever. I knew the truth of what it had taken to create this life. I knew of the loss, the sacrifice.

When our eyes met, Anne had tears in hers, but she looked so very happy.

"*You're a mammy,*" I whispered with a grin, and a sob escaped her as she nodded, more tears coming. I leaned down and kissed her damp forehead.

"Time to let them rest now," Nan told me.

The fresh, cool air of the hallway was a relief as I closed the door behind me. I took some steadying breaths that made me cough. When I rounded the corner, William and Breck were both on their feet, staring at me expectantly.

"A girl," I managed, not realizing until then how tired I was.

William nearly sprinted past me on the way to his wife and daughter. I rubbed at my eyes with a finger and thumb as I stepped further into the room. I'd never been aware that birth was such an extreme event. When all three of my younger siblings had been born, we'd been sent away to stay with friends of the family. All I knew was that one day, Mammy had a round tummy, and then a week later we came home and had a new baby sister.

My hand fell to my side just as Breck's arms came around my shoulders and he hugged me close. I embraced him with my own arms slung loosely across his lower back, one hand gripping my other forearm.

"That was terrifying," I admitted.

He laughed quietly.

"I can imagine. Another new experience you can cross off your list." Breck's hand came up to the back of my head as I tucked my face against his neck, breathing him in.

"I'm not sure that one was ever on the list to begin with," I mumbled.

"But you're glad to have helped someone you care for," he reasoned, his fingers working lazily through my curls.

"Aye. That's true." My eyes had closed, and the comfort of being in Breck's arms was sending me dangerously close to falling asleep standing up right there in the middle of the sitting room. I nuzzled against his neck. "Take me to bed?"

"Together in your room for the first time, and you only want to sleep?" he teased as we untangled from each other. Confident that everyone else in the house was still preoccupied, I laced my fingers with his and led him toward the stairs. I thought vaguely about how Breck's silent bare feet made it much easier to sneak him up with me.

"Wake me up in a couple hours and we can discuss crossing that off the to-do list, as well," I whispered over my shoulder with a smirk. When we reached the top of the stairs, Breck pulled me back with our joined hands, his free one coming up to the side of my face as he kissed me. I closed my eyes and kissed him back.

"Anything you want," he offered before our lips met again. *"Happy birthday, mo ghrá."*

CHAPTER THIRTY-FIVE

I didn't make it to the stables in time to step between Henry and Ant Byrne a week later. My favorite redhead had thrown the first punch, landing a solid hook on Ant's jaw. By the time I reached the scene, Wally and another stable hand were trying to break them up, but Henry didn't stop until I had my hands on him, dragging him away from the fight.

My stomach gurgled uneasily when I got a look at Henry's face. His nose was bleeding. His lip was split and starting to swell. He sniffed and ran his sleeve across his mouth, wiping away most of the blood, and he inspected the fabric briefly before he shot a look in the direction I'd pulled him from.

"What has gotten into you?" I asked, incredulous.

Henry wasn't done. He turned around with a frustrated shout and slammed his fist into the solid wood of a stall divider. Luckily the horses were turned out, otherwise it would've startled them as badly as it startled me. I lunged for his arm before he could do it again, holding his wrist and elbow tightly. He shoved his shoulder into me, trying to push me off. "Henry, *stop!*"

We struggled for another moment until Henry finally gave up and I let him go.

"Pete—" he started, but then stopped. I thought his voice might've cracked with emotion. "You can't stay here." He sniffed again.

"What?" My brows dipped in confusion. This was my job. This was my home.

"You're not safe. He told me he's gonna come after you and, and, and—" Henry turned his head and heaved onto the smooth stone floor. He'd swallowed too much blood. I gagged hard and looked away, reaching for Henry so I could pull him all the way outside. I didn't have enough time to worry about what he'd said as I thought loudly, so loudly for Breck to bring Finna at once.

They found us sitting near a shallower part of the river. A stand of trees and some rocks on either side hid us from view of the stables. Henry had removed his ruined shirt and I'd dunked it into the cold water so he could hold it against his face. Finna got to work right away, instructing Henry to tilt his head forward instead of back so more blood didn't drain into his stomach. He'd broken his hand punching the wall. I felt numb as I watched her working her magic on him, his words finally sinking in.

"Ant knows, somehow. About me," I told Breck without looking at him.

"Okay," he said calmly.

"Henry said he's been saying threatening things about me for weeks. I don't know if he truly means to act on them or not, but."

Henry cut in. "He does, boyo. And I'll kill him." Finna guided his head back down gently.

"If I tell Wally, or William, then they'll have to know the truth about what he's claiming. But even then, there's no guarantee they'll even take it seriously."

"And if they do, Ant is likely to spread rumors to all his loyal followers no matter if they let him stay on here or if they make him leave." Henry's voice was muffled by the wet shirt. He set it down on his legs but kept his head tilted forward. "I know you're not ready to tell everyone, but that's not even me biggest concern. He's gonna hurt you. He told me himself. He said he's gonna make you wish you'd never even seen another man's cock. *Shite,*" he cursed as Finna did something to his wounded hand. "Sorry."

Embarrassment coursed through me, but Finna didn't react to his words at all, and Henry was still too worked up to be shy about saying them. I finally looked at Breck, and he was staring into the distance in the direction of the stables. I took a step closer to him.

"Don't you dare try to do anything irrational," I warned.

"I was just listening," he reassured me, so I had to believe him.

Had Ant already spoken to Wally and told him the truth? I didn't have any idea how he could've come to the conclusion on his own about my preferences. To my knowledge, he'd never even seen me with Breck. My own thoughts were apparently too loud to be ignored.

"He thinks it's you and Henry. He's made up his own assumptions because of the other rumors, and because he sees how close the two of you are."

"Ah, feck that," Henry groaned. "Why would I have taken a wife if I didn't want one?"

"It's what I'm expected to do, Henry. The rest doesn't matter. A man takes a wife and carries on the family name." My stomach was unsettled all over again as I said the words. His bundled shirt returning to the lower part of his face told me he didn't know what to say to that.

Watching Anne and William settle into parenthood had been one of the most wonderful things I'd ever witnessed. Anne was radiant in her new role, taking everything in stride and soaking up each bit of advice she was given, while still doing things the way she thought was best. William was putty around his child. He'd been reserved at first, but only a few days in I'd caught him smiling down at her, and even talking to her. And despite this example, and the example my parents had set for all of us, I knew deep inside that wasn't the life I wanted for myself.

Henry made a few more pained noises as Finna bandaged his hand. I sighed and coughed several times, the weight of everything finally too much. I sat down in the crunchy grass and leaned my back against one of the trees.

"I don't suppose this is the ideal time to tell you," Henry started. I gave him a worried look. "But Sarah and I have made our decision."

I wasn't ready for this. If he had decided to keep things the way they were, that's not how the conversation would've started. He would've just come out and said it, or not bothered to say anything at all. "And?" I asked feebly.

"And in a month's time, we'll be moving back to the estate. Permanently. Sarah worked her charm on her parents, and they've agreed to let us run the place however we want to, as long as we keep up with the renovations and maintenance. It'll be easier to have someone on-site anyway.

They're also still allowed to visit whenever they want to, along with the rest of their family, but Sarah says she thinks that won't be very often at all." His gaze fell to his lap. "We signed some legal documents yesterday."

I leaned my head back against the tree and stared up at the empty branches. A few remaining dead leaves that clung to them fluttered in the breeze. Henry was leaving for good. My hands found the bend behind my knees to keep them from sliding along my thighs.

"I'm going to take me team along. We've decided that we want to open an equine facility. It'll bring jobs to the people there who are still struggling after the illness. There are so many still struggling. Plus, you and I know better than most how an exciting game of polo can bring joy to a place that desperately needs it. I want to breed horses, Pete. The best horses around. People will come from all over the country to see them. Other countries, even. To buy them. It's what I always thought this place could be, if the right people were behind it."

My lungs ached. I tried to take a deep breath and coughed it out harshly, a few more following it.

"There's just one other thing I'll need," he added. I waited for him to continue. When he didn't, I picked my head up to look over at him where he was still sitting by the water. His crooked grin was even more crooked thanks to his swollen, discolored lip.

"What's that?"

"You."

I blinked at him. Blinked again. My forehead wrinkled. "Me?"

"How am I supposed to run the best facility around if I

haven't got the best manager?" My mouth opened slightly, and he continued with a new excitement in his voice that hadn't been there before. "I want you to come with us. I want you to manage the horses and the stables, the whole lot. I'll build the most modern equine facility anyone's ever seen, and you'll be the man who makes it magic." He paused to shrug his shoulders. "What do you think?"

A long silence stretched between us.

"I think your Da is a fool for letting such a clever businessman out of his grasp."

Henry cackled. "And he doesn't even know yet! So what do you say? Think about it?"

I didn't need to think about it. My heart was singing. I felt on the inside the way Elina looked on the outside, shining out rays of light in every direction. This was the opportunity I'd always dreamed of. A chance to prove to William, to myself, that I really was doing something with my life. I looked up at Breck, and he was giving me a little smirk that told me everything I needed to hear, but he said it anyway.

"When shall we start packing?"

My excitement faltered. "What about my family? And Finna?" I turned my attention to where she'd just finished gathering up her supplies. I couldn't take Breck away from her, could I?

"Don't you worry about me, love. My door will always be open, no matter how far away you go."

Breck stretched out a hand for me to take and helped me to my feet. I felt a little unsteady. He didn't let go, and Henry noticed.

"You'll both be welcome to stay with us at the estate for as long as you'd like, though I imagine you'll want to build a home for yourselves. We can discuss the details once we're all settled." Henry was up then, too. He clapped his hand on my shoulder, bloodied shirt draped over his other arm. "You're bigger than this place. I've always known that you are. I want to make a difference in the world, and I want to do it with me best friend."

EPILOGUE

I'd been awake for over twenty-four hours. At least, I was pretty sure I had been. The gas lanterns fixed at even intervals along the wall didn't reveal what time of day it was, and they were the only source of light I had seen since my early morning rounds the previous day had been thoroughly derailed. Fatigue had me fighting to keep my eyes open. I was grateful for the half wall of the stall door that was holding me up. Both forearms were braced across the top of it as I tried my best to ignore the grume that had dried under my fingernails.

The soft snorts and shuffling of hooves in the fresh straw coming from inside the stall were comforting, only to be outdone by the familiar arms that came around my middle from behind. I felt Breck's body press against mine as he tucked his chin into the crook of my neck.

"Hello there, little one," he murmured. I could hear the smile in his voice.

"Another filly," I told him. "Look at the star on her forehead." A perfect splotch of white between her eyes interrupted the dark fur that covered the rest of her. She was nearly the twin of her mother, who was busy licking the new foal's rump. An added nuzzle of affection nearly sent the hours-old filly tumbling on her unsteady legs. In my over-tired state, this was enough to make me laugh more than it should have.

"Have I lost you to the delirium?" Breck kissed my neck with a tenderness that made me swoon. I made the mistake of closing my eyes and leaning into his touch.

"I think I'm asleep right now," I admitted groggily, which made him chuckle.

"This may come as a surprise to you, but you are not, in fact, a horse. Sleeping standing up is not advisable."

"I just want to watch them a while longer. She's a first timer." The birth had gone smooth enough, but that didn't mean things couldn't still go wrong. The long whiskers around her mouth had tickled my palm as I'd helped the filly find the way to her first milk. These stalls in the back of the stables were larger and had been specially made to keep out cold drafts and the unpredictable weather. It was warm, and safe, but somehow it still never felt like enough.

"Horses have been born for thousands of years in much worse conditions than this. You've done your part. Let nature do the rest for now."

I wanted to protest, but Breck's fingers tugging methodically at my shirt were enough of a distraction to make me reconsider. As soon as he had the tails of it untucked from my waistband, his hand found its way to my stomach. I could feel the cool press of his rings against my skin. There was the one on his thumb, another thinner one on his pointer finger, and the last was the one I'd given him.

On the night of our joining, we had knelt together in the

woods and grinned at each other like fools while Fallon wrapped our hands with ribbon. As soon as Eabha had finished her speech, I'd broken fairy tradition again and kissed Breck like it was the first and last time I would ever get the chance. The cheers that erupted around us had been deafening. After Breck had straightened his circlet in his hair, we'd surprised everyone a step further by exchanging matching bands. Finna had helped us take some of the twine I'd used to craft his flower crown and fashioned two real metal rings out of it. Her magic was something I would never understand.

Nearly two years had passed since that night. We'd spent the first year living in the estate with Henry and Sarah, and eventually the twins they welcomed that summer. I'd been mortified when Henry kept trying to convince anyone who would listen that I was responsible for their double luck thanks to the gift I'd given him in the little jar. When I'd asked Finna if there was any truth to his claims, she'd just shrugged with a twinkle in her eye.

Finna had only remained in the village for a handful of months before we convinced her to move closer. Breck had reopened the mill at the estate, running it with the help of two new apprentices. Other locals filled the roles of black-smith, and baker, and many more helped with the construc-tion of the stables and other buildings that made up the facilities Henry and I had designed together. Most of them stayed on to become stable hands or grounds keepers, and a few had been selected to help me with the training of the horses. To my delight, Finna finally took her chance at becoming apothecary for us all.

"Come have some breakfast," Breck said before he kissed my neck again, his little finger teasing the skin just beneath the band of my trousers. "Then we can get you to bed."

"I'm not sure your motives are in the interest of me getting any sleep." I forced my eyes open and turned in his arms. His smirk was telling as he took my hand in his, leading us down the long row of stalls. I stole one more glance back at the mare and foal.

"Food first. Then sleep. And then I'll be waiting when you wake up."

I huffed out a laugh. "As I said. A promise like that will make it hard to get any rest."

I blinked at the morning light as we started along the road that connected the stables with the rest of the estate on the other side of the coastal hills. Two training arenas sat empty at that hour, one on either side of us, but would soon be busy with rhythmic hoofbeats. Henry and I had spent months carving out new riding trails, working to form alliances with other local breeders and trainers, and procuring a plot of land that would soon become our new polo field. Every day, I woke up looking forward to what was yet to come, knowing that I was a part of something bigger than myself.

As Breck and I rounded the corner between the hills, the estate came into view. Pinks and purples stained the sky as the sun was just beginning to work its way above the horizon. I thought of Lucy and her storybooks, full of castles and magic and fairy tales. I thought of my family.

They'd all just been up to visit us for a week; Nan and Lucy, William and Anne, and little Catherine, with her bouncing blonde ringlets and rosy cheeks just like her mammy. They'd brought news of another babe on the way. Watching all the people I cared about splashing in the salty waves together had been something I never knew I needed, but I'd tucked away the memory to keep forever.

"What's got you grinning?" Breck raised our joined hands so he could kiss the back of mine. I would never tire of his lips against my skin. The gulls were already calling down by the water, breaking the silence, and I sighed out a contented breath that didn't make me cough.

"It's everything. This place. Being here. Doing work that I'm proud of. Making everyone else proud. William told me that while he misses me back home, he sees that what I'm doing here is making a difference for people who need it. I've known since we got started, but something about hearing it from him made it feel... I don't know. Real."

Breck made a thoughtful noise and brought his free hand to the crook of my elbow, holding my arm close against his body as we turned from the main road onto the footpath lined with lilac sea asters and wild clover. Finna's new home was already coated with the local flora, as well as all the rest of her favorite flowers, but we were steadily catching up. I felt a twinge in my chest when our cottage came into view.

It was simple, no bigger than what we needed for just the two of us. Breck had thrown the windows open, allowing the constant breeze coming off the sea to ruffle the curtains inside. The briny air had proven to be good for my lungs. I found myself coughing far less often, though I knew Breck's magic had something to do with that, as well. The powerful, minty burn of it had been lasting longer and longer in my chest after our more *intimate* moments.

"Tonight will be most special for the both of you," Finna had said as we prepared to stand before Eabha. We'd decided to get ready together to ease some of my nerves. It helped, for the most part. "When Breckabhainn uses his magic, it will bond the two of

you in a way that nothing else ever will. I find it so romantic," she'd crooned, her hands clasped under her chin.

When I had asked him about it in what turned out to be our final private moment before the festivities began, he'd actually blushed. "Fairies are not supposed to use their magic on anyone else during copulation until they're mated." As the apologetic look on his face grew, my mouth fell open. "Please don't tell Finna I did it before tonight. This is one tradition that really means a lot, and I don't want to upset her."

"You scoundrel," I'd scolded him playfully, hooking a finger under his chin as I kissed him. And even though that night had been wonderful, nothing would ever top our night in the woods, when he really had used his magic on me for the first time, sealing our bond in place.

The breakfast Breck prepared was simple, just oat porridge with honey and apples, but it was exactly what I needed. It was still warm as we sat down to eat after I had washed my hands and arms twice in the basin. I was getting less squeamish with each new foal that I helped birth. I found myself rubbing my palms against my thighs far less often, as well. I had decided that my new life would not be weighed down by all my past worries. Truthfully, there wasn't time for it.

We had built the simple stone cottage so that the back of it faced the ocean. It was a breathtaking view, especially as the sun came up, or when a storm was rolling in. I studied Breck's profile as he stared out the window while we ate, his legs crossed under him in his chair.

He had taken up his role with the Seelie court as easily as we all knew he would, flawlessly combining his responsibilities with helping the humans in our new community. He had a way of always being exactly where he was needed most.

Sometimes it was at the mill, teaching his young lads the tricks of the trade. Other times, he would show up just as another man was needed to hoist a wooden beam up for a new roof. He continued to share his wealth with others, only keeping a paltry portion of his earnings – especially since Henry insisted on my salary being far more than what we needed.

And at the end of the day, no matter where he'd been called off to, he always came home to me.

ABOUT S.O. CALLAHAN

 S.O. Callahan has always been fond of sweet things, namely chocolate and love stories. When she's not writing or reading, she enjoys baking, visiting National Parks and Historic Sites, and traveling with her husband. They live in Georgia and have two very spoiled cats named Ozzy and Beau.

ALSO BY...

ALSO BY S.O. CALLAHAN

Fella Enchanted

FAE & HUMAN RELATIONS: A REGENCY FANTASY SERIES BY SARAH WALLACE & S.O. CALLAHAN

Breeze Spells and Bridegrooms - A new series by cozy fantasy authors Wallace and Callahan

Read a sneak peek now!

PREVIEW FOR BREEZE SPELLS
AND BRIDEGROOMS

Torquil's Tribune

Greetings fair folk and haphazard humans,

For those just now returning to London, welcome back.

Did you miss me?

The summer months are always horrifically dull for this humble writer. So little gossip to share. So little havoc to wreak. We are excessively relieved to see people return to the city. Whose lives shall be changed this Season? Who will fall in love? Who will flirt with scandal? We are, as ever, eager to find out.

It would appear that the Council for Fae & Human Magical Relations is preparing to convene soon, a whole month before the Season begins. To what do we owe the pleasure of a group of blustery and generally useless politicians to our fair city?

Well, the trend of human children receiving low scores on their Hastings Exam has started to reach a crisis point.

Low scores have always been a potential result of the magical testing process, but high scores are becoming increasingly rare. As more and more humans with low Hastings scores reach adulthood, we are seeing the strain on society.

This strain is not caused by those with low scores but rather the way the world treats them. We are seeing more humans rejected for employment opportunities, or reaching the age of majority without a single marriage proposal. As human children are increasingly less likely to receive the desired score, this presents a troublesome insight into our future.

Will the Council find a solution? This writer considers it unlikely. But who knows? Perhaps a hero will emerge from the midst. It hasn't happened since King Arthur's reign but, as they say, nothing is impossible where magic is concerned.

Your esteemed editor,

Torquil Pimpernel-Smith

Roger

Roger Barnes attempted to surreptitiously dab at the beads of sweat gathering on his forehead. The Council's chambers were notoriously hot, even in the waiting area. Some blamed it on the heated debates between councilmembers, but Roger privately believed it had more to do with the placement of the wing. It really did get the most atrocious amount of sunlight. Convening in late summer did not help. Roger had a brief wistfulness for his family's country estate, wind gliding over the pond as he read by a tree. He shook his head and reined in his thoughts. Now was not the time for wistfulness.

He took his notes out of his pocket, reading them for what felt like the hundredth time. The paper was crumpled from so much handling. He didn't need to read the notes; they were memorized already. But he tended to get flustered when he was nervous, agitated, or generally upset. Quite frankly, flustered was practically Roger's natural state. He folded the paper, his hands shaking. He put it back in his pocket, decided he ought to have it handy just in case, and pulled it out again. He tapped the paper against his thigh, decided that wasn't doing the crumpled state any favors, put it back in his pocket, and clenched his hands together.

He could hardly believe he was doing this *again*. Was he really foolish enough to approach the Council for a third time? When an aide appeared at the door and beckoned him in, he concluded that, apparently, he was foolish enough to do just that.

He felt six pairs of eyes follow his progress into the room. He had always believed that an even number of members was an absurd way to assemble a council responsible for big decisions, but no one cared much about his opinions on the subject. In this case, his reasons for approaching were so important that Roger felt overwhelmed by it all. He walked up to the little stand and placed his wrinkled notes down, smoothing out the edges. He looked up and found his father sitting at the end of the table, the lowest-ranking human councilmember, and the only person in the group that did not thoroughly intimidate Roger.

"Well, Mr. Barnes," Councilmember Williams said, his gruff voice making Roger feel even smaller, "to what do we owe the pleasure this time?"

He tried to hide his wince. He glanced at his father, who gave him an encouraging smile. He cleared his throat, "Thank you, sir. I am grateful for the opportunity to approach this august company again." He could tell his voice sounded monotone as he read out the words, but monotone was preferable to stuttering, so he kept going. "I understand that the Council is working to find a solution to the...Hastings score...situation and I-I would like to offer a suggestion."

Councilmember Cricket glanced at Roger's father. "Yes," she mused. "I suppose you would have opinions about that."

"I hope it is different from your last suggestion," Councilmember Gibbs sniffed. "Your last one left much to be desired."

His last suggestion—to raise the testing age to eighteen—had been squashed in record time. It was a pity. He'd really believed in that one. However, he had been significantly less prepared when he'd approached the Council before. His reasoning behind changing the testing age had not been well argued. Perhaps now that the situation was more dire, the Council would be more willing to hear his solution—particularly when his notes were better organized.

"To be fair," Councilmember Applewood put in, "the previous suggestion was not a bad one. But I'm still concerned about keeping families in suspense about inheritance for so long. It would be very taxing, particularly for the children involved."

"Not to mention, valuable time would be wasted that could be spent training heirs in what they need to know," Councilmember Williams added.

"There is little need to go over the subject again," Councilmember Wrenwhistle said coolly. "I take it Mr. Barnes has a different solution in mind this time."

"Y-yes," he stammered. "My proposal is to move away from the Hastings Examination rubric altogether."

There was, predictably, a small clamor at that, mostly from the human side, although there were a couple of fae members who were chattering too. He thought they seemed approving. Councilmember Applewood was looking at him pensively, a smile playing upon her lips. Roger felt a small bit of hope at that expression.

Councilmember Wrenwhistle raised her hand to silence the rest. "That is certainly a bold suggestion. I am curious to hear your reasons and what you suggest as an alternative."

"Well," he said. "My reasons are fairly simple, I think. As you know, the success rate for the Hastings Exams are extremely low. Some families see children with no passing rates at all, even from powerful bloodlines. My belief is that the exam is too narrow in its observations to be properly conclusive. My proposal..." he shifted his notes so the second page was on top, "is to have a more nuanced approach to testing. We only test human children on one spell. If we were to broaden the scope of the examination, we could test multiple strengths at once. I do not have a new model fully drafted yet, but I believe testing for...er...spell force, as we currently do, but also control, attention to detail, and...creativity, would be beneficial."

Councilmember Williams scoffed. "Creativity? What, are we going to have students offer up poems to their examiners?"

"N-no, sir. But it would be good to see students apply principles of basic theory to multiple spells. Sort of a theoretical examination on top of a practical one."

"Roger," his father said, his tone mild, "what do you propose for the fae examinations? I agree that the Hastings Exam may be out of date, but it is the most standard form of testing we have and has the benefit of being the most closely aligned to the fae test, the Sciurus Exam. Both rubrics must be comparable."

"I admit, sir, that I do not have sufficient expertise on fae magic," Roger said. "I would cede to the Council on that part, although I do agree that it is an important part of the issue."

"It hardly matters what the testing rubrics are," Councilmember Cricket sneered. "*We* do not treat our children like outcasts when they don't do well. I think that is the most critical issue at hand."

His father looked like he wanted to agree but Gibbs was quick to say that the fae had issues of their own, thank you very much. Then Cricket argued that whatever issues the fae had, they at least protected their own, which could not be said for humankind.

Roger felt himself wilt a little. This was more or less what happened the first time. He had made a proposal that started a debate, then he had been unceremoniously sent out. It wasn't quite as bad as the second time, when he suggested the testing age be altered. That time he had practically been laughed out of the room. He supposed if he had to choose, watching the Council descend into its usual chaos was somewhat preferable.

Wrenwhistle raised her hand again. The arguing died down, primarily because the fae were pointedly respectful to their Head of Council and the humans couldn't very well argue against silence. When the bickering stopped, she was silent for a long moment before saying, "Your proposal has merit, Mr. Barnes." Roger felt hope kindle in his chest. "But," she went on, quickly extinguishing that brief feeling, "a vague idea is not sufficient. We will give you a fortnight to come up with a detailed proposal, a workable testing rubric. I agree that a comparable model for testing fae magic is necessary, although I appreciate your restraint in overstepping beyond your expertise." Roger thought this was said with some sarcasm but he tried to pretend it wasn't. "So for now we will give you an opportunity to present to us a real solution. Something we can act upon. If your rubric is accepted, we will assign a fae to work with you on a comparable rubric for fae magic. Are we in agreement, Councilmember Williams?"

Williams gave Roger a long look. Finally, he nodded. "I believe that will suffice."

"Thank you, Mr. Barnes."

Roger knew a dismissal when he heard one and wasted no time in leaving. Once outside the room, he allowed himself to process his warring emotions. On one hand, they actually listened to him and hadn't laughed at him outright! That was certainly progress. On the other hand...he had not figured on developing the testing rubric himself. He had ideas, but with his Hastings score, he didn't have much hope that those ideas would be taken seriously. However, his mind was already starting to churn. He strode down the hall, lost in thought.

Wyn

At one point in time, Wyn supposed, the grandeur of the Parliament buildings along the Thames had been quite impressive. Countless spires stretched from the rooftops, tall enough to pierce the dreary, unwelcoming clouds that often collected overhead. Inside, the ogive arches helped draw attention to the stained-glass windows and intricate stonework on the walls and high ceilings. It was easy to let your jaw go slack at such a spectacle if you were not accustomed to it.

Wyn had been visiting his grandmother in the Council's chambers his entire life, effectively numbing him to the beauty of the architecture. Even the meticulously manicured grounds that surrounded him on his brisk walk along the cobbled path had long since faded into familiarity.

He followed his older brother Emrys up the steps, who touched his fingers to the brim of his hat as he greeted the doorkeepers by name.

"*Ugh*," Emrys moaned as they passed through the vestibule, quick to voice what both men were thinking. "Could it possibly be any hotter?" Even the echoing of their footsteps in the long hallway seemed muffled by the stifling air inside the building.

Wyn struggled to ignore the way the damp fabric of his cravat was sticking to his neck. His discomfort wasn't enough to make him regret wearing his thick, wavy hair long enough to reach his shoulders, though. It was a decision he'd made just recently, opting to let it grow out of the more fashionable cut that most men were wearing. His mother could protest many of his decisions, but this would not be one of them.

He took a deep breath and let it out in an impatient sigh.

"I just hope Grandmother makes this quick," he muttered, still trailing behind Emrys toward the chambers. There was an invitation to the first event of the Season with his name on it sitting atop his dressing table. He would wear something far less stuffy than his high boots and heavy coat. With any luck, the evening would dissolve into a more private situation that required no clothing at all.

"When has she ever been known to do that?" Emrys asked with a faint chuckle. "Although, maybe if I show her the way my new clothes are being ruined with sweat stains, she'll take pity and grant us leave."

As they approached the final corner in the maze of window-lit hallways, someone called Emrys' name. Both men turned to look over their shoulders and discovered the familiar smile of Keelan Cricket, one of Emrys' closest friends and the son of another councilmember.

"Go ahead, I'll catch up with you in a moment." Emrys left no room for argument as he pivoted and took off in the direction they'd just come. Wyn rolled his eyes, knowing that was the exact opposite of the truth, and turned the corner— directly into someone else.

"Watch it," Wyn hissed, taking a steadying step backward, trying his best to maintain appearances in case his brother or anyone else had seen. Upon realizing who had run into him, his annoyance flared. Of *course* it would be Barnes getting in his way.

"Apologies," the shorter man mumbled, his hands doing a ridiculous little dance, as though he couldn't decide between reaching for the scraps of paper he'd dropped on the floor or fixing his spectacles that had fallen askew after crashing into Wyn's chest.

Wyn crossed his arms and watched as Roger bent to pick up the papers from where they had fluttered to their feet. His mouth curled into a faint smirk.

"Had to draw yourself a map to find the exit, did you?"

Roger righted himself with a puff of an exhale and quickly folded his papers away into a pocket, fixing his spectacles with an indignant glare. Wyn's gaze slid down to the man's shoes and back up again. Barnes had never known how to dress for his plump figure, nor find a suitable color palette to match the light brown of his skin. Such a pity.

"I've been here just as many times as you, Wyndham," Roger said. Wyn bristled instantly at the casual use of his name. "I know my way around—"

"You will call me Mr. Wrenwhistle," Wyn ground out with a slow emphasis on each word, his jaw tight. The man was a year older than he was, but the fact remained that he wouldn't tolerate the disrespect of being addressed by his first name in public, especially by the likes of Roger Barnes. They might've known each other since they were children, but that did not make them friends.

He felt it then, the familiar tingling, and Wyn knew his magic was seconds away from begging to be set free. It was an issue he'd dealt with for as long as he could remember. Returning to London was most stressful for a fae who struggled with being surrounded by disorder. For Wyn, his melancholy was exacerbated by the stress, resulting in his magic demanding to be felt as his emotions flared.

Wyn drew in a deep, silent breath and held it, eyes sliding shut. He focused on what he could feel. The growing ache in his chest from holding the sweltering air in his lungs. The perspiration clinging in some unmentionable places. The cool, smooth metal of the rings on his fingers. He exhaled as these thoughts filtered through his mind, quelling the surge of emotion that had dared to unwind him right there in the hall.

"Are you…feeling quite the thing?"

The sound of Roger's voice, laced with just enough concern to sound sarcastic, washed away every speck of control Wyn had just regained.

"Do get out of my way," he said brusquely, stepping around Roger and continuing down the corridor.

The heels of Wyn's boots clacked harder than necessary all the way to the final door that separated him from the Council's chambers. He slammed through it with a flourish, coat whipping about his hips as he went. Without needing to read the nameplates hanging outside the offices, Wyn approached his grandmother's and let himself in.

Iris Wrenwhistle lifted her gaze from the papers on her desk, a pleasant look of surprise on her face despite the fact that she'd been the one to request his presence. This was the way she always regarded her grandchildren. She treated every interaction with them like a small gift.

"There you are, darling," she said with a warmth that helped wash away the last of Wyn's twist of frustration. "Where is your brother?"

"Chatting up a friend," he replied. The chair by the window had always been his favorite. He plunked into it like a sullen teenager and crossed his arms over his chest, eyes cast to the floor.

"Ah, yes. It's good to be back in London with everyone, is it not? A little early, but we've got important work to do."

I hate it here, he wanted to tell her. *I hate it more than anything.*

Wyn wanted to be back in the country where he could enjoy the fresh air and sunshine and nights under the stars without the constant bustling and noise of high society. Somewhere he was not continually reminded that, despite his magical aptitude, he was inferior in the eyes of others thanks to the score he'd been given when he was just a child.

"It's good to be back," he agreed, though the lie burned hot on his tongue.

* * *

Want to read more of Breeze Spells and Bridegrooms? Buy it now!